The Cradle and the Cage

The
Cradle
and the
Cage

HASTIE SALIH

The manufacturer's authorised representative in the EU for product safety is Authorised Rep Compliance Ltd, 71 Lower Baggot Street, Dublin D02 P593 Ireland (www.arccompliance.com)

This is a work of fiction. Names, characters, businesses, places, events and incidents are either the products of the author's imagination or used in a fictitious manner. Any resemblance to actual persons, living or dead, or actual events is purely coincidental.

Troubador Publishing Ltd
Unit E2 Airfield Business Park,
Harrison Road, Market Harborough,
Leicestershire LE16 7UL
Tel: 0116 279 2299
Email: books@troubador.co.uk
Web: www.troubador.co.uk

ISBN 978-1-83628-338-6

British Library Cataloguing in Publication Data.
A catalogue record for this book is available from the British Library.

Printed and bound in Great Britain by 4edge Limited
Typeset in 11pt Minion Pro by Troubador Publishing Ltd, Leicester, UK

Dedicated to Juliette and Lana.

1

The journey had been smoother until Yasmine realised that something was delaying their landing. The Boeing Dreamliner had been circling Erbil airport for half an hour now.

She had yearned to glimpse the mountains with their rugged peaks and sparkling streams. How soothing it would be to bathe in the creeks, throw pebbles into the rivulets and taste the sweet oranges her mother had so often mentioned.

Yasmine couldn't wait to be reconciled with her mother's land and heritage. The ancient history of Mesopotamia and Nineveh, the rich soil between the rivers Tigris and Euphrates, the cradle of civilisation were all waiting to be unearthed. Her pristine and idyllic perceptions of this country she had never visited, built up over years, had culminated in booking a flight ticket after finishing college.

Tufted clouds overhead were morphing into a spear and the shimmering beams of sunlight had difficulty peeking through them.

'*Merda*. A drone is targeting Erbil airport,' the Italian seated next to her shrieked, grabbing hold of her hand. Yasmine snapped out of her reverie and turned to face him. Beads of sweat had formed on his forehead.

She held back a scream. *What a start to a three-week, post-graduation holiday.* This wasn't going to be just a recreational break to discover the wonders of her mother's homeland.

But nothing, not even a giant buzzing drone over Iraq's airspace would stop her from trying to uncover the silences that overshadowed her family in London.

The plane circled the airport for a few more minutes until the captain declared that he had received the all-clear to land. A woman behind Yasmine whispered that US military bases grounded in the area were being targeted by the drone. *Thank goodness this drone didn't carry missiles, only surveillance cameras.* Tears were welling up behind Yasmine's eyelids.

The Italian put his trembling hands on his lap and gazed at her curiously. 'What on earth enticed you to go on this challenging journey to a country in turmoil?'

Yasmine straightened herself in the small seat, crossed her arms and looked at him, perplexed. He was beginning to remind her of her mother's warnings of robbers and people smugglers in the mountains. It had been comical drafting a will – at her age, she didn't have much to give away if she died, but her mum had insisted on it.

The drone brought with it a rush of adrenaline which she had last experienced when jumping into a bay from a cliff in Dover. This was during a summer holiday a few years back, but she still heard the shrill scream of her mother to keep away. Yasmine had relished the plunge, the smell of salt and the freezing, unforgiving sea. The waves had lashed out at her, but she had conquered them.

She closed her eyes as she thought of what her mother had advised her the previous week: 'Start the journey to Iraq by visiting the site of the Garden of Eden, or search for the remnants of ancient civilizations and cuneiform writing.' Those words had touched her soul and shifted a yearning inside her.

Amongst all these geographical treasures was her favourite uncle, Aram. She had to see him again. He had been the uncle who had soothed and played with her as a small child until her father had died in a mysterious car accident, after which Aram had hastily returned to Iraq. But she kept telling herself that he was part of her family, just waiting to be found and welcomed back into it.

She wanted to shed light on what her father's death had to do with Uncle Aram's disappearance and why it coincided with whispers between her mother and her partner, Samantha. They always stopped as soon as Yasmine entered the room. *Hmm. Unresolved feelings or unfinished thoughts?*

The plane landed with screeching brakes and she was jolted forwards. She was finally on Kurdish soil in Iraq, her mother's country, the cradle of civilization, but also the largest stateless nation in the world. She frowned. Arbitrary land borders had been drawn by the Allies after the First World War, promises made and broken, lines in the sand with an unabashed disregard for the Kurdish people. Would history blend in with the modernity she was used to in London during her stay with her mother's sister, Auntie Dilly, and Uncle Jamal in Iraq?

The flight from London Heathrow had taken eight hours and the officials at the airport in Erbil made her pay $65 for a tourist visa to enter Iraq's Kurdish region as there was no trace of her Kurdish heritage in her passport and she didn't have a Kurdish ID. Odd that her mother hadn't asked for one. Surely, she might have known that Yasmine would one day want to return to her homeland and fulfil her dreams of connecting with family?

The shuttle bus that took Yasmine to the arrivals hall at the airport in Erbil was teeming with European expats chatting boastfully in English, French and German about their well-paid jobs as engineers, teachers and diplomats in Iraq. Her mother had left her country decades ago, married an Englishman and worked as a GP in London. *Strange that Mum has never returned to Iraq after Dad died.* After his death, her mother had met her partner Samantha, down-to-earth, humorous and Yasmine's second mother, whom she adored. Why was the wider family not mentioned?

When Yasmine had expressed her desire to travel to Iraq, her mother had repeatedly fretted about people smugglers and robbers. Geez. Not once had she revelled in memories of the magnificent Zagros, Azmer and Korek mountains like Uncle Aram had. There had been no answer as to why he had left Britain so suddenly after her father's death. What if he had joined the freedom fighters, the famous Kurdish Peshmerga? Or maybe a romance was involved. She would love to exchange her romantic stories with him. Well, not all of them, of course.

4

Yasmine peered through the window of the slow-moving bus and was met by a pale and parched landscape. November was cooler than the summer months where temperatures often notched above fifty degrees. How had her mother managed to live in that climate? Sulaymaniyah, where her family was from, was only marginally cooler. Her mother had told her that they would sleep on rooftops to catch a cool breeze during the summer months, watching the gleaming stars and listening to the hypnotic sounds of cicadas. For now, Yasmine couldn't wait to feel the winter warmth on her skin. The grey and dreary skies in London could, with all respect, fuck off.

At a kiosk selling SIM cards, Yasmine spent twenty minutes playfully insisting to the vendor that she deserved a good deal, not a rip-off internet bundle designed for tourists – she wasn't entirely a tourist, after all – and it worked. She took a mental note for future interactions.

'Yasmine?' A voice called, milliseconds after she had left through the airport gates. She followed the sound to find a middle-aged woman with neatly coiffed dark curls, a pale complexion and gleaming, kind eyes. Auntie Dilly.

'*Balê, Pura Dilly.* Yasmine's words came out muffled as her auntie stepped forward to give her a big squeeze.

Dilly kissed her on her cheeks three times – the classic Kurdish greeting. '*Chawakum,* how was your flight?' she said, leaning back to get a proper look at her. Yasmine smiled. Her mum would call her by the same Kurdish endearment: *my eyes.*

'It was fine, *pura*. Mum sends her love.'

'*Mashalla*, you're just as beautiful as her.'

Even as she smiled, Dilly's lips stayed plump and her skin wrinkle-free. *She must have had some work done,* thought Yasmine. Despite the poverty in some parts of the country, the beauty industry was booming. In the half hour since she'd landed in the country, she had already spotted a woman with her nose plastered after getting a nose job, and a passenger on the plane had told her that she needed her Botox repeated. Yasmine was so glad she had shaved her legs and threaded her eyebrows before travelling to Iraq.

Oh, how liberating it would be to blend into this country of her mother's, she thought. With her dark, curly hair and brown close-set eyes, maybe she could camouflage into the local environment and feel less watched and more included. Her dark features had always stood out in London, even though it was a multicultural city.

She almost bumped into a man who had his eyebrows tidied up and threaded. They were sculpted like a woman's. Had he had his chest hair waxed off too? He glanced at her. She covered her shoulders with the shawl her mother had given her as she wasn't sure whether Auntie Dilly would expect her to cover up. What would her uncle and auntie think of her tattoo on her forearm? She pulled her sleeve down over her arm.

She quickly explained to Dilly that her Kurdish wasn't very good so it would be better to speak in English. Dilly nodded and embraced her tightly.

'I miss your mother.' Dilly raised her well-groomed eyebrows. 'Beautiful woman, inside and out.' She sighed. 'I don't know how she hasn't found another man for herself yet. We must try to find her someone.' She grinned. 'I have a few in mind.'

Yasmine couldn't help but laugh. The Middle Eastern auntie stereotype was in full force. If only Dilly knew about her mother's partner, Samantha. To be honest, why was her mother still so highly secretive about Sam? Her mother had become something of a role model to Yasmine's friends when she had unwillingly been outed in university. But she was closeted at work. If her mother, Sozanne, could gather the courage to come out to her sister, surely Dilly would eventually accept her for who she was, even if that had to come with time.

'Are you hungry?' Dilly glanced at her curiously. 'Our maid, Cecile, has cooked some *dolma* and *fasulye* for you.' Yasmine's tummy rumbled. 'It'll take us half an hour to get home, is that okay?'

'That's fine. You have a maid?'

'Yes. She's wonderful. She's Somali, but she speaks Kurdish and English, and I've taught her to cook our traditional meals.'

Amazing. It was Sam who did most of the cooking in London and she didn't excel in Kurdish food. Yasmine's mouth started to water at the thought of *yaprach*, rice-stuffed grape leaves.

'Can she teach me too?' Yasmine asked, pulling her heavy suitcase along.

Dilly looked surprised and started to laugh. 'I think we're going to have fun with you.'

'I'm sure you will,' Yasmine replied, wondering how far their differences would amuse her auntie, before they unsettled or annoyed her.

She looked up at the sky. A few days ago, drones had been shot down where US forces were stationed. Tensions were high. Northern Iraq was embedded between Turkey, Iran and Syria, none of which were sympathetic towards Kurds. This wasn't the first time drones had been used in Kurdistan.

In 2014, the leader of ISIS, Abu Bakr Al-Baghdadi, had declared a caliphate and had set his eyes on Erbil, the treasured capital of Kurdistan. Yasmine had read that the Kurdish Peshmerga militia wouldn't have been able to drive back ISIS without the help of US fighters and drones, which had dropped laser-guided bombs on a plethora of Islamic State targets.

As if following Yasmine's train of thought, Dilly said, 'Don't worry, *chawakum*. You're safe.' She put her arm around Yasmine and squeezed her hand, then waved at a Mercedes waiting nearby. 'It's been many years since we saw your mum. How is she?'

'She's fine. Busy working. If it wasn't for Samantha, I don't know how she'd cope.'

'Who's Samantha? Her maid?'

'Um, no, it's her friend.' *What a farce. Now I'm forced to take part in it.*

'I'd love to visit her but it's so difficult to get a visa nowadays.' Dilly stepped towards the Mercedes. 'This is your uncle, Jamal.'

A man with a handlebar moustache got out of the car. *'Choni, bashi?'* he said in a loud, raspy voice.

'Bash'm, spas,' she responded quickly, saying that she was fine.

His grip was firm as he shook her hand. He was

wearing billowy grey trousers that tapered at the bottom, with a matching jacket over a white shirt, and a thick strap of golden fabric around the waist.

'Excited?' he asked. 'This city has been waiting for you. Our holiday apartment is on the twenty-second floor so you'll be able to take it all in. At night, with all the bright lights, you'd think it's Las Vegas.'

London was full of high rises and bright lights. She'd be much more compelled to explore the city's history and the surrounding nature. 'That sounds amazing,' she said with a polite smile. 'Can you see the citadel from your apartment?'

'Yes. It's not far and the main bazaar is nearby. We can go and see it tomorrow,' he said as he loaded her suitcase into the boot and she and her auntie got in the car.

Yasmine nodded a little sleepily. The citadel in Erbil was one of the oldest continually occupied towns in the world, her Uncle Aram had told her. It was up to two millennia older than the Great Pyramids of Giza which she'd seen with Harry last year. She frowned. This wasn't the time to think about her on-off boyfriend Harry. She would FaceTime him later on.

Her uncle and auntie smiled at each other as she asked her questions. *They must be so proud of their culture,* she thought. *Family starts with heritage. Isn't that what I've come for?*

'Uncle, how long have the Kurds been living in and around the citadel?'

'I'm glad you asked, Yasmine.' He took a deep breath. 'The Kurds consider themselves descended from the Medes, an ancient Iranian people. They use a calendar dating from 612 C.E. when the Assyrian capital of Nineveh was conquered by the Medes.'

'Jamal, stop teaching her all these facts.' Dilly gently prodded her husband. 'She's tired, can't you see that?'

'She asked about our history,' Jamal answered indignantly.

'No, Jamal.' She laughed. 'Yasmine asked about the citadel.'

'She can't wait to find out about our surroundings and history.' He looked at Yasmine with a roguish expression in his eyes.

'Um…' Yasmine was at a loss for words. She didn't want to side with either of them. They were so different in their attitude towards their surroundings, and yet united in their loving relationship. Or were they?

Uncle Jamal had already started talking again. 'We are the descendants of various Indo-European tribes who migrated to the Zagros Mountain region four thousand years ago.'

'I'd love to see the mountains,' Yasmine cried out.

'We'll take you wherever you'd like to go,' Auntie Dilly chimed in, turning to face Yasmine at the back of their jeep.

'Our national anthem states that we are descendants of the Medes and if I were to translate more of our anthem … *Kurdish youth have risen like lions…*' Jamal took his hands off the steering wheel to make a claw-like impression of lions rising up.

Dilly shrieked and implored him to keep his hands on the steering wheel. Yasmine couldn't help stifling a giggle.

'Oh, okay. I'll sing a bit of the anthem then,' Jamal said, putting his hands back on the steering wheel. '*Kes nelê Kurd mirdûw e, Kurd zîndûw e.* Let no one say the Kurds are dead; the Kurds are alive.'

His hoarse voice filled the car with an ebullience Yasmine hadn't expected so soon after arriving in the country. She chuckled, especially when Auntie Dilly added, 'And their flag shall never fall.' *Hmm, but what about the family flag?* Yasmine couldn't help thinking. Would three weeks be enough to resolve her queries?

Anyway, it was soothing listening to Uncle Jamal's singing after his explanation that the Western Allies had carved up the Middle East like a lamb, cutting Kurdistan into four pieces, namely Iran, Iraq, Turkey and Syria.

'I'll teach you more lines of our national anthem after the visit to the citadel, Yasmine.'

'Thanks, Uncle. The citadel and bazaar sound like a great place to explore,' she replied enthusiastically.

The citadel is just the right place to start making enquiries about Uncle Aram. She remembered his stories about the citadel and working in a coffeehouse on its grounds, but she said nothing about her plans to Jamal and her auntie. They were most probably just as secretive as her mother.

When they arrived at her uncle and auntie's flat, Jamal parked the car in the underground garage and they took the lift up to the twenty-second floor.

Yasmine put her suitcase in the spare room they had prepared for her and walked into the sitting room. The panoramic view of Erbil was spectacular. The massive Erbil citadel dominated the skyline, with every street in the city radiating from its centre.

Jamal came over to where she was standing and followed her gaze. 'The citadel is the oldest continually inhabited place in the world.'

A shiver ran down Yasmine's spine. The citadel was where she would start to follow Uncle Aram's tracks the following day. But first, she had promised to FaceTime Harry. He had always sought out stability, order and consequence. There was little space for excitement in that.

2

Yasmine took the elevator to the ground floor and walked into the garden of the gated compound her auntie and uncle lived in. A few boys were shouting as they played football. They kicked the ball close to where she was standing. She ran towards it and kicked it back, thinking about Harry and how he had screamed when Ronaldo scored a goal against England. She chuckled.

In springtime, when she had met Harry, delicate yellow daffodils, bright-pink cherry blossoms and deep violet bluebells adorned parks and lakes in her favourite local park. Harry and she loved strolling through it. Yasmine took a deep breath. Life was simple in London. Everything was at your doorstep – food, water, electricity and gas. Here, in her mother's country, she was far away from predictability and safety. Harry offered her all this, but that was all. She frowned and took out her phone as she walked around the compound.

'Yas, where have you been?' said Harry. 'I was worried sick about you.'

'Hey, babe. I'm sorry, I've been a little all over the place. I've been trying to sort a few things out and organise something.' She kicked the ball over to the boys on the compound again. She had to let off steam.

'Oh? You should have mentioned it, angel. Do you need my help with anything?'

Harry sounded hurt over the phone, but she had to tell him, sooner rather than later. 'I don't think you can help me much with this.'

'Uh, okay. What do you mean?'

'I have something to tell you. I'm at my aunt's house in Erbil, Iraq. I needed to do this now that I finished with my studies.'

'Oh…' She heard Harry's Labrador, Benny barking in the background. She would miss that dog. 'You don't think it's a bit weird that you booked it and travelled to Iraq without, like, mentioning it to me?'

'I've been hinting at it for ages, Harry. I can't say that I've ever picked up any enthusiasm on your end for my plans. You didn't even ask me any questions about it the last time I tried to bring it up.'

'That's not fair,' he said. 'You know how hectic things were when I was going through the Master's applications—'

'Yes, well you left it pretty late down the line to mention your plans to move up to Manchester.'

'What? That's not true. I told you about my applications.'

'Yes, after you'd already sent them off.' Yasmine felt her heart pounding. 'Anyway, that's not important now. I've been thinking about how things are going between us, and how I've been feeling in the relationship over the last few months. We're heading in such different directions, babe.' She let the sentence sink in, then said, 'Maybe it's better to close a chapter and appreciate what we've had before things change even more, you know? The last thing I want to exist between us is resentment.'

He hadn't seen it coming, she could hear that in his voice. 'You want to end things? Over the phone?'

Her eardrums felt like they were about to explode. 'I mean … you did, with your ex. Remember?'

There was silence at the other end.

'Is that all *you* remember, Yasmine?' He sounded hurt.

She remembered the warm breath on her neck from Harry's kisses, the way he used to hold her whenever she got anxious through uni. But his gentleness, his reliability, his predictability, all lost their colour and warmth when she thought ahead to the future.

'I'm sorry. This obviously isn't easy for me to say, but I owe you honesty about how I really feel. You wouldn't have changed my mind about going to Kurdistan and I wouldn't have changed yours about Manchester. And that's okay. We're in our twenties, Harry. It's like, every year we're gonna keep coming back to a crossroads between different life paths until we figure out what we're doing, you know? And that's something I need to do alone.'

'No, Yasmine,' he said, sounding breathless. 'That's just you.'

The conversation went on for a couple of hours in slow, painful circles. Harry was willing to try long distance, Yasmine wasn't. Harry felt that her words came out of nowhere, Yasmine thought it was clear that they'd been building for months. Harry knew where he was headed over the next few years, Yasmine's future sprawled as vast and open as the sea. Harry's tone was defeated by the end of the conversation. 'It sounds like you've already made your decision about us already, huh?' She searched for the right words to say next, but Harry was faster. 'Good luck with everything, Yasmine.'

Suddenly she realised he had gone.

Yasmine covered her face with her hands. *What a shit situation. Is there no one on my side?* Even her mother had been obstructive about this journey. She wiped a tear that was escaping from her eye. Her sleeve would do. She bit her lip until she winced with the pain.

Her mother's secrets couldn't wait. She hoped it wouldn't be like opening Pandora's Box. She watched the boys playing football on the lawn, focusing on scoring and winning. They most probably knew all about their families and whereabouts. No missing family members. Her eyes welled up. Her uncle hadn't even said goodbye to her. It was as if he had vanished into thin air. Why didn't her mother care?

She had to find him.

3

t last, her adventure was about to unravel. She
had waited for so long, graduated, worked as a
barista and finally saved enough money to fly to
Iraq. Yasmine quickly scrolled through a Wikipedia page
on Erbil's history and took some notes on her phone as her
uncle drove her to the citadel.

*Erbil — important centre for Christianity during Sasanian
period and under Abbasid Caliphate. Then comes rise of
Islam from the year 600 onwards, until the Mongol invasions
of the mid-13th century.*

*Today, Erbil = capital of the Kurdistan Regional
Government in Iraq, KRG.*

*KRG formed in 1992 after genocidal campaigns of
Saddam Hussain + Baathist regime aiming at Arabization
of the region led to large-scale Kurdish uprisings. KRG is
the only region where Kurds have autonomy (as opposed to
Kurds in Turkey, Iran, Syria).*

Population estimate of all Kurds = 35 to 40 mil.

Her mother was one of these people, living in the diaspora.

Great, her notes would be full of new ideas and personal revelations by the time she returned to London. She would write a few articles on her trip as soon as she got back, maybe get some extra cash for them. It would be easier than working as a barista. She tapped her foot impatiently as they neared the citadel.

Yasmine was dubious whether autonomy in the region she had entered had brought much success. Her uncle had told her that the Kurds were still reliant on money being sent from Baghdad, Iraq's official capital, and salaries were only sent over every couple of months, which meant that often people would go months without an income. Recently, the Kurdish government had refused to receive its share from the federal budget on the grounds that it wasn't enough.

Before long they reached the citadel, and, stepping out of Uncle Jamal's car, she craned her neck to take in the towering construction. It stood tall and strong, like a silent guard protecting the vibrant city of Erbil, the beating heart of the Kurdistan Region of Iraq.

She had read that the ancient citadel, known as Qelay Hewler, was included in the World Heritage List and had passed through Sumerian, Assyrian, Sassanid, Mongol, Christian and Ottoman hands. It was previously known by its Aramaic name, Arbela. Yasmine chuckled as her mother had initially wanted to call her Arabella. Thank goodness, her father had decided to give her a different name.

'Here we are, Yasmine,' Uncle Jamal said. 'You look fit enough to walk up to the citadel. It's about thirty metres above this bazaar. Dilly will accompany you.' He gestured to his wife with a smile but didn't put his arm around her as he would at home.

Public displays of affection were frowned upon here. Yasmine tried to remember the other rules her mother had told her. One of them was not to mention her (now-ex) boyfriend. *Oh Harry...* he had sent her a string of messages since they'd spoken. He said he'd felt it was unfair to give up on the relationship after eighteen months of being together. Things at home hadn't been easy for him this week, either. His parents' arguments had hit a breaking point and his dad filed for a divorce a couple of days ago.

The thought of what he must be going through right now made her heart hurt. He needed someone to be there for him, for sure, but she knew she'd made the right decision to part ways. Their realities couldn't be more different as she readied herself for her stay in Kurdistan and the journey into her mother's past.

Walking past the bazaar, she found herself looking at all the middle-aged men who resembled Uncle Aram, half hoping that he'd just be there, ready and waiting for her at the first stop she made in the city. Aram had been a caring fatherly figure for her but one day, he had mysteriously disappeared. Shortly afterwards Samantha, her mother's partner, had entered their lives.

Many of the men walking along the narrow pavements stared back at Yasmine. They were somehow aware that she was a tourist in her own country. How could she have imagined fitting in here? Every step she took would attract attention. She paced up the steep, dusty path to the citadel with long strides, happy to stretch her legs after her previous day's flight, while her auntie took it at a more relaxed speed. Uncle Jamal had gone to meet his friends at a cafe by the bazaar. The walls of the citadel were largely refurbished, standing tall and strong. She wondered how many enemies had tried to capture this fortress.

A map showed several smaller museums within the complex at the top. 'Which one shall we start with, Dilly?' she asked as she turned to her auntie coming up behind her, trying to catch her breath. *Note to self: slow down, Yasmine.*

'Anything, my love.'

'What about the gemstone and fossil room?' Uncle Aram had told her how pretty fossils in the citadel were when she was a child.

'Fossils?' Dilly looked at her curiously. 'Sure. I didn't think you'd be interested in them.'

As they entered the small courtyard, Yasmine spotted a man in the same traditional Kurdish costume her uncle had worn the day before. His face was tanned and his beady eyes followed her cautiously.

'*Salaam u alaikum,*' he said, looking at Yasmine's trainers. No doubt he had already identified her as a Westerner.

'*Wa alaikum u salaam,*' Auntie Dilly answered as they strolled into the small room display.

Soon her auntie was busy texting someone in the corner. She must have seen these fossils many times before. The turquoise stones were crafted finely. Yasmine gazed at the starfish fossil and green malachite from Zaire. Her muscles started to twitch as she caught sight of the white calcite and large white snow quartz. Uncle Aram had loved fossils and it had been his dream to put one he owned into the museum in the citadel.

She stopped abruptly in front of one of the glass cases. A blue stone was sliced into two parts and displayed a yellow interior. Surely it wasn't … it couldn't be the one Aram had shown her when she was a child? He had told her about the preserved remains of plants and animals buried in sediments. Had the fossil he'd cherished been blue or green? Yasmine tried to concentrate on memories that were slipping through her mind.

Yes, it was the missing one. Aram had compared it to the blue Kurdish sky, devoid of grey clouds. It was the one missing from her mother's house after Uncle Aram left! She felt a tinge of excitement crawl up her spine. *What a discovery so soon after arriving in Iraq.*

'Auntie Dilly, I just need to get some fresh air. I'll be back in two minutes.'

Dilly nodded, looking slightly irritated.

Yasmine slipped outside the small display room and into the courtyard. The guard looked up at her as she pretended to eye the brick walls.

'You must have lots of schoolchildren coming here on scientific trips.'

The security guard stopped chewing his gum and took in her blue jeans and white blouse. His hands looked coarse and his teeth were yellowish as he smiled at her. 'You are from England?'

'Yes, *effendi,* but I'm here with my auntie,' she replied, feeling flushed with expectation and fear. 'My uncle must have been here. His blue gem is in the display glass cabinet.'

The man looked at her confused, his opaque eyes narrowing. She showed him the photo of the blue stone she had taken on her mobile and decided to be more forceful with her next sentence. 'Aram Kazzaz. You must remember him! He used to work here' She saw him flinch and look away. Surely, he remembered Aram. 'I'll give you ten dollars, if you can tell me where he is.' She didn't want to sound desperate, but she didn't want to lose too much time. Her auntie would be coming out into the courtyard soon.

The guard raised his eyebrows and grinned. 'Twenty dollars.' He started chewing his gum again and tried feigning a lack of interest in the matter, looking at his tobacco-stained fingernails.

Yasmine shuddered. 'Okay. Twenty dollars.' She hesitated. 'Did he sell the stone?'

The guard shifted his position in the wooden chair and took the note Yasmine was offering. 'Yes,' he said, standing up to scrutinise the dollars.

'When was he here?' Yasmine asked, looking past him and into the courtyard. She didn't want to appear too eager, otherwise the guard would increase the price.

'That will make another twenty dollars, Miss.'

Yasmine frowned and nodded, irritated.

'He came with another man two months ago.' He looked at her distastefully. No doubt he saw her as a spoiled Westerner.

Yasmine counted the dollars she needed to hand over to him. 'Where was he travelling to?' She put the dollars behind her back and raised her eyebrows, almost taunting him.

The guard hesitated, then replied, 'Sulaymaniyah.'

'Why should I believe that?'

The guard laughed. 'Because we ask everyone who sells a precious stone here to give us some details, not just for our statistics, but also because they may be crooks.' He laughed disdainfully, then took a long puff from his cigarette. 'He said he needed the money for a wedding. Is he your father?'

Yasmine recoiled. 'I already told you, he's my uncle.' She hesitated, realising that her voice sounded hoarse. 'My father died when I was young. Aram Kazzaz became like a father to me.' *Why am I oversharing?* She quickly handed over the dollars.

'Are you sure you want to find him?' He smirked. 'What's your name?'

'You don't need to know,' she said firmly as she turned to go back into the showroom, but her auntie was already sauntering out of the small fossil room.

'Yasmine, what have you been doing out here for so long?'

The guard smiled smugly as he put the dollars into his pocket. 'I know your name now.'

Yasmine bit her lip, stumbled towards her auntie and embraced her tightly.

Dilly almost fell backwards and laughed. 'You're very affectionate, Yasmine. You must be missing your mother.'

Yasmine felt more relieved than emotional. 'Just happy to see you. Can we leave now?'

Dilly wiped Yasmine's forehead with her hand and led her out of the courtyard, saying 'I guess we'll need a good qaswan coffee in the citadel café now.' She eyed her niece curiously. 'I don't think going to the citadel the day after you arrived in Erbil was such a great idea. You should have rested a bit more.'

'Oh no, Auntie Dilly. This trip came at the right time.' Yasmine tugged at her auntie's sleeve, almost pushing her out of the courtyard and away from the Kurdish guard's scrutiny.

They strolled towards an open café at the back of the citadel and sat on the wooden bench with red embroidered cushions. Yasmine looked around her. Red tassels were hanging from the rug used as a ceiling for the café. It cooled the place down and she felt her muscles relaxing.

She hadn't expected to find a clue to Uncle Aram's dwelling so quickly. There was no turning back. She had to find him, no matter what obstacles lay in the way. A piece of her family's past was missing. Uncle Aram would surely help her.

An archaic red kilim was hanging from a wall to her left. The design was similar to the kilim her mother had brought over from Iraq, the one that she loved walking on barefoot. How many stories had been woven onto that rug?

She used to dream about her mother's homeland when wiggling her toes on her mother's rug, feeling like Aladdin, about to fly off into an adventure. And now, she was finally in her mother's country. She did miss her home in London, but the urge to demystify her family connections had overcome her. Yasmine straightened her posture and put one of the cushions behind her back.

She took in some ancient kitchen utensils hung up on the wall opposite her. Old pans, spoons and forks were displayed proudly. Hmm, the Kurds certainly had a tight connection to their past. Thank goodness the kitchen didn't have an aura of sadness around it like other areas in Iraq with tragic stories of the past.

Yasmine said, 'Auntie, I'd love to take a jeep to Sulaymaniyah, next.'

'Goodness. What's the rush?'

'A journey to the past.'

Dilly looked at her puzzled as they sipped the hot *chai* the waiter had brought them.

After a few minutes, they made their way to the bazaar as it was what they had planned to do after the visit to the citadel. She was being propelled into a tsunami of family secrets imbued with despair but she relished in the light-headedness.

4

She couldn't believe her eyes. A man with a giant Samovar on his back roamed the street opposite the citadel, offering tea in small *istikans*. Yasmine almost stopped to ask for his chai from the amazing giant metal self-brewer but thought better of it when she caught sight of the bustling market. She hurried into one of the numerous ancient alleyways surrounding Qasari bazaar. The dome-shaped ceiling gave the bazaar an eerie look. Yasmine looked around her cautiously. She inhaled clouds of fruity shisha smoke which calmed her racing pulse. Dilly had trouble keeping up with her.

'Slow down, Yasmine,' she chortled. 'I've been diagnosed with something called fibromyalgia and my muscles can't keep up with yours.'

Yasmine took her auntie's hand, excused herself and looked around her in wonder.

Stalls were filled with colourful spices, sweets, cheese and yoghurt. The strong smell of grilled nuts made her mouth water.

She didn't know in which direction to glance. Hissing

gas lamps and whistling errand boys filled the air. She inhaled the various scents of shisha smoke billowing out of well-lit corners of shops within the bazaar. This was more exciting than the shopping malls in London. And the sizzling kebabs. Her stomach rumbled.

'Would you like to buy some jewellery, my love?' Dilly asked, smiling. 'A golden belt for your wedding?'

Not again. A wedding is the last thing on my mind.

She tried to hide her pained and perplexed feelings, linked arms with her auntie and pushed her towards the food stalls opposite them. 'I don't need *almas* at the moment. Let's have a look at the food stalls.' She turned towards a table laid with pickled cucumbers, red beet, purple turnip, garlicky carrots, olives and pickled red onions in blue bowls. Her stomach felt tight. She turned the other way, pulling her auntie along. Dilly turned to look at her, a quizzical expression on her face.

'I'd prefer to have a look at the nuts, dried fruit or honey.' Yasmine couldn't help sounding stern as she turned into a different alley. A bearded man in traditional brown salwar trousers was following them, feigning interest in the stalls they were passing.

He turned into a different alley with her and stopped when she halted to look at a stall with mixed nuts. Yasmine felt her pulse race again. Since speaking to the guard in the citadel, she seemed to have become a person of interest. Why? She glanced at Dilly who was tasting the pistachio nuts on display.

'We'll buy some of these. They're delicious and healthy, especially the—'

Yasmine pushed Dilly aside, nudging her into a

different alley of toiletries just as a crowd of young tourists came between the man and themselves. Dilly dropped the nuts and found herself in the jewellery section of the bazaar.

'*Bismillah*, Yasmine, what's got into you?' Her eyes were a mixture of anger and despair. 'I just asked you if you wanted to buy some jewellery and you ignored my proposition, only to pull me there a few minutes later.'

Yasmine looked around her. The man had disappeared into a different alley. She heaved a sigh of relief.

'Sorry, Auntie. I've had a long flight.' She yawned in mock fatigue.

Dilly eyed her warily. 'Okay, Let's go to a tea house. Some qahwa qaswan will sort you out. Mam Khalil's tea house is one of the best.' She grabbed Yasmine's arm. *Was Dilly afraid she would rush off again?*

They passed through the stalls with colourful fabrics on display. Dilly stopped shortly and said, 'We need to buy you some fabric for a Kurdish costume. In March, we'll be celebrating Newroz, our New Year.' She beamed proudly. 'It's a great occasion with displays of fire on the mountains, lighting up the whole area around them.'

'Maybe next time, Auntie. I can't keep my eyes open.' She rubbed her eyes with her sleeve. She hadn't counted on a stranger following her so quickly. She flinched. *Did he have anything to do with the guard she had questioned in the citadel?*

'Goodness me. Your mother didn't tell me how sensitive you are. What else hasn't she told me?' Her auntie sounded irritated. 'Okay let's go to the tea house now. I still have some nuts at home. No need to buy them here.'

They walked briskly past the carpenters' alley, the alley of flowers, kitchen sinks and bronze taps, footwear and stalls brimming with toiletries such as shampoos and hair dye for men and women.

She was surprised to see small Eiffel Tower trinkets on display. Vintage toy car models, belts and scarves were strewn across stalls, using up every free space available. Yasmine checked all the alleys for the man who had followed her. He was nowhere to be seen. Her mouth felt dry.

Suddenly, a young man stepped in front of her. She jolted backwards. *Has he been following me?*

'Would you like to try some qahwa qaswan, Miss?' He handed her a small trinket.

She held back a scream, steadied her breathing and looked up. This man wasn't the bearded guy who had been following her. This one had kind eyes and had taken a step back. She was thirsty for anything. She nodded, accepted the drink and put it to her parched lips.

'Mmm. It's delicious. What's in it?'

Dilly answered whilst sipping her own offering of chai.

'It's an ancient Kurdish drink made from the roasted and ground terebinth fruit, rich in antioxidants, caffeine-free and a natural aid for digestion.' She patted her tummy triumphantly.

'Would you like to buy some?' The young man asked shyly.

'Of course.' Yasmine smiled at him. He had azure, blue eyes, like Harry's back home. She felt a pang of regret that he couldn't accompany her on this trip, certainly not as a boyfriend. Anyway, they had broken up for the time being.

I might have put him in danger in this country where kidnapping is an imminent threat, and he's not as adventurous as I am.

Her mother had even offered to get a Peshmerga freedom fighter to accompany them if they went together. No, Yasmine had needed to do this trip alone. Whatever happened, she didn't want anyone else to get hurt. She shook her head involuntarily, trying to banish images of injuries.

Kahlil's Tea House was next on her agenda. Dilly bought some samples of qahwa qaswan and they strolled to the tea house. Thank goodness their stalker had disappeared into the crowd. Yasmine wiped her forehead with a napkin the tea boy had given her. Enough excitement for today.

Dilly walked into the tea house and was greeted by a waiter who appeared to know her. He asked her how *kak* Jamal was and led them to a side table that was quieter than the other ones.

'What a cool place to take a break from the hustle and bustle of the bazaar,' Yasmine said, eying the curved roof nooks and pictures of family and celebrities displayed on the walls. *And what a relief to be sitting in a safe place after being followed by a stranger. Does Uncle Aram have anything to do with my stalker? Was this an invitation to follow him, or a warning to stay away?*

'Yasmine, this café is the oldest café in the city,' her auntie said, smiling at her. 'It was built in the 1940s and the photos on the walls date back to different eras in Iraq's history.' She looked around her proudly.

They sat at a wooden table in the corner of the teashop

and ordered their chai. Yasmine was acutely aware that they were the only women in the café.

'We seem to be going back in time,' she said, tying her hair back with a rubber band. Hopefully, that would make her look less conspicuous. She certainly stood out with her white Skechers, flannel trousers and perplexed expression.

'Yes. Our heritage is exhibited on the walls.' Dilly gestured towards the photos. 'That's why the elderly come back to this place.'

'Hmm. That's one of the reasons I came back to Iraq,' she said, smiling. No need for Dilly to know her other reasons for now. 'But the history of the Kurds in Iraq has been fraught with conflicts, hasn't it?'

Dilly sighed. 'Yes. In fact, you should have seen the memorial for those who lost their lives in the 1988 chemical attack on Kurds in the town of Halabja by Saddam's army. You know that five thousand Kurds were killed in one day?'

Yasmine realised a tear was about to escape Dilly's moist eyes. She handed her a tissue. 'I know, Mum commemorates that day in March every year.' *It is never easy belonging to a persecuted people.* She looked around her. Everyone was busy talking so no one could hear them. Anyway, the *Mukhabarat* Secret Service didn't exist anymore now that the dictator Saddam Hussain was dead. Or did they? She brushed that thought aside.

Dilly followed her gaze. 'First we spent our childhood watching newsreels of the Iran-Iraq war in the 1980s and then the Gulf war in the early 1990s.'

Yasmine nodded, willing her to continue talking. 'My mum doesn't like talking about that time.'

'No wonder. Our mother used to cry a lot when our brother Yousef was ordered to fight in the Iraq-Kuwait war.'

'Hmm. Mum told me he died there.' She kept quiet for a few moments, then said, 'But Grandma had another son, Aram. She must have been happy to have him around.'

Dilly pursed her lips and took another sip of her warm tea.

'Why does everyone keep quiet when I mention Aram?' Yasmine put her *istikan* down abruptly and glared at her auntie.

Dilly shuffled in her chair and kept quiet.

'When I was little, Uncle Aram used to carry me on his shoulders and sing me songs in Kurdish. Although I didn't understand them, I still remember the joy in his eyes.'

Dilly remained silent and stirred her chai again after putting two cubes of sugar in it.

'Well, don't you want to tell me what the problem is?'

Dilly looked up at Yasmine and said, 'He was a very mischievous boy.'

Yasmine had to suppress a laugh that was brewing in her throat. 'You're vague. What do you mean by 'mischievous?' Her auntie was beginning to exasperate her.

'He used to climb trees and fall off them.'

Yasmine started to laugh. *What nonsense.* She tugged Dilly's sleeve. 'You can't be serious. Is that all it took to be called *mischievous*? I would say bold.' *Thank goodness Dilly doesn't know what I was up to in university.* The four years of study in St Andrews had been a mad whirl of the

32

usual student binges, some pleasant and unpleasant sexual encounters, and a questioning of the next phase in her life.

Her auntie shrugged and looked away. Then she looked at her directly and said, 'You do know that a djinn sits on each shoulder?'

'Pardon me?'

'Djinns report your good and your bad deeds, Yasmine.'

Yasmine let out a hearty laugh. It was such a relief to laugh out loud, especially after being followed by someone she didn't know.

'Auntie, I'm not going to be enslaved by imaginary djinns. I'll tie them up together.' She hesitated, noticing Dilly's eyes widen in shock. 'Then I'll breathe some life into them.' *As if a djinn has nothing better to do than record people's misdemeanours.*

Dilly cried, '*Kwah neka*, God forbid.'

Yasmine peered out of the window of the *chai khana* and gulped. *No, it can't be him again.* The bearded man who had been following them was walking past the tea house. She ducked behind her auntie, then sank under the table.

Her auntie had her back to the window. She stamped the floor, saying, '*Bismillah*, Yasmine. What are you doing down there? The men around us are looking at you.'

'Um, Auntie Dilly, I dropped my tissue,' Yasmine whispered, staying underneath the table for a while longer. 'And when I picked it up, I noticed lots of ants underneath the table.'

Dilly widened her eyes when Yasmine picked her head up again. *What must she be thinking about this niece of hers, coming from Britain and afraid of ants, but not of the perilous djinn?* Dilly opened her mouth but closed it again. 'Listen Yasmine, we have frogs in our garden in Sulaymaniyah.' She eyed her fearfully and asked, 'Does that mean we have to lock them up?'

Yasmine let out a hearty laugh. 'No, auntie. I love animals, just not ants.'

Dilly looked at her suspiciously.

'I think this conversation should be continued somewhere else,' said Yasmine. 'Let's go. I'll explain later on.'

Dilly looked startled by the sudden end of the conversation but heaved a sigh of relief.

Yasmine raised her head and turned towards the sound of the singing Muezzin calling for prayer.

The men around them continued their games of *tawla,* backgammon, and drinking their chai, but some of the other men left to visit the mosque for their prayers.

Dilly called the waiter to pay the bill.

No doubt, her auntie would have preferred a cosier chat. Yasmine decided to be more careful with her in future. She didn't want her complaining to her mother. There were more pressing issues to sort out. She would need to plan her next steps carefully without causing havoc in a bazaar. If her follower in the bazaar was Aram's friend, why had she run away? Could it be that she was frightened? God forbid. She had never been afraid of anyone. Even the menacing man in the citadel hadn't scared her. Well, not for long.

This incident in the bazaar only made her more desperate to chase Uncle Aram.

5

'The Jeep is ready to go,' Uncle Jamal said loudly, signalling Yasmine and his wife to hurry up and get into it. They had put some water bottles, fruit and nuts in the sturdy vehicle in case the car broke down or they were held up. *Who the heck will hold us up?* she wondered. *Smugglers? Wolves on the mountains?* Yasmine watched her auntie move towards the car.

'How did I agree to this journey, Yasmine? You've only stayed in Erbil for a few days!'

Yasmine ignored the stiffness that infused Dilly's voice. 'I couldn't wait to visit the mountains, Auntie.' She watched her pack another suitcase into the boot, remembering that her mother had told her how she and her sister had run up to the mountains for refuge when Saddam had begun his Arabisation Anfal campaign. *Thank goodness they survived, otherwise I wouldn't have been born.*

Uncle Jamal started to explain that the Kurds were deported to the south where it was more arid than the north. Many didn't survive the journey. Saddam's government provided the Arab settlers with weapons, loans, agricultural machinery and credits. All names were changed to Arab names. The Anfal campaign was named after the eighth sura in the Quran. Over 180,000 Kurds were killed and deported in 1988.

'Uncle Jamal, did the Anfal Campaign get recognised as genocide?'

Jamal wiped his forehead. 'The Iraqi parliament recognized Anfal as genocide in 2008 and the military commanders who carried out the heinous campaign were handed death sentences. Ali Hassan Majeed, known as 'Chemical Ali,' was hanged in 2011.' Yasmine didn't want to upset her uncle anymore so she kept quiet but he added, 'Yet thirty-five years after the massacre, Anfal survivors say they still haven't received compensation from Iraq.'

Yasmine shook her head. She was relieved that she had been born in London, far away from beheadings, rapes and torture. *But what do these mountains portray now? Safety or danger?* Her uncle had not hired a Peshmerga freedom fighter to accompany them on their journey to Sulaymaniyah as this would have cost more, however, he trusted the driver for protection.

Kak Ahmed was the son of one of his cousins. He kept an AK47 in the boot of the jeep. Yasmine had winced when he'd opened the boot to display the rifle. She didn't want to touch it and she would never want to use it. Mum had abhorred violence and Samantha always took spiders out of their house when she was frightened of them. Their house was a sanctuary until her father died, but Samantha had filled the void, caring for her mother and loving her unconditionally after Aram left with no explanations.

Yasmine tried concentrating on what Uncle Jamal was telling her. The Kurdish land rights had not been settled satisfactorily since the 1923 Treaty of Lausanne as they omitted the clauses of the 1920 Treaty of Sèvres, which promised the Kurds an autonomous state of Kurdistan. These clauses were never ratified. Land-grabbing was still happening today. Yasmine nodded but didn't jot anything down in her notebook. She had read about these treaties in uni.

Jamal's voice sounded joyous when he told her that the Kurdish Regional Parliament was established in 1992 and that, after decades of dictatorship, the people in Kurdistan were able to vote for their representatives for the first time in their history.

After driving through the iron-reddened mountains of Shaqlawa, they finally stopped by a turquoise stream to have a rest. Yasmine was relieved as the roads had been a bit bumpy.

'We need to buy some flip-flops and wade our way through the waters to reach Gali Ali Beg, our highest waterfall,' Dilly said, reaching out to one of the coffee vendors.

Yasmine was mesmerised about the canopy of colourful, hanging umbrellas as they waded through the walkway. The umbrellas were held together by a rope and converged into a giant umbrella. They looked commercialised, unnatural, but also blocked the glaring heat out in summer.

After a few minutes, they reached the cascades. Yasmine looked up in awe. The thunderous sound drowned out the noise around her. The water was untouched, unspoiled in its entity, the roar seeping through her frozen body. *But why do I feel cold, unfeeling? Am I a typical child of the diaspora, only loosely connected to her motherland?* She yearned to feel attached to this country, to the people, to herself.

It wasn't just her Uncle Aram, the missing link. She felt there was an association, a relationship, maybe even a danger she needed to explore. She would bide her time. Her distance to trauma was safer than her mother's, of that, she was sure. And yet, she had a recurring nightmare, one where she would reach out to a man, thinking he was her Uncle Aram, only to realise that his face was darkened by something, maybe the nightlight. She would hear a hollow laugh but couldn't decide who was laughing. Since coming to Iraq, she had woken in the mornings with drenched pyjamas, and it wasn't the heat that had caused this.

Uncle Jamal patted her on the shoulder. He was trying to explain something. Yasmine turned towards him absentmindedly as he said, 'These rocks behind the cascades date back twenty-five million years and are a convergence of the Arabic and Iranian plates on the Zagros mountains.'

What a legacy. No people smugglers yet, she thought as she watched some children squeal with joy when their hired boat got closer to the cascades.

'No one can destroy these waterfalls,' Uncle Jamal said. 'They can try to bulldoze our lands, but they can't change the shape of water.'

Yasmine nodded, enjoying his explanation and imagery. She felt her muscles relax as she wriggled her toes in the flip-flops, feeling the tickling water of the waterfall cool her feet.

'Time for some fresh fruit and coffee, Yasmine.' Her auntie had come back to join them, holding a glass of honey she had bought from one of the vendors.

'Just a few more minutes, Auntie.' Yasmine inhaled the pure air, took in the lush foliage and closed her eyes for a moment. The surrounding pale and parched earth had formed an oasis. Would she be able to rise from the dryness of her life to join a fertile spot, a refuge, a sanctuary from the hollowness of her being? And would her estranged Uncle Aram help her fill in the missing jigsaw pieces of her family?

Far away from London, she could find unity with nature, pee in the fields and in spring pick nergiz flowers to her heart's content. But what dangers were lurking behind the mountains? This land had born so much bloodshed and torture. It was time for peace, for protection. Yasmine had entered the country for excitement and a challenge, but an uneasy feeling was overcoming her.

She opened her eyes again. Her uncle and auntie had already moved on towards the vendors selling baklava.

Hmm, a place of safety and happiness in the midst of troubles. She didn't even know what the troubles were, but she shivered when she thought of the journey she had taken leading her to an unknown destination with a hazy outcome.

It was time to get back into their jeep. Yasmine took off her flip-flops and dried her feet. She had never felt so close to Mother Earth as when she had waded through the streaming water around the Gali Ali Beg waterfall.

They all climbed back into the jeep and Yasmine fell into a trancelike state until they reached their next destination.

'Time for a break and chai,' Jamal craned his neck to tell Yasmine and his wife who were sitting in the back of their jeep. 'Your legs must be stiff by now.'

Yasmine stopped tapping her feet in the car, trying to blend in with the music of Fairuz, one of the Lebanese singers her mother admired and occasionally listened to when cooking in the kitchen. Yasmine's ears were not used to the sorrowful Middle Eastern music but it accentuated the melancholy of the region.

She got out of the jeep and walked up to the edge of the Rawanduz Canyon, taking in the panoramic view of the valley. The rock formations rose to the sky steeply. Another layer of a mountain was peeping behind it. The valley bore some green bushes and a stream trickling down through the valley.

'Wow. This is beautiful,' Yasmine said, turning towards her auntie.

'Yes. The name of the canyon comes from Rawn, a famous poet of the area, and Duz, which means citadel or tower. As children, your mother, Aram and I used to come here with our parents. Our mother loved the dusty roads and lush green valley.'

This is the first time she's mentioned Aram of her own accord. Yasmine probed further. 'What did my mum and Aram think about the area?'

'Your mum loved it and wanted to go down to play in the valley. But Aram…' She looked at the vertiginous rock formations and hesitated. 'He hated it. He shouted at our father, saying the river in the valley looked like a snake moving through it.'

Yasmine looked at the river. 'Hmm. That's an unattractive way of looking at it.'

Her auntie shifted her position. 'There was a big fight here. Our father berated him for not seeing the beauty in the canyon and for not joining the Peshmerga freedom fighters.' She hesitated. 'Aram screamed at him, saying he wasn't a coward but that he wanted to stay with our frail mother.' She paused and scanned the horizon to collect her thoughts. 'There was a scuffle. Our father pushed him towards the edge of the canyon. Our mother ran towards Aram and shouted for them to stop arguing. She thought he would fall over the fence and into the canyon.'

Yasmine shuddered and realised that Uncle Jamal had already gone to the nearby houses to get some *chai* from a vendor. She could talk to her auntie alone. *Mum has never mentioned these fights between Uncle Aram and his father, but then she has never talked much about her previous life in Iraq.*

'What happened next?' she whispered.

Dilly looked transfixed. 'As I explained, our father pushed Aram towards the canyon.'

Yasmine's heart pounded. She placed a hand on her chest to calm herself.

Dilly shook her head. 'Our mother grabbed hold of our brother and pulled him away from the edge although a metal fence stood between our brother and the canyon.' Yasmine held her breath. Dilly bit her lip, then said, 'Aram wasn't allowed to get back into the car. He had to find his own way home and it was dark."

'Did he hitchhike?'

'In those days, it was even more dangerous than now. Robbers were in the area. Smugglers were waiting to get their claws into young men like Aram…'

Dilly was about to continue her story when Jamal came back from the nearby vendor. He was beaming and held a tray of steaming chai in four istikans. He said, 'You can count on me for saving my dehydrated family.'

'It's not now we need saving,' Dilly said tersely.

Uncle Jamal stopped in his tracks and frowned. He laid the tray on the wooden table and moved it away from the edge of the canyon.

Yasmine stood still, not daring to move closer to the canyon. Decades ago, it had been the beginning of a family rift.

6

After navigating through some precarious hairpin turns on dusty roads, their jeep wound its way through the mountain towards the white Bekhal waterfalls. Yasmine's stomach churned. She looked forward to stretching her legs and wading through water again. Her neck felt tight after learning about her Uncle Aram's family fights in the canyon.

'I've never seen so many majestic waterfalls in such a small area,' Yasmine said, looking up in awe at the roaring waterfalls that seemed to fall out of the mountain. The water rushed in her ears, pounding like a heartbeat, flowing through her arteries. *Life wasn't stagnant here. It was forever flowing.* That was if the people weren't attacked by surrounding countries, or by members of their own family.

What other stories would she get out of her auntie? She needed to tread carefully. Some memories would be painful for Dilly. Her Uncle Jamal didn't seem to be in the full picture. In Erbil he had always been doing chores outside the house or meeting up with his friends.

Did her auntie and uncle ever have any pillow talk? *Surely, they don't just fall asleep the minute they put their heads on their pillows.* Dilly had told her that she had never seen a man undressed before she met her husband. In fact, she had thought that he had shaved his genitals for the honeymoon. Yasmine didn't know whether to laugh or cry. Geez. She didn't want to imagine them in bed anymore and glanced at the waterfall instead.

A boy of about twelve or thirteen climbed up the wet rocks in flip-flops. He flung a plastic bottle into the water. The surrounding of the waterfall was littered with some other plastic bottles and bags. *The tourism industry needs to sort this out.* Plastic would be deathly for fish and the climate. She remembered the climate change demonstration she had attended in London. There were no demonstrations taking place around the mercurial waterfalls in Kurdistan.

The people here were most probably more frightened of attacks from neighbouring countries, not climate change.

The teenager's father appeared to talk to him assertively, whereupon the boy picked up the plastic bottle and gave it to his father.

Yasmine smiled at the teenager. Why had her mother never mentioned her own father? Had she too been thrown out of the car in the canyon? Surely, Yasmine's grandfather hadn't been that abusive. And what did she know about her grandmother? Hardly anything, only that she hadn't been able to go to school for long and couldn't read or write well. Hmm. She'd need to meet her one day when they finally arrived in the city of Sulaymaniyah.

'Let's sit down somewhere and drink some chai, one of our favourite pleasures.' Dilly nudged Yasmine to follow her towards the café perched on the platform a few metres above the base of the waterfall.

'*Gulakum*, my flower, I hope I didn't frighten you with the story of Aram having to find his way home alone on the canyon?' Dilly touched Yasmine's sleeve gently.

'No, Auntie. You must have endured a lot in the eighties and nineties, during Saddam's Anfal genocidal campaign of terror.' *It was better to talk about politics to distract from the personal problems of the family.*

'Yes, we did. I remember our meals in the house were often interrupted by sirens. We would have to run and hide in our shelter underneath the house.' Dilly kept quiet for a few moments. 'We would open the trapdoor and go down the steep stairs, often accompanied by other neighbours who would knock on our door.' She smiled. 'Aram was the only one who would defiantly stay upstairs.' She took a sip of her chai and added, 'By the time we came back up again, he had eaten up most of the dolma.' She giggled. It was good to see her retell an amusing story amidst the horror of conflict and war.

'So, Aram was a daring brother?'

'Well, not only daring, but provocative at times.' Dilly had a distant look in her eyes.

The waiter came towards them with the kebabs they had ordered. Yasmine made a place for the plates. 'Did you just mention Aram?' The waiter looked at Dilly curiously. 'Aram Kazzaz?'

Dilly kept quiet for a moment.

'I'm only asking because he left his job here all of a

sudden. He looked so much like you.' The waiter was almost apologetic as he stood embarrassed at their table. Dilly looked at him with a guarded expression in her eyes. Surely it wasn't her resemblance to Aram that shocked her.

'Do you know where he went?' Dilly asked quietly, picking up her knife and fork.

'Well, he said he had work to do in Sulaymaniyah.'

'What kind of work?' she asked cautiously.

'He didn't say. But he did mention that he would get much better pay with his new job.'

Dilly almost dropped her fork but caught it at the last minute. *What kind of job would freak her out like that?* Yasmine picked up her cutlery. She needed to get to Sulaymaniyah as soon as possible.

7

The chemical attack on the Kurdish town of Halabja on 16th March 1988 by Saddam Hussain's regime destroyed the morale of the Kurdish parties fighting for their rights. Dilly explained that this was the reason why Kurds took five minutes of silence on that day every year to remember the estimated five thousand people who died of poisoning.

At the time Halabja was gassed, the first phase of Anfal genocide was already being played out with attacks on the PUK (the Kurdish Patriotic Union of Kurdistan) party. They were hidden in the mountain villages of Sergalu and Bergalu. This is where Dilly wanted to drive past. *The family must have some history here.* Yasmine watched her auntie sniff and wipe her tears away as they drove past orchards, farms and very old trees. Jamal didn't seem to notice her distress.

'Some of these oak trees are four hundred years old,' he said, peering at them in awe. Yasmine gasped when she caught sight of the twisted branches of the oak tree. She had never seen trees that were that old in Britain. *How ancient, symbolising wisdom, courage and endurance of the Kurdish people. Thank goodness Saddam hadn't destroyed them too.*

Dilly cleared her throat and said, 'This is Sergalu, the village where Aram was born.'

Yasmine flinched. *Had he been affected by the poisoning of this village?*

Dilly blew her nose and said, 'Our mother had to ride a donkey on her own to get to a house where she could have her baby.'

'Why was she alone?'

'Our father was in prison because he belonged to the Peshmerga freedom fighters.'

'Oh, I didn't know that.'

'Didn't your mother tell you?'

Yasmine kept quiet.

'Anyway, don't worry. We're going to the Shingelbana Holiday Resort near the Korek Mountains.' Dilly brushed away the painful memories with a swipe of her hand. 'We can stay overnight and drive to Sulaymaniyah the following day.' She looked at her with a mixture of pity and hope in her eyes. *She must be wondering what else her mother hadn't told her.*

Uncle Jamal didn't stay in the village, most probably not wanting his wife to cry when looking at the graves on the roadside. He drove through the village quickly until they reached the Shingelbana holiday resort. Yasmine closed her eyes for a few moments. *How could mass graves and a holiday resort lie so closely together, yet separated only by a few decades?* She opened her eyes again as they entered the gates of the resort. Yasmine took in the view of various villas on both sides of the road.

'Wow. I didn't expect to find villas up here.'

Dilly smiled for the first time since leaving the village of Sergalu. 'We're sharing a room and Jamal and the driver will take the other one.'

Yasmine turned to look at her uncle. He was deep in conversation about the song they were listening to, remembering old times. She had no memories of this country or her heritage. Her mother had tried to assimilate in Britain as fast as possible, most probably in order to keep her family as far away from trauma as possible. *And yet, it's here that I'm drawn to, the gap in my heritage and in my roots. Would it be dangerous to defy Mum's eclipse of part of her family? It's too late to ponder on that now.*

After settling into their villa and putting their clothes into the bedside cupboards, Yasmine sat on her bed and took her trousers off. She was about to put her leggings on when a high-pitched scream filled the room.

'Ya, Allah. What's happened to your legs?'

Yasmine dropped her leggings and scrutinised her legs. There was a small scratch on her left leg.

'Don't worry, Auntie, it doesn't hurt.'

'Even if it doesn't hurt,' said Dilly in an irritated voice, 'we can't take you to a *hammam* like that.'

Yasmine looked at her auntie in disbelief. Surely, she was joking. 'It won't get infected. It's just a scratch.'

Dilly jumped up from her bed and said, 'It's your hairy legs, Yasmine. *Stachferallah*, didn't your mother teach you how to remove the hair?'

Yasmine peered at her legs. She'd used the hair removal cream before travelling but stubble was peeping out now.

'You make me laugh, Auntie. I used hair removal cream but it's only just beginning to grow back.'

Dilly came closer to inspect the scene of crime and said, 'It's not cream you should be using. The hair has to be torn off with honey and patches.'

Yasmine stopped laughing. *Hell no.* She wouldn't agree to this torture. She had tried the honey patches as a teenager and had had to stop the removal as it had been too painful to bear.

'Let's talk about this another time, Auntie. We need to do some exploring now.' She pursed her lips and looked at Dilly defiantly who muttered something in Kurdish, whilst looking away from her unsightly legs.

At the end of the day, they left the villa to get a cable car around the resort. Yasmine squealed with a mixture of delight and fear. But the best part of the resort was the breathtaking view of the snow-capped Korek mountains. *A natural winter paradise, not like ice skating in London's Winter Wonderland.* The Kurdish mountains lay dignified around the resort, watching its inhabitants peacefully. *No need to worry about man-made beauty ideals such as waxing.* Yasmine heaved a sigh of relief.

She chuckled as she briefly patted her right buttock. Hidden behind her trousers was a tattoo of a dove soaring into the blue sky, a symbol of freedom and love. *If a dove can spread its wings, I can too.*

8

Yasmine grinned. Her notebook was gathering more information with every day spent in the country:

Sulaymaniyah, a city in the east of the Kurdistan region of Iraq, wasn't far from the Iran-Iraq border. It was named after Sulaiman Baban, who was the first Baban prince to gain control of the province of Sarezûr. The city, also known as Suli, was always a centre of great poets such as Nalî, Mahwi and Piramerd. The population was estimated at 1.5 million Kurds.

As Uncle Jamal drove through the city, he explained the history of Suli in a proud way but stammered when he spoke about the Red Prison – *Amna Sureka*. It *was* one of the headquarters of Iraq's secret intelligence agency, Mukhabarat. He added that in this establishment, they tortured and imprisoned Iraq's Kurds and Assyrians from 1986 to 1991.

He glanced at her sideways as he tried dodging the hooting cars in his way. 'Saddam Hussain commanded the extermination of the entire Kurdish population in Iraq, thousands of Iraqi Kurds and several thousand Assyrians were murdered.'

Yasmine flinched. Her mother had spoken vaguely about the prison. Now, Yasmine would most probably be visiting this notoriety. Auntie Dilly leaned over to embrace Yasmine and added, 'Don't let Jamal dampen your enthusiasm.' She patted her hand and said, 'They couldn't exterminate all of us. Thank goodness, the Jewish population had to leave for Israel in the fifties before the Anfal killings happened. They would have been the next to be exterminated by Saddam's Baath party.'

Geez. So much death and destruction. It would be better to focus on the oak trees and the glimmer of hope and resilience they offered.

Yasmine heaved a sigh of relief when they arrived at their destination. She climbed out of the jeep while Jamal shouted across to the neighbours, an elderly couple and their son who were having lunch in their garden full of budding pink Madagascar periwinkles.

She smiled hopefully. Maybe the neighbours had a daughter her age. As she entered her auntie's house, she counted the 'evil eyes' hung in almost every room. The huge, blue amulets were pinned to the white walls aiming to ward off bad spirits. She went upstairs and unpacked her small suitcase in the bedroom that had been allocated to her. She peered at the hairbrushes and combs on the dressing table opposite her bed.

Photos in silver frames caught her attention, especially a black and white one of her mother and auntie, presumably in their early teens. They had their arms around each other and were smiling at the camera.

Strange that there had been no mention of Auntie Dilly for a few years. They looked so serene in the photo.

Next to that photo was another black-and-white one of an old lady holding a baby in her arms. This must be the grandmother she had never met. She bore a toothless smile, but there was something sneaky in her expression. Her mother had told her that she had worked as a midwife. Hmm. That would make her a bearer of joyful news. But where was Uncle Aram's photo? It was as if he were a phantom. She'd ponder on the missing photos later on.

Yasmine walked towards the window and peered at the lush garden. She watched Jamal push a swing… *How exciting it must be as a trapeze artist, free to swing in different directions.* It had been somewhat restrictive walking around in Erbil's bazaar.

It would have been refreshing for Dilly and Jamal to have children playing on these swings. They would have made loving parents. Yasmine hadn't been told why they never had babies and she didn't want to pry or hurt them.

A lone pomegranate tree stood at the far end of the garden. The sunny weather in Sulaymaniyah would be just the right climate for the tree to bear its fruit.

She opened the window of her room and watched Dilly water the plants and fig tree whilst talking to them. '*Gyanakam*, darling fig tree, you look beautiful. And how you've grown.'

The fig tree would thrive on such tender endearments. A warm feeling overcame her as she sat on her bed trying to sort out her conflicting thoughts on the surroundings of the city. The street vendors selling seeds, nuts and baklava on her way through the city had been very friendly when they had stopped for some bottles of water. But she shuddered when she thought of the neighbouring country, Iran. Mahsa Amini – otherwise known by her Kurdish name – Jina Amini, had been killed by morality police allegedly for wearing a loose headscarf. Some female demonstrators around the world removed their hijabs or cut their hair as acts of protest.

And yet, the critical responses of the Kurds in Sulaymaniyah were muted, as Dilly told her that it was because they still depended on trade, including food from Iran. Food was a basic need, contrary to morals. *How wretched that they couldn't demonstrate against misogyny.* Yasmine kicked off her shoes, furious at the double standards of men and religion.

She hugged herself. At least there had been large demonstrations against the killing of Jina Amini in all the other European countries.

'Yasmine, are you ready?' her auntie shouted from the adjoining bedroom. 'We're all set to drive to Serchinar for dinner. We don't need to cook now.' She sounded relieved. 'You'll love this resort.'

Yasmine flung her suitcase under the bed and ran downstairs to join Dilly and Jamal. She would unpack later on. 'We've got time, Dilly. What's the rush?'

'We don't want to be roaming the streets when it gets dark.'

Yasmine turned to look at her auntie but no explanation was given. They had been to other cities in the dark. What was wrong with this one?

When they arrived in Serchinar, they parked their car

further away from the park and walked into it. Yasmine stopped on the bridge overlooking the small lake.

'Your mother and I used to love this park.' Dilly looked into the distance smiling. 'I used to point out the handsome boys to her.'

Yasmine looked at her auntie curiously. 'Did mum choose some too?'

Dilly frowned. 'No. Oddly enough, she didn't. Maybe because her head was always in her books.'

'What kind of books?'

'Anything she could get her hands on. She had to go to our local library because we didn't have enough shelves.' Dilly let out a laugh and added, 'I was better with my hands and loved embroidering and making jewellery. That's what Jamal said he adored about me – I saved him a lot of money. Ha ha, I didn't have to buy so many clothes and jewellery.'

Hmm. Harry would have liked that too. To spend less money on her. Yasmine raised her eyebrow. Her auntie continued talking about the card games she used to play with her sister and brother. Aram would usually win.

Yasmine's gaze swept across to the other side of the lake. A woman in high heels, almost Yasmine's age, wearing a mini-skirt and red crop top was talking to an older man in shabby clothes. He started gesticulating. The woman shook her head and started to walk away. The man followed her and took her by the arm. She broke away, kicked off her heels and carried them as she ran towards the bridge. Yasmine gasped. She ran towards the slight young woman. Her auntie was still talking about the olden days and wasn't aware that she had left her.

'Are you okay?' Yasmine asked, catching her breath as the woman ran into her on the bridge.

The young woman looked up at her, wide-eyed and trying to catch her breath said, 'You speak English?'

'Um. Yes, I grew up in London.' She quickly added, 'Is that old man bothering you?'

'Please, don't ju…judge me.' The woman stuttered, holding on to Yasmine's sleeve and hugging her tightly, causing her dangly gold earrings to sweep into her face. 'If he catches up with me, he'll k…kill me.' Her mascara was smudged due to her tears. Her accent was Iranian. She cocked her head to one side like a robin and her long auburn hair lay exposed in the wind. It wasn't just her hair that lay uncovered, unprotected. Yasmine looked at her, mesmerised by her red earrings and bright red lipstick. The blush she had used looked like dried flower petals.

The old man walked up to them. '*Ghahba!*' he wheezed, hardly audible, as he grabbed the woman by the arm again.

Yasmine held her breath. She knew the expression as her Uncle Aram had used it when he was annoyed with his girlfriend. It meant *prostitute.*

'Now look here,' Yasmine said, taking the young woman's hand. She looked more like a girl than a woman. 'You can't force this lady to come with you.'

The old man glared at her. 'It's none of your business, you meddling tourist. Go back to your mummy.'

The young woman pushed the man's hand away and stepped behind Yasmine, wiping away the tears that were streaming down her face.

'It *is* my business,' Yasmine heard herself say. 'This woman is my sister.'

The old man looked at her disbelievingly. Yasmine saw her auntie approaching them and tried to sound assertive, waving at her. 'And this is our mother.'

'Yasmine. Why did you run away all of a sudden?' Dilly looked annoyed, eyeing the old man and the young woman suspiciously.

'She was being accosted by this aggressive tramp.'

With hatred in his eyes the old man looked around him and spat at the ground. 'I'm taking her to the police station.'

The young woman started to wail, tugging at her long, curly hair. 'He asked me for my services.'

'And you accepted,' the old man snarled.

'No, I didn't because you said two other men would be included.'

Dilly took hold of Yasmine's arm and retorted, 'Stop this interfering now. What would your mother say to all this?'

'You're not her mother?' The old man growled, staring at Dilly. 'Then go away. This is private.'

'Yasmine, your mother wouldn't like this.' Dilly said exasperated.

'She'd be happy to help. You don't know my mother like I do.' Yasmine answered defiantly, stepping closer to the man. She could smell tobacco on his breath and added, 'I'll call the police myself if you come any closer. I witnessed you grabbing hold of this girl.'

The old man was about to say something but saw Jamal coming towards them. 'You'll regret this. I know where this prostitute comes to every day.'

'I don't want to be killed. Pl…please, Yasmine.' The young woman held onto Yasmine's jacket, almost ripping the sleeve. She had remembered her name. 'I'll do anything for you, clean, cook…' She started crying again. *Was she stuttering because of the crisis in which she found herself or did she always stammer?* Yasmine let the girl hold on to her and felt her heart pounding through the thin fabric she wore.

Dilly tried pulling the girl away from Yasmine but almost stumbled whilst trying to do this.

'Auntie, it's just for a while,' Yasmine said, her eyes welling up. 'Please let her come home with us.'

Dilly looked at the girl with a mixed expression of disgust and pity.

'I'll ask my mother to help us with some money.'

Dilly raised an eyebrow.

The old man looked bemused and seemed to forget his urges for a moment.

Dilly turned to look at him and said slowly, 'We've made our mind up. Go away. My husband is just coming over to us.' The tramp hesitated. Dilly added, 'He knows more policemen than you do. You'll be in trouble if you try to contact them.'

The old man gazed at Jamal who was back from the grocery store and quickening his pace to join them.

'You'll regret this.' The old man's face was reddening with rage. He limped away before Jamal joined them.

'What's going on here?' Jamal asked, eyeing the young woman suspiciously.

'Please Uncle Jamal. We need to take this woman home. She's in danger.' She stepped forward and said urgently, 'The old man wants to kill her.'

Jamal took in the high heels in the young woman's hand and glanced at her mini skirt. She was holding on to Yasmine's jacket again.

'We need to talk to your mother, Yasmine,' Jamal said quietly. 'This was supposed to be a day out, not a danger to our reputation.'

'Uncle, it'll only be for a day. Please.'

He glanced at the crying woman and looked at Dilly who nodded slowly. 'Okay, just for a day… Until we decide what to do.'

The young woman clasped Yasmine's hand and squeezed it. They walked briskly back to the car, taking a different route to the one the old man had chosen and bought some kebabs on the way.

The oldest trade in the world, and the saddest transaction, Yasmine thought, clutching the younger woman's hand protectively.

Tara sat at the dining-room table; hands outstretched as if trying to connect with her new family. This was the name she had given Yasmine after the altercation on the bridge in Serchinar.

'I know you're forming an opinion of me right now,' Tara said cautiously, half in Kurmanji-Kurdish and half in English, looking at Dilly and Jamal as they stood around her with folded arms. 'But I can explain what happened.'

'I don't want to hear about it,' Jamal said, turning towards the door, almost tripping on the carpet.

'Wait,' Yasmine said quickly. 'Let's hear her out. She looks younger than me…so vulnerable, Uncle. Please.'

Jamal stood in the doorway, then looked back at

Tara who had started to sob. Dilly gave her a tissue and Yasmine put her arm around her.

'Okay. But we need to phone your mother afterwards.' Jamal looked at Tara with a mixed expression of pity and disgust.

Tara gripped Yasmine's hand.

'Uncle Jamal, people aren't a homogenous collection. They have each had a different journey.' Yasmine couldn't help raising her voice.

'I'm sorry to have caused you such tr...trouble earlier on.' Tara stuttered, 'but, yes, my travels have been terrible.'

Jamal stopped at the doorway and turned around to face Tara.

'My father disowned me when I told him that my umm, unc...uncle put drugs in my drink and *umm... abused me.*'

Jamal coughed and muttered something Yasmine couldn't understand. He averted his gaze.

Tara's eyes were downcast. *Why should she be embarrassed?* Yasmine felt sick. Tara dabbed her eyes with the tissue in her hand, leaving black streaks under them.

'What's that scar on your forehead?' Yasmine asked.

Tara picked up her head, 'My father threw a b...bottle at me and I couldn't dodge qui...quickly enough. I had to run away from Iran with no money except a purse with some coins from my m...mother.' She put her head in her hands. 'I couldn't even say good...goodbye to my mother.'

Dilly shook her head and said, 'I think Tara needs some rest and a good meal. I'll make lentil soup. She looks too thin.' *Geez. That's an easy way out.* Her auntie scuttled towards the kitchen, leaving the two women and Jamal alone. Yasmine was happy her auntie had used Tara's name. She was an individual made of flesh and blood, not just a woman belonging to a group of horizontal workers.

Tara looked at Yasmine with pleading eyes. *So, this is the underbelly of Kurdish society.* Her mother hadn't told her enough about this.

She heard herself say, 'Tara is a human being. Why do we always have to talk about reputation?'

Jamal retorted, 'This isn't the time to start these discussions.'

'It never is, Uncle. We're all a result of our upbringing and conditioning.' Jamal looked confused. He most probably didn't know what conditioning meant and Yasmine didn't know what the Kurdish word for it was. She continued, 'Tara has a heart and soul.' At this point, Tara started to cry again and got up to hug Yasmine.

Jamal stood helplessly and waited for Tara to stop crying. 'Okay. She can stay for tonight. But she'll have to leave tomorrow.' He turned towards the door and said, 'We'll phone your mother as soon as possible. I know what she'll think of all this. Unbelievable, the danger you've put us in, Yasmine.'

Jamal left the room and Yasmine motioned Tara to sit back in her chair. She patted her back and whispered, 'Don't worry. I'll help you.'

9

The next morning, Yasmine crept downstairs. Tara was trying to get comfortable on the sofa which was too small for her long body. She had changed into Yasmine's tracksuit and had washed her face. As Yasmine entered the sitting room, the young woman sat up and smiled at her, but smile didn't reach her eyes. Yasmine walked towards her gingerly and sat on the chair opposite her.

'I'm so grate…grateful to you, Yasmine. I don't know how to …repay you.' She frowned. 'I haven't got any m… money or possessions, only a cat that follows me around on the umm str…street you found me in Serchinar.'

'What's the name of the cat?'

Tara let out a shy laugh. 'I named her Diva.'

Yasmine gave out a hoot of laughter. 'Oh, why's that?'

'Because she loves being the centre of attention.'

Yasmine nodded and pulled the thin bed sheet over Tara's knees. She spoke softly and stopped stuttering when mentioning her cat. In another life, she would have been a silver birch tree. How much of this job of hers would she be able to cope with? *When would she snap?*

'How can I repay you, Yasmine?'

Yasmine smiled at her, 'Tell me your story, Tara – or whatever other names you have.'

Tara let out another laugh. 'How did you know I have other n…names?'

'You need to have them in such a dangerous job.' *How old had she been when she started this work? It must have been her last resort.*

'How old are you?'

Tara looked away and whispered, 'Sixteen.'

Yasmine didn't ask how she had gotten into the oldest job in the world. They needed to get to know each other better first.

Tara looked at her shyly. 'Why are you h…helping me, Yasmine?'

'Um… When I was your age, I was almost assaulted.' She hesitated and took a deep breath. 'After being spiked in a London pub.'

She looked away from Tara and planted her gaze on the soft teddy bear, the Paddington Bear she had bought Dilly as a present from London. Harry had given her a Paddington Bear whilst in hospital recovering from her spiking incident. After the spiking, it was this spectacled bear with his blue duffle coat and old red hat that had helped to soothe her.

Thank goodness, her friends had taken her home to her mother on that terrible day. What would have happened if she had stayed alone in the pub? What kind of a person would need to spike a girl? She glanced at

Tara. The same type of person who would use a girl like poor Tara.

She tried blotting out the memory of her waking up in hospital with her two mothers at either side of her. They had stayed in hospital till she woke up from the effects of the spiking. *Am I channelling my feelings and efforts into Tara? Geez. I should have faced my demons or gone into therapy many months ago, before delving into this big journey.* She turned to face Tara, who had started speaking again.

"My friend Maryam was k...killed in Dohuk.' Tara sniffled into her tissue. 'Killed by her own father when he found out that his brother had abused her.'

Yasmine bent forward to hug her. She had only heard about honour killings in newspaper articles and never experienced anyone who'd witnessed it in her entourage. Surely men's honour didn't depend on women.

Tara said, 'I don't want to be killed. But this life is not for people like m...me. I don't know if I can continue like this.' She started to cry again and pulled another tissue out of the box on the table.

'Maybe my mum can help us.' Yasmine was surprised that she had used the word 'us.' *Are we in this together?*

'Why would your mother help me?'

'She's a doctor and she helped me when I was drugged.'

Tara took her hand and said, 'I'm so...so...sorry someone drugged you.' She held her face with both hands.

Yasmine said decisively, 'We'll phone my mother soon.'

Tara wrinkled her nose. 'Why should she want to help me? The doctors I've met here don't c...care. I daren't go for my STD checks because the last doctor I consulted, in...insulted me and added that I was a d...danger to men.' She gritted her teeth. 'Doesn't he know that it's a m...man who led me to this kind of life?'

Yasmine reached out and held her hand while Tara buried her face in Yasmine's shoulder.

Tara may have crossed boundaries after her odyssey, but what about the men who had transgressed humanity? If no one helped Tara, she would die in this country.

10

Her mother roared into the phone, 'How could you interfere in this woman's life?'

Yasmine shifted in her chair. It was uncomfortable without a cushion. She should have prepared herself better for the anger that was to come her way.

'But Mum, I wasn't interfering. I was helping her when she was in danger.' There was silence on the other end of the phone. 'You of all people should know that.' *No mention of the spiking I'd experienced.* Her mother wanted to forget that, but Yasmine couldn't brush it aside. A plethora of unwanted shadows in her previous life invaded her mind.

She sat still, waiting for her mother to respond, but it was Auntie Dilly who spoke first. She stood nearby pretending to polish the kettle and said in mock-agreement, 'Yes. She's a doctor. She should understand. People are always in a difficult situation when they come to see her.'

Yasmine shook her head. Her auntie had no idea

about the spiking ordeal she had been through. She glared at her and said, 'There are other reasons for her to be understanding of this situation.' Her auntie looked at her curiously.

'Okay, Yasmine. Where is she now?' Her mother had started speaking again.

Yasmine heaved a sigh of relief. 'She's upstairs – she can't hear us. You have to help us, Mum. Please.'

'Has she got any family?'

'Yes, but they're all in Iran and her father wants to kill her because of what his brother did to her.' She buried her face in her hands. *Honour killings! What about the father's honour as a murderer? Or Tara's uncle's reputation as a sexual predator?*

Her mother had started to speak again. 'Right, you need to find someone to help her to get out of the country and out of Dilly's house. You're all in danger as long as Tara stays there. One more day and then she has to leave.'

Yasmine watched Dilly drying the dishes and said reluctantly, 'Okay, Mum.' At least she had one more day until she decided what else to do.

Dilly put the plates back into the kitchen cupboard methodically and turned around, looking relieved.

'How's Sam, Mum?'

'She's fine, sweetheart. We're both worried about your escapades. You were supposed to get closer to your heritage and culture, not deal with all these other problems.'

'But Mum, this also belongs to our culture.'

There was a crashing noise as Dilly dropped one of the cups she was putting away. '*Stachfarallah,* this doesn't belong to our culture,' she said in a shrill voice. 'This woman is an exception.' She glared at her.

Yasmine touched Dilly's hand gently. It was better not to argue about heritage now. She didn't want to irritate her auntie any more than she already had.

'Yasmine,' her mother said, 'I need to go now. I've got three home visits and a meeting with our asthma nurse in an hour.'

'Okay, Mum. Thanks for being available now. Love you.'

'Love you, darling. Be good to your auntie and uncle.'

Yasmine ended the call and turned to look at her auntie, whose mouth was set in a straight line. 'Auntie, I can cook for us now.'

Dilly hesitated.

'Better still, Tara can cook for us. She learned how to cook our food in the household she was working in before...'

'No. I don't want her to cook for us,' Dilly exclaimed, pushing the washed cups away from Yasmine. 'I'll do some dolma now. I need to keep myself busy to forget all these problems.' She hurried towards the fridge and brought out some vine leaves, peppers and aubergines. 'Allah will hear our plea. He's merciful. Yasmine, you need to speak to Tara. See who can help her when she leaves us.' She turned around to face Yasmine, saying, 'All this is Kismet — it's her fate.'

Yasmine felt her parched lips with her tongue. Tara's fate was not predestined. What nonsense.

The phone call to her mother had taken a few minutes and she hadn't dared to move during that time. Now, she had to go to Tara and explain that she needed to leave. *Is there anyone who can help this girl?*

She slowly climbed the stairs and opened the door to her bedroom where she had told Tara to stay during the phone call. When she entered, Tara was sitting on her bed with a razor blade, pointing it towards her wrist. Yasmine gasped and ran towards her, knocking over Tara's red heels as she did so.

Tara was sobbing as Yasmine slammed the door behind her. She grabbed the razor blade as nimbly as she could and threw it underneath Tara's bed, then she ran her fingers through Tara's hair. It was thinning and a few grey hairs were peeping through the back.

'You've already got grey hair, Tara,' Yasmine said, trying to defuse the situation with a bland statement although her stomach was churning.

Tara put her head on Yasmine's shoulder and continued sobbing. Then she started hiccupping. Yasmine kept quiet and waited for Tara to compose herself.

Tara said, 'It's in our fa… family. My mother started getting white h…hair in her early twenties.'

'When did you last see her?' Yasmine asked carefully, stroking Tara's hair.

Tara furrowed her brows. 'I think it was th…three years ago.' She started to cry again.

'Would you like to see her again?'

Tara wiped her eyes with the tissue Yasmine had had in her pocket. 'Of course. But I daren't. My father would k…kill me.' She looked at the ground.

'Hmm. Okay, what about starting a new life in another country?' Yasmine tried to keep her voice steady, although her mind was going around in circles, making her feel dizzy.

'What country? Most people h...hate me.' Tara looked at Yasmine directly. 'And my pass...passport was stolen by a customer.' Yasmine was overwhelmed by the feebleness in Tara's voice. No, there must be a way out of this rut Tara had been flung into.

'Some countries are better than others,' she replied fervently. 'Do you know anyone who could help you?'

Tara cocked her head and sighed. 'There was a cl... client on the street where I work... I mean worked,' she said coyly.

'Yes?' Yasmine bent forward as Tara's voice was very low.

'He went to the other girls, one spec...specifically.'

'What did that have to do with you?' This girl was beginning to speak in riddles!

'One day, one of my clients threw me out of his c... car...I refused to take his friend into the h...hotel. That wasn't part of our deal.' She covered her face with her hands. 'My face was bruised and I could b...barely walk.'

Yasmine held her hand. There was no end to the awful stories this girl had experienced. 'Did anyone help you?'

Tara picked up her head. 'Yes. The man I mentioned. He saw me trying to h...hobble to the hotel room. When I fell down again, he walked over to help me up. He even took me up to my room.'

'Oh no.' Yasmine covered her face for a moment.

'It's not what you think, Yasmine.' Tara took Yasmine's hands down. 'He didn't want any services from me. He just wanted to help. And to talk.'

Yasmine almost laughed. It reminded her of films she had seen in London. 'What did you talk about?' she asked.

'How I got into this st…state.' Tara let out a laugh. 'And I asked him the same thing.' Yasmine waited for Tara to collect her thoughts. 'I told him that I was running away from my f…father who had disowned me.'

'What about your rescuer?' Yasmine asked.

'He told me that he was thrown out by his traitor of a sister who n…never wanted to see him again.' She hesitated. 'He didn't tell me why.'

'Hmm. Well, he seems to be helpful. What was his name?'

'His name was Alan, I think. Anyway, that's the n… name he was known by. Why?'

'He may be able to help us.' *There I go, using the word 'us' again. As if Tara and I were a team, have something in common.*

'Okay. Here's my plan, Tara,' Yasmine said slowly. 'When you have to leave Auntie's house today, you could find him on your street again.'

'And then?'

'Tell him you know someone who could offer him money to help you.'

'Who on e…earth would that be?'

Yasmine smiled. 'Me.'

Tara's eyes filled with tears. 'Why are you helping me, Yasmine?'

'Let's say I never had a sister.' *There was another reason. But no need to mention the spiking again.*

Tara had such a broad smile on her face, that Yasmine had to grin too. She reached out to embrace her.

'We'll meet again in the National Museum of Sulaymaniyah where my auntie is taking me tomorrow. Bring Alan with you. I'll have some money on me then.'

Tara sat up again. 'I won't be allowed unless I'm wearing decent clothes.'

Yasmine looked up and took in her crop top and tight-fitting red skirt.

'You can take these jeans and I'll find you a blouse. I'll get you a wig from my auntie. You may need it if you have to hide. My auntie has a couple of wigs. God knows why.' She waved her arms emphatically, laughing at the same time.

In the meantime, I need to convince my auntie that I'm interested in getting to know the worthy heritage of her country. She laughed. *Did the underbelly of a society not belong to its culture? What bigotry.* She wouldn't keep quiet.

11

Yasmine felt a lightness in her chest, imagining the help she could get in this museum, not for herself, but for Tara. There was a man that could help them both, that is if he appeared in the museum as planned. Geez. How would she feel, speaking to a man who visited brothels?

When Yasmine stepped out of the car opposite the museum, her auntie said, 'I'm so happy you want to explore your heritage here. It's just the right place to come to.'

Yasmine stood on her tiptoes to see the museum more closely. She smiled wryly. There was no need to tell Auntie Dilly about her plans.

'The Sulaymaniyah museum is the second largest in Iraq and the largest in Kurdistan with collections dating from prehistoric to modern times.' Dilly beamed at Yasmine.

'Sounds great. Thanks for the lift, Auntie.' Yasmine nodded, feeling impatient. 'I can already see the sign above the archway to the museum. It says 'Kurdistan –

the Cradle of Civilisation.' *Poor Tara would know more about this.*

Thank goodness Dilly couldn't read her thoughts.

'Tell me all about your impressions of the museum later on. I need to get some things from the bazaar.' And with these last words, Dilly walked off in the direction of the bustling market.

Yasmine entered the museum and walked slowly through the large rooms, glancing around her from time to time. Would Tara appear today or not? And would she bring the helper guy with her? He sounded weird, helping Tara when she had been in difficulty with the tricky punters, even though he was a user of sex workers' services himself. *What an oxymoron. Is he a psycho?* Anyway, there was no turning back. Tara was in danger and needed help.

Yasmine stopped to read a plaque on climate and environment change. About thirty-five to 18,000 years ago, Sulaymaniyah was much colder and covered by tundra and steppe vegetation with some trees. Red deer, horses and wild goats roamed the streets. Yasmine smiled. She had seen goats and horses on her way here but no red deer. *What a shame.* They would have soothed her from the whirlwind of events that were distressing her after meeting Tara on the streets of Serchinar.

She moved over to the other plaque nearby. It was translated into three languages – Kurdish, Arabic and English. *'The earliest known writing systems were developed in the Middle East around 5,000 years ago.'*

Yasmine looked into the glass cabinet underneath the plaque. Small wedge-shaped cuneiform tablets were displayed. She continued reading the plaque above them.

'Legal theory flourished, expressed in codes of legal decisions such as the Code of Hammurabi.' Yasmine decided to tell her auntie about this Code. She was sure to know about it and be very proud of it. *I'll need more than the Code of Hammurabi now. And how long will it take to get rid of the codes of honour here?* She couldn't help shaking her head.

After a few minutes, Yasmine looked behind her. The museum was half full, but Tara was still nowhere to be seen. *Hopefully, she's still alive. The tramp who had tried to accost her should be beaten up.* Tara had told Yasmine that the other female workers received thousands of dinars for their services. But Tara only got five or ten thousand dinars — barely a US dollar — maybe because of the scar on her face after her uncle had thrown a bottle at her in a drunken rage. *How could she live on that?* There was no other job available.

Yasmine brought her thoughts back to another plaque further down the room. 'Literature and history.' One of the earliest and important works of literature revealed in tablet fragments was the Epic of Gilgamesh, King of Uruk. Yasmine remembered how her mother had proudly told her about this epic as it was the oldest story in the world.

Excavations had unearthed many public and private archives and libraries, such as the famous library of the Assyrian King Ashurbanipal. Yasmine frowned. She had missed an exhibition of King Ashurbanipal in the British Museum a few years ago as she had been too busy studying for her A-levels. *How exciting to finally be able to research Iraq, but also be stepping into the footsteps of my forefathers.*

But then, there was Tara's fearful and doe-eyed look, trying to survive in a society that used her and cast her out at the same time. What horrifying fate awaited her? Yasmine closed her eyes for a moment.

She remembered the time when she had climbed a mountain in Wales, how exhilarating it had been. But then, when she had encountered a rusty sign that said DANGER, KEEP OUT, she had ignored it and strolled onto a cliff edge, slipping all the way down a treacherous mudslide. Would this happen again?

She opened her eyes and walked towards the final plaque. If Tara didn't appear soon, she would need to leave and meet her auntie in the café opposite the museum. *What a waste of time. Well, no, it's not. I've learned a lot here.*

The plaque of Scripts and Languages stated that the four main written languages of historical Iraq were Sumerian and Akkadian, both written in syllabic cuneiform signs, and Aramaic and Arabic, written using alphabets. Apparently, Akkadian, Aramaic and Arabic were Semitic languages whereas Kurdish was an Indo-European language.

Cuneiform signs were written on clay tablets for over three thousand years until Papyrus and paper gradually replaced them. *Thank goodness. Clay tablets would have been too heavy to carry around.* Yasmine let out a chuckle. *How thrilling it would be to grab hold of one of the tablets.* For a moment, she contemplated doing just that, but the sight of a female guard walking around the museum stopped her dreaming about touching the tablet's smooth surface.

She felt a presence behind her and clutched her handbag. Then, she smelt the *La Vie est Belle* perfume she used occasionally. She turned around quickly and almost bumped into a woman wearing a wig with curly brown hair.

'Tara. At last.' Her heart skipped a beat in relief. 'What kept you so long?' She tugged at her friend's sleeve, hoping she didn't sound too desperate. Surely, it was Tara who needed her more.

'Sorry, Yasmine. It took longer than usual to w...walk here.' Tara wiped her forehead.

Yasmine looked at her shoes. 'Well, you're not wearing your heels today.'

Tara let out a laugh. 'No, I'm not. But I had to walk s...slowly because my feet were hurting me. The heels are too tight.'

Yasmine laughed. 'Get rid of them.' She hesitated, then said, 'Is that my perfume you're wearing?'

'Um, yes. I borrowed it.' She looked at Yasmine sheepishly.

'Ah. Is that why it's not in my bedroom anymore?'

Tara looked around her and stifled a giggle.

'Anyway, where's your helper, Alan?' Yasmine followed Tara's gaze.

'He's at the entrance, under the archway.'

'Okay, let's go there,' she said warily. 'I've finished with the museum now.' She grabbed hold of Tara's hand and walked slowly towards the exit of the museum, avoiding the female guard who was watching them from the other side of the hall. 'By the way, what did Alan say about helping you?'

Tara pursed her lips, then said, 'It depends on what you offer him.'

Yasmine winced as she followed Tara. *What kind of a man is this Alan, using a sex worker and protecting another one.*

As they approached the entrance of the museum, Tara walked towards a slim man with a goatee beard. He was wearing black jeans and a brown jacket with the lapels turned up. He had shoulder-length hair and was taking a few puffs of a cigarette whilst looking down at his shiny shoes.

The man slowly picked up his head to face Yasmine. She could hear his sharp intake of breath and immediately smelt tobacco. His posture stiffened. He stared at her for a split second. 'Did your mother,' he gulped, trying to compose himself, 'put you up to this?'

Yasmine blinked at him, confused. *What was he talking about? Her mother wasn't even in the country. What did she have to do with this business?*

Now she knew what the expression 'blood curdled' meant. Her blood seemed to stagnate. A heavy feeling in her stomach dragged her down. Her mind was fuzzy.

She blinked as she faced Alan, otherwise known as her Uncle Aram, the uncle she had last seen in her mother's house in London when she was a child. She stared at him, trying her best not to tremble. He had put on weight. His eyelids were drooping, as one would expect for his age, his gleaming brown eyes had lost their shine. He would be in his early fifties now, younger than her mother, but he had definitely not aged as well.

Aram cleared his throat. 'So, we meet again, eh? Underneath the Cradle of Civilisation.' His laughter didn't sound as light as it used to. It had a layer of sarcasm and bitterness.

Yasmine felt frightened and glanced at the front door of the museum. His sister, Dilly, would be entering it any minute. Her mind started racing – Aram, Dilly, her mother – saints or villains? It didn't make sense. She saw Aram's lips move. Of course, he had started speaking again. The shock was mutual.

'Admit it. Your mother put you up to this,' Aram said again through gritted teeth.

'No…not at all. She isn't even he…here.' Yasmine stuttered. *This was how Tara would stammer when anxious. Never in her wildest dreams had her favourite uncle presented himself in this way.*

'What do you want?' He hesitated. 'Or rather more, what have you got for me?' He smiled suddenly, glancing at Tara who was watching them wide-eyed.

'Is this your uncle?' she blurted out.

'Yes, I'm her long-lost uncle. Banished from the house of good reputation.' He laughed.

'You weren't banished,' Yasmine said slowly, regaining her confidence. 'You walked away without saying goodbye.' *I must sound so naïve. I need to get a grip of myself.* She tried standing on her tiptoes to match his height.

Aram came closer. She could feel his stale breath as he said, 'Didn't your mother tell you why I left so suddenly?'

Yasmine inched away whilst looking at him directly. 'You tell me,' she said, trying to raise her voice to match his.

'Ah, I like that, the fighter spirit. Not like your mother – passive and...' He had an inquisitive look in his eyes.

'Please stop,' Tara said, trying to hold Aram's arm. 'I didn't want to cause t...trouble.'

'Your name is "trouble",' Aram spat out, glancing at her for a second.

Tara stepped towards Yasmine who instinctively put her arm around her. *Why am I here, getting involved in another woman's fate?* Yasmine had no time to put her thoughts into chronological order. She looked at Aram disgusted. *But what was I expecting? What had Mum been hiding?*

'Where's the money?'

Yasmine flinched and turned her thoughts back to her uncle. His eyes had widened, the razor-sharp smile had returned.

'How are you going to help Tara?' Yasmine tried to sound bold.

'In the only way possible – with money.' He laughed as he turned his trouser pockets out.

'I mean, how can you help us?'

Aram cocked his head. 'Let's see... Maybe get her a false passport.' He let that proposition dangle in the air before continuing, 'And smuggle her out of the country.'

Yasmine felt her hands shaking. *What would Mum say? Getting involved with people smugglers, one of them being my own uncle.*

'I ... I need to speak to my mother first.'

'Ah, Baba needs to speak to her Mama first.' Aram imitated her voice.

She stood still, feeling small, no matter how high she had felt standing on her tiptoes.

Aram grinned and said, 'Here we are, standing underneath the words *cradle of civilization* and yet Yasmine isn't out of her cradle yet.' His laughter echoed loudly.

'How dare you say that!' she retorted. 'I came all the way to this country.'

'Only to be mollycoddled by my other sister, Dilly.' Aram laughed, keeping her in his sight.

Yasmine was about to turn towards the wide-open door at the exit when Tara grabbed her arm and pleaded, 'Please Yasmine, I can't continue like this. I would rather d…die than continue my um… job.' She started to sob.

Yasmine glared at her uncle who stood cautiously, watching her move back towards Tara.

'I need time to think about this.' She tried to sound tranquil and collected, but felt the rage rise up in her.

'Okay. I'll give you two days to think about our problem.' He folded his arms and waited for her reply.

So now it's 'our problem.' He has included himself in our team, a team of illegal dealers. Never in her wildest dreams had she expected to find her uncle here with sex workers. Did her mother know about this? She looked away from Aram, the very man she had been looking for, a substitute for her father. The memories of him cuddling her when playing hide and seek in the garden in London crumbled. Menacing visions of him playing with the sex workers took their place. Yasmine couldn't breathe. She took Tara's hand and stuttered, 'Let's go and have some chai with *decent* people.' She tugged at Tara's sleeve.

Tara stood still and said bluntly, 'Your auntie doesn't want me.'

Aram started to laugh. 'Ha ha. Yasmine, you're already with decent people – me and Tara.'

Yasmine pushed past him and turned towards Tara saying, 'I'll speak to my auntie.'

Tara hesitated, looking at Aram and her undecidedly, with tears in her eyes. Aram put out his arm for her to hold onto, grinning at Yasmine. Tara took Yasmine's hand instead, avoided his gaze and followed her towards the exit.

The cradle of civilization was becoming the death of civilization. A cage. Yasmine hurried towards the open door. She needed fresh air before speaking to her auntie and mother. These events were happening too quickly. She was on a train rushing ahead and struggling to grasp the images of the countryside and people surrounding it. Dizziness engulfed her. She ran outside to inhale the fresh air she so badly needed before tackling her auntie in the nearby café.

12

illy was sitting at the front of the café. A waiter was speaking to her, probably taking her order. She noticed Yasmine entering the café and waved, then caught sight of Tara trailing behind her. Her smile vanished. She finished chatting to the waiter and stood up to approach the two young women, a scowl on her face.

'*Haram.* What is *she* doing here?'

'Auntie, let me explain.'

'You've brought us nothing but problems, Yasmine.'

What a fucked-up way of looking at life, Yasmine thought, glancing at Tara, the abused girl and outcast who reminded upright citizens of the vice amongst them, too abhorrent to acknowledge.

They stood at the doorway. Dilly's face looked ashen; despite the faint red blush she had applied. The waiter came over to them and asked whether they wanted to sit down or leave. He looked at Tara curiously, paying particular attention to her wig. Yasmine hesitated but decided to lead the way to the table she had been sitting at.

Tara followed her quietly with downcast eyes. Yasmine

avoided the glances they got from the other visitors of the café.

At the table, Dilly took a deep breath and said, 'What's going on, Yasmine? You said you would be at the museum.'

'I was there, then I met Tara.'

'Just by accident, I suppose.' Dilly folded her arms. Yasmine sat down and beckoned Tara to do the same. The visit to the museum had shaken her. Under different circumstances, she would have mentioned Aram. After all, he was Dilly's brother. But something held her back. His menacing allure was confusing. Had he forgotten their childhood fun and games?

Yasmine kept quiet. The waiter came back and they all ordered the same qahwa qaswan coffee, not daring to stray from Dilly's proposal of her favourite drink.

Yasmine's mouth felt like sandpaper. She sipped the glass of water the waiter had left them on their table. Shit. She should think of an excuse as to why Tara met her in the museum.

'Was Tara doing research in the museum too?' her auntie asked, looking at Tara disdainfully.

Tara looked at the floor. Yasmine began to feel annoyed. *Why do I have to justify myself when Dilly is keeping bigger secrets about her brother?*

'Dilly, why didn't you tell me your brother is here?'

Dilly sat up in her seat. The colour drained from her face. 'What? Whose brother?'

'Your brother, Dilly.' Yasmine waited for this to sink in. 'You know his name.' She felt emboldened by the confusion on her auntie's face.

Silence ensued. Then her auntie stuttered, 'I didn't know he was here. I...I thought he had returned to Erbil.' She looked away, unable to meet Yasmine's eyes.

'Aram is very much here. The waiter in the Bekhal waterfalls alluded to his whereabouts. Remember?'

Dilly frowned.

'Now it's my turn to ask what's going on.' Yasmine reached out to touch her auntie, but Dilly didn't take her hand.

While her auntie was weighing up her response, Yasmine said, 'Either there are gaps in your memory concerning Aram or you're hiding something from me.' She watched her expectantly, well aware that she was hiding something from her auntie, too.

'Some things are better left unsaid.' Dilly sat up in her seat, eying Yasmine warily.

'We're a family, Dilly. What can be so awful that you can't share it with me?'

Dilly turned towards Tara and said scornfully, 'She doesn't belong to our family. We can speak when she leaves.'

Tara looked up and nodded. 'S...sorry, Yasmine. I'll go now.'

Yasmine glanced at both of them and said tearfully, 'For the time being, Tara.' She took out the eighty dollars she had in her pocket and surreptitiously handed them over to Tara underneath the table, without her auntie noticing. She mouthed the words *hotel* and squeezed Tara's hand.

Tara wiped a tear going down her cheek and said, 'Thank you for trying to help me.' She glanced at both of them before hurrying out of the café.

When she saw Tara had crossed the road outside the café, Yasmine turned towards her auntie and said, 'Now we're alone, please explain what happened between my Uncle Aram, Mum and you.'

Her auntie took a deep breath and replied, 'Now is not the right time to speak about those matters.'

Yasmine looked at her wide-eyed. *It was never the right moment to speak about family matters, either for her mother, or for her auntie. God. I'm going to be more open with my children if I ever decide to have any.*

Her auntie had started speaking again. 'We need to speak to your mother first.'

Yasmine opened her mouth to remonstrate but Dilly said, 'She's your mother, I'm your auntie.' And with that, she refused to answer any other questions. It was time to leave the café. What a mess she was in.

13

After much deliberation and cajoling in the morning, they had agreed to FaceTime her mother in the evening at seven o'clock English time, which would be nine o'clock Iraqi time. *What a relief.* Yasmine bit her lip. *That gives me time to convince Dilly and Jamal that Tara could be in grave danger.*

She sat on the highchair next to her auntie in the kitchen. Yasmine wondered how Tara had spent the night. Hopefully, a stint in the hotel would give her enough energy to continue. *What exactly?* They hadn't mapped out a plan yet.

Uncle Jamal came into the kitchen and picked up his cup of tea. Dilly was sitting at the table, peeling some potatoes. She looked up at Yasmine. 'You're used to eating potatoes in England, instead of rice.'

Yasmine looked at her and laughed. 'No, I still like eating rice, especially yours, Dilly.'

Dilly looked up. There was a faint smile on her face. *She must be gleeful, thinking that Tara will disappear out of their lives soon.*

Jamal watched them quietly, then said, 'Yasmine, we could visit a photography exhibition nearby so you could switch off from your worries.'

Yasmine smiled. Her uncle was trying to show her the entertaining part of Sulaymaniyah. She hesitated. Tara was as much a part of the city as the buildings in it.

Her uncle stepped closer to her. 'You should see us on Eid, when Ramadan finishes.' He beamed at her. '*Walahi*, our wives cook on huge pots and pans over a large fire, preparing food for hundreds of people.'

Yasmine nodded.

Her uncle added, 'I'm so proud of our women.'

Yasmine couldn't help scowling. *Is Tara not someone to be proud of? Why should she be condemned as a perpetrator of sins when she's just a victim? No. She is a heroine to withstand and survive so much aggression.*

Her uncle watched her cautiously for a few moments, then said, 'I think it's good for you to visit the Amna sur Museum, part of your heritage.'

'That's a great idea, Jamal.' Dilly stopped peeling the potatoes and turned to look at Yasmine. 'It's daunting but you need to see it. We've got plenty of time before we call your mother this evening.'

Why is this museum daunting? Yasmine nodded with half a smile on her face. *Daunting* places matched her frame of mind at the moment.

'Okay, Let's get ready,' Jamal said. He paused, then added carefully, 'This Museum is a prison that was built in 1979 and finished in 1985.'

'A prison?' Yasmine asked, picking up her weary head.

'Yes. It is an important historical site for commemorating the resistance of our countrymen—'

'And countrywomen,' Dilly added, throwing her husband a reprimanding glance.

'Yes, yes. Resistance against our Baath dictator party occupiers and oppressors.' Jamal looked past Yasmine at the photo of his brother on the wall next to the door. Yasmine remembered that he had been martyred during the ethnic genocide in the nineties. This museum wasn't going to be as jovial as the previous one, but Jamal looked eager to show it to her. Hopefully, Aram and Tara would not show up here. She needed a break from these encounters.

The visit to the museum would buy her time to think about a strategy in approaching the subject of Tara with her mother again, especially now that Aram had reappeared. Anyhow, *why should she be hesitant in mentioning this encounter when her mother had been silent about her brother for more than a decade?*

Yasmine was getting to learn about her society and family here, no thanks to her mother. She clasped her hands tightly. There wasn't any need to be afraid of speaking to her mother that evening, but there was the issue of getting Tara a passport and smuggling her out of the country. Her mother had been furious about a programme on TV portraying smugglers as callous Kurds. Many women and children had died trying to cross the perilous English Channel. How would she convince her mother about rescuing Tara? She couldn't be left to her own devices. What future lay ahead for her in Britain?

It was true that there were laws in place protecting

refugees, but they were still being attacked and vilified. Plans had been underway to send them to Rwanda and taxpayers were annoyed about the amount of money that would have to be spent on this plan. Yasmine shook her head. Thousands of Rwandan Tutsis and some moderate Hutis had been killed brutally and women had been raped before Yasmine had been born and yet British politicians had wanted to send asylum-seekers to that country.

Her mother and Sam had told her that people who originally came to the UK to seek asylum made up 0.6% of Britain's population. Thank goodness, the Rwandan Scheme had finally been abandoned. What if Tara could escape to Germany? But then she didn't speak the language. *What a quagmire.*

Yasmine took one of Dilly's peppers on the kitchen table and took a huge bite.

'Goodness, Yasmine. You must be hungry!' Her auntie looked at her surprised.

Hungry for explanations, Yasmine thought, glaring at her auntie impatiently. 'Let's go, Uncle Jamal.' She watched him reaching out for the small cucumbers. 'We need to be back on time for the phone call with Mum.'

Jamal raised his eyebrows, no doubt wondering why she was so eager to go when just a few moments ago she had seemed uninterested about other matters and reluctant to speak to her mother.

A feeling of unease crept upon Yasmine. *I feel as though I'm stuck in a whirling vortex of a complex society and I'm not sure whether I can swim against it or whether it would be easier to be left trapped inside.* Yasmine groaned, picked up her dusty rucksack, and strode towards the door.

14

S he glanced at the huge grey plaque at the front of the museum. It stated: *National Museum Amna Suraka – Not to be Forgotten.* Large dark green tanks stood outside the Museum. Yasmine shuddered. Roses grew in the flowerbed underneath the plaque as if to defy the gravity of contents and memories of the museum, whatever those memories portrayed.

The sections of the buildings were lined up – Museum Offices, Peshmerga Museum, Kurdish Genocide Museum. *This isn't going to be easy.* Her neck muscles tightened. Other sections were the Exodus Museum, Anfal Museum, Martyrs of ISIS war Museum, Mine Museum, Heritage Museum and Jails and Torture Section. *Shit. What kind of state will I be in when I leave this museum? I should have agreed to the photography exhibition Uncle Jamal had offered, but it's too late now.*

Would it be like the Chamber of Horrors in Madame Tussaud's? Yasmine couldn't help trembling. Her mother had mentioned the jails in Sulaymaniyah but had never been explicit about the torture. Yasmine glanced at her uncle. *I'm not alone. I'll be okay.*

The first hall was illuminated with hundreds of lit up mirrors, each symbolising the dead Kurdish victims of the Arab Baath regime under Saddam Hussein. *Thank goodness this isn't starting with a chamber of horrors,* Yasmine thought, looking around her at the reflective mirrors. She peered at the small mirrors, each one reflecting fragments of herself. Despite the illumination of the hall, her skin prickled. *If ever I encounter a haunted place in my nightmares, this will be it.*

In the following section of the Museum, Yasmine read the writing on a white plaque hung up for visitors to see: *March 3rd, 1991, is considered a turning point in our nation's struggle for freedom.*

Jamal followed her gaze and said, 'The 1991 Iraqi uprisings against Saddam Hussein lasted a month after the ceasefire following the end of the Gulf War against Iran.'

'Why after the war with Iran?' Yasmine asked, surprised.

'Because Saddam was perceived to be more vulnerable and weaker afterwards.' Jamal paused. 'However, during this one-month period of unrest, thousands of Kurdish people died and millions were displaced.'

'That sounds terrible, Uncle. Did any of our relatives die?' she asked gently.

Silence ensued. Jamal looked at her indecisively, then said, 'Humanity was asleep. However, the United Nations passed the resolution which resulted in the no-fly zone for our undefended nation in Iraqi Kurdistan.' He looked at the floor. 'But it was too late for thousands of Kurdish women and children. Their husbands had either died during the war or the following uprising.'

Was my grandfather one of the people who had died here many years ago? Her mother hadn't openly grieved about it. How weird.

As they strolled into the next section of the museum, photos of mass exodus, women carrying infants, plastic sheets, self-made shelters and tents appeared. Barbed wire was placed in front of these photos. *Geez. The atmosphere is getting worse.*

The sharply pointed wire twisted around at short intervals reminded Yasmine of concentration camps and oppression, but also of Amnesty International's logo – a candle surrounded by barbed wire. *The candle represents hope.* It would bring some light into her soul, or better still, into Tara's spirit.

Colourful newspaper articles were displayed. Yasmine read the front page of *Paris Match* stating '*Kurdes L'Horreur*' and written next to it: *Les Photos commentées pour nous par Danielle Mitterrand.* Her mother had adored Danielle Mitterrand; the French President's wife was a friend of the Kurds, having visited them many times. She was touched by the French sympathy, deciding that her next trip would be to Paris, the city of love. For a moment, she suppressed a chuckle. Who would she go with? No time to think about Harry now.

Jamal stood in front of a photo and drew in a sharp intake of breath. This was out of character. Yasmine stared at him, not knowing what to do.

The photo revealed an old lady with a white turban and a walking stick. She only had one leg and no shoes.

'I can't stand this,' Jamal started sobbing. Yasmine

hesitated, then put her arms around him. She had never seen him cry before.

'It must be very difficult, Uncle.'

'It is, especially, when it's a photo of your auntie,' Jamal almost choked.

Yasmine stifled a gasp and squeezed Jamal tighter, not daring to move away from the photo.

'I loved her so much,' Jamal sobbed. 'She couldn't keep up with us running up to the Iranian mountains. We begged her to let us carry her but she refused, insisting she would manage on her own.'

Yasmine peered at the photo again. 'What happened to her?'

'We never saw her again. We heard that Saddam's henchmen got hold of her and put her into this prison.' Jamal covered his face. 'She died here. Her corpse was left to rot and thrown to wild dogs.' Suddenly, he looked up at her and said, 'Thousands of people demonstrated against the war between Israel and Palestine. Who demonstrated against the genocide of the defenceless Kurds?'

'Uncle,' she gulped, 'of course we cared. My mother was at one of those demonstrations against Saddam Hussain.' Yasmine felt slightly sick and wished they could leave the Museum soon. This may have been educational, but it was getting too personal. *Geez. Had I really asked for this trip?*

Her uncle took her hand and said, 'You must see more of this, your heritage.'

She took a deep breath and followed him into the other rooms of the museum. *This wasn't the kind of heritage I had been looking for.*

94

The next room displayed a map with the title '*The Anfal Campaign: February – September 1988.*' On it, Yasmine could see where chemical attacks had taken place and the known mass execution sites. Resettlement complexes were also highlighted. She couldn't shed any tears although she was shocked, maybe because she belonged to the second generation of displaced victims. She turned to look at her uncle who was still sobbing.

Yasmine caught sight of another highlighted plaque with the words 'Ali Hassan Al-Majeed is the one who said about his Anfal crimes: '*Was it possible to leave those goats in peace? Looking after them? Serving them? No...Never. The best way was to bury them by bulldozers.*'

She quickly led her uncle to a different room. Being compared to goats being bulldozed would make him cry more. *What obscenities ethnic cleansing led to.*

The next image was more hopeful. It was a photo of a Kurdish Freedom Fighter tearing up an ISIS flag and waving a Kurdish flag instead. Next to this was an array of flags displaying countries which had made mines used in Kurdistan. She was shocked to find flags of twelve countries, one of which was also involved in de-mining the same region they had targeted.

The hypocrisy of war, she thought, inspecting a small grey mine displayed in a glass cabinet. The specification noted that the mine was four centimetres high and fifty-six centimetres wide. She had only seen mines on television when Second World War ones were found by chance. *Hopefully I'll never encounter one.*

Her mother had interviewed some mine victims with lost limbs in a hospital she had visited in Erbil decades ago. *At least they survived.* Of all the patients her mother had treated in London, none of them had been mine victims. It would have triggered her. Thank goodness, she had emigrated to Britain.

Jamal kept his distance from the statues, especially the one of an ISIS soldier in black attire wielding a knife. Her uncle's hunched shoulders brought about a tenderness towards him that Yasmine hadn't felt with Uncle Aram, even before she had met him here in Sulaymaniyah.

She peered at graphic photos of ISIS soldiers beheading their victims. In one of the photos, a man was about to be thrown off a high building. Yasmine remembered this story. Her mother had told her about the reason for his death. It was a gay man who was thrown off a high-rise. She shuddered as she thought of what a politician had claimed in London: 'One cannot come to Britain claiming asylum for *simply* being gay.' Being gay was still deathly in many countries. And what about gay families? Were they not entitled to life? *What would have happened to my mothers?*

Yasmine suddenly felt homesick. She wanted to speak to her mother again, to feel her tousle her hair when she was anxious and to embrace her tightly when she came back from work.

'Uncle, can we leave now?' she said in a low voice.

'Not yet, my dear. I wanted to show you your Uncle Aram's cell.'

Yasmine jumped backwards and stared at Jamal. Had she heard the name correctly? No one had told her that Aram had been in an infamous prison. *How could I turn back now?*

Jamal shuffled towards a batch of cells in another part of the museum. Yasmine shivered as she followed him.

'This was Aram's cell,' Jamal stated flatly. Yasmine peered at a damaged, white-tiled room with a broken lock. She didn't dare move.

'Aram told us that he had been kept standing in this room for hours and every time a security officer passed by, they would put out a cigarette on his skin.' He covered his face. 'Those barbarians!'

Yasmine felt her muscles freeze. The damp air in this prison made her tremble even more. The mould was the least of her problems. The lack of oxygen drained her energy reserves. She wanted to leave, but she needed to find out more about her uncle, the man who used to play with her joyfully as a child. The man who was now involved in people trafficking.

Cautiously, Jamal moved to the next caged cell.

'A hundred and fifty men were kept here. They were detainees waiting for their release. But their suffering continued because they had to sleep in turns for some hours.'

He turned to glance at Yasmine. 'Three brick spaces were not enough to sleep all the time.'

Yasmine nodded and peered at the various rugs on the bare floor. They didn't resemble the beautiful kilim her mother had brought back to Britain.

I've only ever slept in a comfortable bed. How lucky I am to have been born in a different era and a different part of the world.

'What about women? Were they kept here too?' She licked her parched lips, hoping that the women had been spared.

Jamal looked at her sadly. 'Yes. They were imprisoned in the next room which housed about fifteen to fifty women, some of whom were pregnant.' He hesitated, weighing up his next words. 'They delivered here.'

Yasmine gasped as Jamal stopped talking for a few moments. Then he continued, 'The babies and children were isolated to force the mother to admit the crimes they never committed.'

Yasmine couldn't help scrunching up her face. Did the perpetrators have no babies or children of their own? Or were the imprisoned women lesser moral beings than the soldiers' own wives?

Yasmine and her uncle stood closely together, each an island of grief. She reached out and took his hand and squeezed it gently. She felt so close to him at this moment of horror and sorrow. Their hands branched out simultaneously; they were rooted in the same earth despite having different memories.

When they left the women's section, Yasmine winced as she caught sight of the white statues of a mother and toddler hugging. What if her mother had been imprisoned in this notorious prison? Yasmine would never have been born. She wiped the tears trickling down her face.

She followed her uncle towards another part of the prison, hoping the journey into her heritage would end soon. She couldn't bear much more. But it would be worse for Uncle Jamal, having this previous prison at his doorstep. At least Yasmine could run back to her safe place in London. But no, she didn't want to return yet. She had a few rescue missions – Tara and… She frowned.

Could it be that she was trying to rescue herself, and if so, from what? She brushed the thought aside.

Her uncle explained that the corridor leading to the last section of the museum was stained with blood because the detainees were pushed against the wall when they were transferred to a red-lit room. Yasmine read this horrific news on the plaque hanging on the wall. Blood had always scared her, but now it was the violence entangled with it that made her own blood boil.

Her uncle told her there was a final room, then they could go back to daylight. Yasmine heaved a sigh of relief but as she entered this room, she realised why the lights were all red. *It was the chamber of horrors, a red-lit room of torture.*

The statue of a victim was laid on the bare floor, legs bound together on a pole held by two henchmen who were standing next to him. A statue of the third henchmen was portrayed holding a stick and beating the victim's feet.

'That's enough, Uncle.' Yasmine said, feeling her stomach churn.

He nodded and held her hand as they left the final and worst section of the museum. Yasmine felt a bond she hadn't experienced with Jamal prior to this visit. Both of them belonged to a nation hated unto death and surrounded by enemies.

Outside the rooms, she breathed in the cool air. Her lips felt parched again and she badly needed a drink and a break.

'Uncle, can we please sit down in the café on these grounds? I don't think I can wait till we get back home.'

He looked at her apprehensively and nodded. 'Of course. I need a drink myself.'

They sat outside and waited for the waiter to come and take their orders. Both of them were quiet.

Yasmine peered at the large tanks again. She had never experienced war. But this museum was a visceral reminder of how devastating it was, even after it came to an end.

'Uncle, when did Aram come out of this prison?'

Jamal squinted. *Is the thought painful, or is he simply keeping out the bright daylight?*

'As soon as Saddam was killed, his cowardly henchmen retreated, and we were allowed to go inside this prison.'

Yasmine nodded, encouraging him to continue the story.

'We looked for him but couldn't find him. It was only after a man called out Dilly's name, that we realised Aram was still alive. He had grown a beard and was so thin that Dilly didn't recognise him at first.'

'And then?'

'We took him home to our house and fed him.'

'What did he tell you?'

'He didn't want to talk about his ordeal, so we didn't probe him.' Jamal frowned. 'Did your mother not tell you about this?'

'No. She was already in Britain. I don't know why she won't talk about him.'

'You can't ask her on the phone but you do need to talk to her when you get back,' Jamal said, picking up a tissue that had fallen on the ground.

Will Mum ever tell me the full story? But now is not the right time. She needed to plead for Tara's life who was very much in danger of being killed in this country. Uncle

Jamal and Auntie Dilly were witnesses of crimes of the previous generation.

Tara was a victim of the present generation, an abused and used woman whose death would no doubt not be missed by anyone but Yasmine herself.

I won't let Tara be erased.

15

Dilly had texted her mother that a problem had arisen and that they needed to talk to her. *So now it sounds like I'm the problem.*

Yasmine put her laptop on the kitchen table, ready to FaceTime her mother. Dilly and Jamal were in the sitting-room, waiting to come in as soon as Yasmine had spoken to Sozanne. *I hope this won't end up in an argument.*

She took a deep breath as she glanced at the clock on the wall. Three o'clock. Her mother would have finished morning surgery and home visits. She would be sitting at home with Sam on her afternoon off and planning the weekend, maybe a trip to a West End Musical. *How I miss those.*

She waited for her mother to appear on the grainy screen.

'Hello Yasmine.' Her mother was smiling but the creases around her eyes had spread. 'How are you? I miss you.'

'I'm fine, Mum.' *Well, I have to start off that way, don't I?* 'I miss you, too, but I'm visiting some museums here and taking notes.'

'Oh, are the notes for your diary?'

'Kind of. I'm thinking of writing some articles on women's' rights.'

Her mother looked surprised. 'When you come back, of course.'

Yasmine raised an eyebrow and said, 'Are you worried I'll cause a problem here?'

'Well, you do have to be careful how you express yourself there.'

'Are you afraid I'm going to make people feel insulted?' Yasmine asked curtly, although she knew that censorship was widespread.

The answer came quickly. 'No, darling. Just be careful.'

My mum's always trying to be invisible, especially when she's outside the house with Samantha. Yasmine shook her head, realising that she preferred being loud and clear to the extent that her situation was becoming dangerous.

'Mum, Let's get straight to the point. Jamal and I went to the Amna Suraka Museum today.'

Her mother looked at her warily. 'Oh, that must have been challenging.'

'Um, it wasn't only demanding.' Yasmine hunched her shoulders.

Her mother nodded and waited for her to speak again.

'Uncle Jamal started to cry,' Yasmine blurted.

Her mother picked up a glass of water on the table in front of her. 'He can get very emotional.' She sipped the water and added, 'The museum is a portrayal of a dark phase in Kurdish history.'

'But, Mum, the museum is not only a dark place in our nation's history.' Her mother looked puzzled. Yasmine decided to come straight to the point. 'Aram had been in one of those prison cells.'

Her mother's eyes widened. She put the glass of water down and clasped her hands as if to compose herself. 'Who told you that?'

'Uncle Jamal. Why? Did you want to hide that fact? Like many other things?' She felt herself trembling. She drew in slow, steady breaths. *How many more mysteries am I supposed to unearth in this city?*

Her mother kept quiet for a few seconds, then said in a cold voice, 'I don't want to hear that name.'

'Why Mum? We need Aram now.'

'What?' her mother shouted into the screen, losing her well-guarded composure.

Yasmine sat up on her wobbly chair and replied, 'What Aram must have endured in that prison!' She trembled. 'How could you have kept such an important matter away from me?'

Her mother looked down at her desk. 'It was to protect you,' she answered slowly.

'I don't need protecting, Mum, but I do know someone who does.'

Her mother looked up again, cautiously.

'I met a young woman here who needs our help.'

'Where did you meet this person?'

'In Serchinar when I was on a walk with Dilly and Jamal.'

'Oh my God. Is it that woman you were talking about last time we spoke?'

'Yes, and she's in danger.'

'What kind of danger?'

'Well, walking the streets is a danger to her.' Yasmine cleared her throat. She would need to explain a bit more. 'She had to resort to work on the streets to survive.'

Her mother took a deep breath. 'What's her name?'

'Tara. But she may have changed her name.'

'She's a sex worker, Yasmine,' her mother said curtly.

'Mum, Tara said she only had to do that for two weeks. She needed to eat to survive and without any other job—'

'How do you intend to help her?' her mother interrupted tersely.

'That's where Aram comes in.'

'What? How can he help?' Her mother put down her glass and water splashed on her desk.

'He has connections to smugglers. He can get us a fake passport—'

Her mother gasped, looking at the door of her consulting room, most probably checking that no one had entered the room. 'This is impossible, Yasmine. You're endangering our family's reputation with all this. And for what?' She waved her hand, knocking over the glass of water again.

Not that word again – reputation.

Yasmine waited for her mother to compose herself, then said, 'To save a life, Mum. You of all people should know how difficult it is for an Iranian Kurd. Remember what happened to Jina Amini?'

Her mother glared at the screen again. 'You can't compare the two! How do you know it would be easier for Tara here with us?'

Yasmine nodded. 'I know, Mum. But we can't let her die here! You're a doctor and supposed to be compassionate.'

She waited for her words to sink in. 'Please help us with money. You don't need to get involved with Aram.'

Her mother winced, ignoring the plea. 'How are Dilly and Jamal?'

'They want to speak to you, too.'

Her mother nodded and looked as if she was going to burst into tears. Yasmine felt sorry for her. But it was Tara who needed her now.

Yasmine stood up and hurried out of the room. It was Dilly's turn to speak to her sister.

16

After the phone call to her mother, Dilly became cheerful again as if a big problem had been solved. Her mother had told Dilly that Tara wouldn't pose any more problems for the family. How infuriating! *But It might be better to keep quiet about the matter for a while.*

Yasmine started helping Dilly more in the kitchen. She even cooked her signature dish, chili con carne, which brought Dilly out in a hoot of laughter. She mock-reprimanded Yasmine about not being able to cook a typical Kurdish dish such as dolma, the filled vine leaves, but had attributed this to Yasmine's busy life studying in university. *If only she knew about my studies in other areas of life, such as boys and alcohol – some pleasant and not so pleasant sexual encounters.*

'*Mmm*, Yasmine, your chilli con carne is delicious,' Uncle Jamal said, getting a second helping from the stove.

'She's ready to marry, Jamal,' said Dilly, looking up at Jasmine expectantly.

'I don't intend to marry.'

'What? Why?'

'I mean, it's not my ultimate goal in life.' She hesitated. 'I've so much more to explore before settling down.'

Jamal licked his spoon and said, 'Our marriage was arranged when I finished studying at Sulaymaniyah University.' He glanced at his wife. 'I first met Dilly at my parents' house.'

Dilly turned to look at him and smiled. 'I still remember his dark, curly hair and shy glances in my direction when my parents weren't looking.'

'I'm not shy any more,' Jamal said, touching his wife's hand gently. 'Dilly was gorgeous and,' he hesitated, 'not as complicated as the rest of her family.'

Hmm, he's right about my family and Uncle Aram. Yasmine had yet to meet anyone else from her mother's family. A visit to her grandmother was on the cards. *How trustworthy is she going to be?*

'Oh, stop it, Jamal,' Dilly retorted. 'Don't say anything against my family. They brought me up.'

Jamal raised his eyebrows and poured himself another glass of water, then glanced at the microwave and cried, 'Dilly, it's happened again.' He was trying to heat up his wife's apple cake and the microwave had stopped halfway through.

Dilly laughed, walking towards him. She glanced at Yasmine and said, 'The power surges here kill the microwave.' She prodded Jamal and said, 'You should know by now that our humming generator will kick in.'

Jamal held his wife's hand and replied, 'Our generator is overworked and a new one will cost a lot, at least one hundred thousand dinars.'

'Geez.' Yasmine chipped in. 'That sounds like a lot of money.'

'It's about seventy-five dollars,' Jamal said. He must have realised that she was still hopeless at calculating prices in Iraqi dinars.

Dilly tapped Yasmine on the shoulder and said, 'Don't worry. We hardly use the microwave because I cook every day.'

Jamal laughed, 'I'm a lucky man.'

Yasmine smiled at him. In uni, she had used the communal microwave so often, that she was afraid she would turn into one.

Jamal looked at his reflection in the door of the microwave and ran his fingers through his dark hair. 'Dilly, has my hair started to turn grey?'

Dilly laughed, saying that he reminded her of Mullah Nusreddin, a witty character in the folklore of the Muslim world and a twelfth century hero of humorous short stories and anecdotes of pedagogic nature. He was a courtier of the king.

'Do you know of Mullah Nusreddin, Yasmine?'

'Oh yes, my mother told me some of his stories. His stories were crazy and wise at the same time.'

For a moment, she missed her mother's warm embrace and heartfelt stories in the evenings when she was getting ready to go to sleep.

'Auntie, tell me the story Jamal reminds you of.' She took her auntie's hand and squeezed it.

Dilly glanced at her husband with a glint in her eyes. 'Okay, I'll tell you a story. Fayaz the barber was trimming the mayor's hair and told him that it was beginning to turn grey.'

Jamal came towards his wife and mock-punched her gently.

'The mayor was furious and ordered Fayaz be put in jail,' she continued, 'then asked his court attendant the same question. This man told him that his hair was completely black, whereupon the mayor put him in prison too as he insisted that he was lying.'

Where is this story leading?

'Finally, the mayor turned to Nusreddin and asked what colour his hair was.' Dilly prodded Jamal's tummy and continued, 'Nusreddin replied that he was colour blind and couldn't answer the question, but he said that he couldn't help thinking that to a bald man like himself, any colour would be a blessing.'

Jamal laughed, saying he hadn't heard that anecdote before. He hugged his wife and promised not to mention his greying hair again. Yasmine smiled as they jumped apart, realising that she was watching their embrace.

It was during this ebullient atmosphere in the household, that Yasmine decided to meet the other member of the family again, Uncle Aram, but not in the 'red prison' where he had spent a few months and been tortured. She told her auntie and uncle that she needed to take a few more notes for an article she had been assigned. It was for the alumni university newsletter. Her auntie believed her and was visibly relieved to see that Tara had left them. *Only she hasn't. And she won't.* Yasmine planned her next steps with a tingling sensation in her stomach.

17

The next time they met, Aram wore a light brown suit. He had shaved his beard and had polished his shoes. Yasmine met him at the entrance of the museum and they walked in together, uncle and niece, as if they had never been apart.

'So, Yasmine, what have you been up to with your oh-so-reputable Uncle Jamal and Auntie Dilly?'

'Um… Cooking Kurdish dishes,' she replied, omitting the trip to the prison, where he had spent the worst years of his life. She wasn't sure if they had been the worst years. He had been through so much turmoil and she definitely wanted to know more about his life.

Aram snorted at the mention of cooking and stifled a laugh.

'When I was in the bazaar in Erbil, I realised I was being followed.' She looked at Aram directly, trying to gauge his reaction. 'Did you send someone to stalk me?'

He laughed sarcastically and grabbed hold of her hand. 'When I heard that someone was asking about me in the citadel, I wanted to know who my stalker was.'

Yasmine took her hand away.

Aram's eyes narrowed and he gave her a razor-sharp smile as he said, 'We live in dangerous times and I have to keep myself safe.'

Yasmine snarled at him, 'For all I know, you could be a thief or a killer.'

Aram widened his eyes again in mock-fear.

He was trying to provoke her. Stay calm. She let out a *pfft*, shrugged and turned to peer at the clay tablets in the glass cabinet. Aram waited for her to start speaking.

'You know why I wanted to see you again, Aram?' She turned to look at him again and omitted the word 'Uncle'.

'Yes… You want me to help you save that *ghaba,* your prostitute?' His sarcastic tone sounded sinister this time. *Why was he taking on that derogatory tone? He was using Tara's friends and their services.* Aram raised an eyebrow. 'Ah, I see you judge me because I help the other women.'

'I don't think you're helping them, Aram.' *What a misogynist.* 'You're taking advantage of them.' She surprised herself at the audacious tone she had applied.

He laughed and said, 'All men use them. It's what most men want, but they can't admit it.'

Yasmine's thoughts went to Harry. She felt a pang of regret. He had been faithful and yet she had left him to look for Aram and their heritage. It was turning out to be a hunt, but who was the hunter and who was hunted? *If this is the city where adventure is to be found, it's getting ugly. The harder I try to fit in, the more I crash into my limits.*

'Who are you trying to help?' He jabbed her in the side. 'Tara or yourself?'

Yasmine looked at him confused as he cackled and moved away, not waiting for an answer. An image imposed itself on her. She tried to fight against it – a woman with an angular jawline in red stilettos, ambling out of a bar in Soho, with a black handbag dangling from her left arm. As Yasmine passed her, hand-in-hand with Harry, the woman smiled at her. Her make-up had been applied perfectly – green eyeshadow, black mascara and bright red lipstick.

Suddenly, the woman fell. She had stumbled on the uneven kerb. Two men in black bomber jackets across the road ran up to her.

'Shit,' one of the men shouted. 'She's got stubble on her chin. She's a man!'

The other person laughed and said, 'Were you hoping for a quickie?'

The first man pushed his friend aside and retorted, 'I wouldn't want to do anything with this piece of shit,' He looked at his friend, red-faced.

Yasmine had stopped and told Harry to wait. She had felt her stomach churn as she watched the two men. The woman had tried to get up from the pavement. She had picked up her broken stiletto and was about to throw it at the man insulting her. Her face was beautiful – a fine jawline, brown curly hair, tattooed eyebrows and wide eyes.

The man jumped in front of the woman and grabbed her arm. She gasped as he twisted it, shouting, 'I want to see if she squeals like a woman or a man.'

The woman had shouted for help, doubled up in pain and had slumped onto the curb.

How can I forget this? I should have intervened before the assault continued, then she wouldn't have been beaten up so badly.

Yasmine closed her eyes, trying to shut out the image of the woman being carried away by a stretcher from the nearby ambulance. *Was I a coward?* She winced. *Never again.*

Aram jabbed her in the sides again and repeated, 'How many women are you trying to help? Tara, someone else or yourself?'

Yasmine's thoughts came back to the present. 'Where is Tara now?' she asked, scowling at her uncle.

'Where she belongs. On the scene.' Aram laughed again and added, 'Did you think your eighty dollars would last so long? The hotels wouldn't even take her in.'

What has changed my uncle from the fun-loving person he used to be back in Britain with my mum? Was it only his time in prison? Was it his overbearing father? She looked at him puzzled.

'Uncle,' she said, trying to use a lighter tone. 'Why did you leave us so suddenly in London?'

He scrutinised her and said, 'Indeed. I should never have left, but your mother took in that other wicked woman—'

'Sam isn't wicked,' Yasmine retorted, feeling her face heat up. Surely that wasn't the only reason he had left the country so quickly.

'Well, your mother was selfish. She preferred her to me.' He pouted. 'But I'm family. Blood is thicker than water."

Yasmine was taken aback. *Mum had a right to her*

chosen family. And family is beginning to get a different feel to it.

'Let's sit on the bench near the exit, Uncle.' She still needed him. She took his hand gingerly. It felt rough. He had an empty expression in his eyes but followed her out into the corridor. They both sat on the bench. *I'll need to tread carefully.*

'Uncle,' she said, lowering her voice, 'Jamal and I were in the Amna Suraka Museum recently—'

Aram pulled his arm away and fixed her with an expression of fear and anxiety. 'What did Jamal tell you about the prisoners?'

'Well, he didn't need to tell me a lot. I could clearly see the cells in the Chamber of Horrors.' She paused to gauge Aram's reaction.

'He told you, didn't he?' Aram snapped at her. His eyes revealed a mixture of loathing and fear.

Yasmine touched his hand gently. 'He didn't tell me the details.' She looked at him fearfully.

'Aha,' he growled, 'so you want to know what they did to me, how they enjoyed torturing me?'

'No, no. I just want to hold your hand.' She placed her hand on his sweaty one.

Aram pulled his hand away. 'Like your mother wanted to. Then she threw me out of the house, like a rubbish bin, only she didn't come back to collect me.' He glared at Yasmine.

'Uncle, I don't know what passed between you two … or in the prison cell you were confined to … but I do know that I want to help.'

Aram took a deep breath. He wiped his clammy

forehead and said, '*I* don't need help, but your *friend* Tara does.' He chuckled grimly. 'So, have you decided what you want to do? Let her continue sleeping on the streets like your mother did to me?'

'What do you mean? You were a man when you left our house. Surely, you had friends to help you.'

'I didn't have any friends – I had to leave the country,' he replied, suddenly subdued.

Yasmine waited for an explanation but Aram didn't offer any. He shifted his position on the bench. His whole persona seemed to shift with him. Yasmine shook her head. She wasn't getting any answers from anyone. Gaps in her memory and gaps in her knowledge were widening. *I came to this country to widen my horizons, only for them to be blocked.* She clenched her hands and turned to face him again.

'Okay, Aram.' Again, she didn't call him 'Uncle'. 'How can you help Tara?'

He looked at her sideways and said, 'Your mother would be proud of you.'

She looked at him confused. Her mother would be furious. But she couldn't let another victim be overlooked. Tara needed help. She looked similar to the woman she hadn't helped in Soho many years ago. That woman had ended up in hospital. Tara would survive, thanks to her. And Aram, she conceded reluctantly.

'Okay Aram. What can we do to help Tara?'

He grinned and replied, 'We can start by getting her a false passport.'

Oh God. This could be my descent into crime.

Yasmine shuddered but had no other alternative to

116

offer. Aram looked very pleased with himself and patted her on the shoulder. It was the first time she had seen him happy.

18

It took Uncle Aram about half an hour to drive up the winding Azmar mountains, so close to the perilous Iranian border. Yasmine sat at the edge of her seat, shivering. Would they arrive at the viewpoint of the mountain in one piece and would Tara be there as Uncle Aram had arranged? *Damn, she had better be there otherwise there is no hope of her escaping the country.*

Yasmine wiped her clammy hands on her coat. The tingling in her limbs made her appreciate the night lights, sparkling like jewels in the valley below them. The city of Sulaymaniyah was laid out like a glittering bowl. Even the dragonflies were luminescent. This was where her mother had grown up. A surge of affection for the city crept up on her.

Aram glanced at her sideways. 'You know we have the Azmar, Goizha and Qaiwan mountains in the northeast. They're all majestic, but it's the Azmar mountains I love the most.'

Yasmine turned towards him, eager to hear more about this place her mother had called home.

He hesitated before speaking again. 'When I was in the Amna Sureka prison in the valley, I used to look out of my tiny prison cell, spot the Azmar mountains and dream of my first sweetheart, Leyla. She had the most stunning eyes.'

Aram's voice was softer than Yasmine had ever heard before. What had happened to this first love of his?

'Where is she now?' Yasmine asked carefully.

'She was taken by one of Saddam's henchmen.'

'Taken?' She looked at her uncle, wide-eyed.

'Yes.' His hands gripped the steering wheel, the knuckles white. 'Do you want me to spell it out? She was raped.' His face darkened. 'That's what men do during wars.'

Oh God, oh God. Poor Leyla. Yasmine gripped the glove box and gasped. And the way Uncle Aram spoke. So detached. She covered her ears.

'You're shocked?' Aram said, his lip curling into a sneer. 'You know nothing of life here. At least your beloved Tara, the prostitute, does her sex work voluntarily. She's lucky.'

What the fuck? *What kind of a sexist misogynistic uncle is he?* For a while, she had thought he was being kind, helping Tara escape from a life of exploitation and abuse. Now she wasn't so sure. Was this uncle of hers a sick psychopath? She kept quiet.

After a few seconds, Aram started coughing.

Yasmine looked for a water bottle to give him. She found one in the glove box and gave it to him. He snatched it off her. Yasmine felt her heart racing. *What would Dilly say if she saw me with Aram in the car?* She had told her that she was visiting a friend from uni in the Titanic Hotel to celebrate her birthday.

'Um, leave me alone now,' he said. 'I'm okay. Almost there.'

Yasmine was relieved when they finally arrived at the viewpoint of the mountain.

'You can wait for me here,' Aram said. 'The bench isn't very comfortable but the view of the city is amazing.'

'Where are you going?' she asked with a tremor in her voice. *I mustn't show him how frightened I am.* He looked like a goth in the shimmering moonlight.

Aram laughed. 'Getting some tea from the tea cart over there.' He pointed to a cart about fifty metres away. She nodded.

When he came back, he had two cups of tea and some nuts in his hands.

'Where's Tara's cup of tea?' Yasmine asked, trying to sound calm. Aram had promised she would be here with them.

'Ahh, it will get cold if we buy it now.' He winked at her. They sat down on the bench with a wooden table attached to it. 'Do you know what else I was thinking of when I looked up to the Azmar mountains from my prison cell in the city down below?' he asked.

Yasmine shook her head, then replied, 'Freedom?'

He waited for a few moments, then said, 'My sister.' There was a mixture of fear and disgust in his voice.

'Which one?' Yasmine asked, dreading his answer.

'Your mother.' He looked at her directly, searching her face for any emotion. She tried to keep a straight face and kept quiet. 'Why did you come up here, Yasmine? You could have been satisfied with a tour of the bustling shopping mall, the skyscraper hotels and landscaped parks. You refused to visit the Chavy Land amusement park in this city.' He laughed. 'We could have taken the cable car up to the top of this mountain.'

Why indeed had she agreed to meet Aram up here, far away from the safety of her auntie and uncle?

'I wanted to see the flip side of my mother's country, her society, not just the shiny, polished side.'

Aram let out a snort. 'Did she never tell you about it?'

Yasmine pursed her lips. She hadn't touched her chai yet, even though it was cold up in the mountains.

'Okay, Yasmine,' he said, picking up his chai. Let's talk about Tara who belongs to the underbelly of this country.' He started to laugh, then said, 'I'm teaching you things your mother should have taught you.' He glanced at her menacingly. 'By exploiting men, Tara will regain her sexuality.'

Yasmine looked at him open-mouthed. Perpetrator, victim, rescuer – who could differentiate them? Certainly not Aram. *Here I am, a feminist, having to listen to a misogynistic and twisted man who just happens to be my uncle.* She fought the urge to faint. There was too much at stake. She still needed him.

A woman in black jeans and a hooded, black cardigan appeared from behind Aram. Yasmine tried to make out the expression on her face but it was dark. She waited to see if the woman would come closer to their bench. She wore white trainers that were clearly visible.

'Tara?' Yasmine whispered.

'The woman ran up to her and embraced her so tightly that Yasmine had to pull away.

'I'm so glad you came, my only f...friend in this country.' She looked close to tears.

'Your only friend?' Aram asked through gritted teeth, thumping hard on the table they were seated at.

Tara turned to look at him and added in a quivering voice, 'I meant, my only girlfriend.'

'Sit down, Tara,' Aram said, waving towards the place next to him on their bench. *His tone always commands obedience, as if he's afraid of losing control.* Yasmine watched the young woman quickly sit down. Her movements were much brisker without her heels.

'Okay, first of all, we'll need a passport,' Aram said after a few moments, looking at Tara triumphantly, aware that he had exerted enough control over her. *Geez. As if he hasn't done enough of that already.*

'I've got one,' Tara said excitedly, then added more quietly, 'oh...but it was stolen!'

Aram grunted. 'That's no use. We need to get you a new one – but that will cost you a lot.' He glanced at Yasmine and grinned, waiting for her to intervene.

Tara started to sob. 'But I haven't got much m... money. I want to stop working on the streets...' She turned towards Yasmine. 'Last week, I was beaten up by a client. He said he wanted to hear if I squealed like a woman or a girl. I didn't know what he meant.'

Aram looked bemused. Yasmine stiffened. *Why do men want to know how a girl squeals? Didn't the man in Soho ask the same question when the transwoman he had beaten up had fallen to the ground? Tara looks feminine.*

'Look,' Tara added, 'the bruises around my ch...

cheeks.' She came closer to Aram to show him her bluish-green marks on her face.

He raised an eyebrow and shrugged, saying, 'We need to get a photo of you without these bruises and cuts.' There was no emotion in his voice. 'And the passport must have the correct holograms and perforations with a passport chip.' He held Tara's arm tightly. 'That's why it'll cost a lot. For a British passport you'll need to pay $40,000.'

Tara sniffled into her tissue and said, 'Then I'll have to go home, back to Ir…Iran and my father will kill me.' She started to sob again.

Yasmine shook her head – *Tara has been sentenced in a court from which she's been excluded.*

Aram smiled but his smile didn't reach his eyes. 'You do know that we demonstrated for women's rights after the killing of Jina Amini?'

Tara nodded but her hands trembled. Yasmine moved closer to her but didn't want to embrace her in front of Aram. It was so wrong that he was speaking to them about women's rights. *How dare he. But I have to stay calm, for Tara's sake.*

Aram continued, 'You can go to Iran now if you'd like. It's half a day away from where we're standing.' He laughed. 'I've been there and I can show you the way.' Tara winced when Aram cried, 'Jin, Jhian, Azadi.' He turned towards Yasmine and asked wryly if she knew what the slogan meant.

'It means – women, life, freedom,' Yasmine replied bleakly, realising that Aram simply wanted her to see that escaping back to Iran would be fatal. *As a misogynist, he has no right to use that slogan.* Yasmine stared at Aram, feeling her cheeks heat up.

'Or Tara could get a false passport, and once she's safely in Britain,' Aram said, pretending to tear up something, 'she can shred her passport and say she's an unaccompanied minor.' He smiled, feeling triumphant with his explanations. *But is this an opportunity or a trick?* Yasmine felt sick. She would need time to think about the matter. *Isn't it a criminal act?*

Yasmine was used to omitting information when talking to her mother about this matter. *But Aram is expecting me to be complicit in arranging a fake passport.* If found out, this would entail at least five years imprisonment in Britain. And she could forget her dreams of working as a journalist for any newspaper or broadcasting company. *What have I got myself into?*

'I'll give you a few days to think about how much Tara's life is worth, Yasmine,' Aram said, revulsion and loathing in his voice.

Yasmine refrained from putting her face in her hands. There was no way she would show Aram how helpless she felt. She bit her lip. She would bide her time.

And with that, the meeting ended with Aram driving the two young women back down the mountain. The air was thick with tension.

19

Yasmine waited for her auntie to come down for breakfast. She had boiled some eggs, removed goat's cheese from the fridge and boiled the kettle. What a simple life her auntie and uncle led. Her auntie loved making jewellery and embroidering; her uncle went into his office nearby, hoping to sell houses or flats.

Neither of them had a professional job like her mother, but they were happy and were a pillar of the conservative society in Sulaymaniyah. Her mother, on the other hand, lived a conservative life on the outside, but her life at home was anything other than that. She lived with a woman.

Yasmine ruffled her itchy scalp. She hadn't eaten well for a few days, worrying about Tara and the next steps for her rescue.

'*Bayanit bash.*' The kitchen door opened and Dilly walked in sleepily, wearing a white dressing gown.

Yasmine smiled. 'Good morning, Dilly,' she chuckled. 'Your dressing gown is inside out.'

Dilly looked at her gown and laughed. 'You're up early. Did you sleep well?'

'Yes,' Yasmine lied. She had been up half the night procrastinating about Tara's next steps after sneaking back into her auntie's house and had been restless the remaining part of the night. The only dream she remembered was being locked up in Belmarsh Prison. That might have been easier than being locked up in the 'red prison' or Iran's notorious Evin prison, which Tara would be thrown into if she returned to Iran and survived her father's honour killing.

'You look tired. Do you want us to have a joint call with your mother again?'

Yasmine looked at her auntie, dazed by her intrusive thoughts. 'Um… No, I'm just worried about Tara—'

'Not again! 'Dilly cried, exasperated. 'She's left us. Where's her family?'

'Her family disowned her when they realised, she was … um … different. Not a virgin. They wanted to take her to the doctor for a virginity test.'

'Yes, well, some people respect conservative Middle Eastern values.'

'Oh, well, why are boys allowed to have relationships while girls have to stay virgins till they marry?'

'*Stachferallah,*' Dilly exclaimed. 'Our next-door neighbour, Hawar, didn't have any relationships until he married.'

Holy shit. Yasmine threw up her arms in desperation and said, 'Oh, so you believe that Hawar, a thirty-year-old man, preferred playing cards with his mates till he married?'

She had heard about hotels in Erbil with single women going in and out of rooms of men wearing wedding rings on their fingers, who had made promises to their wives they had no intention of following. Tara had told her how much they earned, hundreds of dollars. And the pimps were not only men, but there were also madams, too old to service punters anymore. Tara had told her that the young girls servicing the men were saving money for their children, running away from abusive fathers or brothers who raped them, or earning money for drug addiction.

Dilly's voice sounded shrill when she started talking again. 'Yasmine, I think we'd better stop this conversation. I don't want to know what your mother lets you do at home, but you had better be careful here.' She crossed her arms and glared at her niece.

Yasmine's heart fluttered. She had to be prudent as she was planning on rescuing Tara in a few days. This was no time to be belligerent with her auntie. She would just be making her suspicious of her moves.

'Sorry Auntie. Maybe you can teach me how to do dolma now?' She smiled at her and looked at the fridge, willing her auntie to open it and bring the minced meat out.

Dilly straightened her posture. This suggestion appeared to be something she enjoyed doing and was proud of. 'Good idea, Yasmine *gyan*. Your mother doesn't have time to get dolma ready. She's so busy with work.' She hesitated, then asked, 'Does that friend of hers – Sam – visit you often?'

Yasmine narrowed her eyes and said, 'As often as she can.'

Dilly nodded with a mixed expression of curiosity and wariness in her eyes. She went towards the fridge.

Mum's relationship with Sam was not for Yasmine to lay out.

20

Once again, Yasmine was up on the Azmar mountain, not for a picnic, to watch the sunset or for a secret meeting with a love interest as some young couples did, but to meet Uncle Aram.

Prostitution, sex trade, murky stuff. *What am I getting myself into?* She looked around her. Dark-grey clouds drifted above her. She put her hood up as it was drizzly. *When will Aram arrive with Tara as arranged?* He was the only one still in contact with her friend.

Yasmine sat on the same bench where they had met Tara at a few days ago and eyed the tea cart a few metres away. Other customers were queueing to get some chai. She would wait for Tara.

Yasmine's taxi driver had driven off, happy with his tip. She had hired him near the Titanic hotel in the valley so that she could be sure he wasn't a rogue driver ready to assault her. Anyone who saw her would easily guess she was a tourist, with her manner of walking self-consciously and looking around her like a lost squirrel.

Aram had told her that Goizha Mountain was the

closest hill outside Suli and was a popular spot for locals to picnic, but he preferred The Azmar ones. Those were the mountains he had turned to when incarcerated in the Amna Sur red prison during the Kurdish Uprisings. From there, he would dream about his childhood sweetheart, Leyla. Would he have been a more peaceful man if Leyla had survived the prison? Yasmine frowned. She would write an article on this notorious prison once she got back from Iraq. She needed to process the torture that had taken place there, once and for all. But ultimately, it was Uncle Aram's wound and he would need to overcome it somehow, otherwise… Yasmine tried to process her thoughts. Otherwise, what exactly? Would her uncle become a killer as well as a thief and punter?

Someone tapped her on the shoulder. She jumped up, turned around and stood face to face with Aram. Her skin was clammy.

'Feeling frightened, Yasmine?' her uncle chortled, tugging at Tara's sleeve. She stood shivering next to him, her hood pulled up and a black scarf tight around her neck.

'No, Aram, it's cold and you're late.' Yasmine tried to sound light-hearted.

He laughed. 'Has Dilly given you a curfew?'

'No, she hasn't. We discuss everything together. She trusts me.'

Well, that isn't entirely true. But I can negotiate with Dilly. Will I be able to reach an agreement with Aram? She looked at him warily. He was carrying a black man bag and his black duffle coat looked as if he had been sleeping in it. *Scruffy, not tidy like Uncle Jamal.* She suddenly felt a pang of remorse. Dilly and Jamal had no idea what she was about to negotiate. Her mother and Sam would be furious.

'Right, have you got the money I asked for?' Aram stood, legs apart, waiting for a response. His eyes were dull.

'Have you got the passport?' Yasmine looked in the direction of his bag.

'Not yet, I need the money first. My contacts at the airport won't get the passport without some money.' He eyed her rucksack, most probably hoping the dollars were in it.

Yasmine's stomach started to churn. Her lips felt parched whenever she met Aram, despite the cold air.

'How do I know I can trust you?' She looked directly at her uncle.

'You don't,' he sneered, 'but you have no choice. Your beloved Tara can only claim asylum in the UK after physically arriving on UK soil. She can't get a visa and there are no safe routes into the country.' He laughed out loud. 'That's where I can help them cross the channel in small boats.'

Yasmine hesitated, clasping her rucksack. Her uncle followed her gaze and added, 'I see you need to get the money out of your rucksack. I'll go and get some chai from the cart.' He chuckled. 'The vendor is getting to know us. This is how rumours start. 'He leered at her.

Yasmine put her hand in front of her mouth. *I mustn't vomit.*

Aram strode towards the tea cart, waving at the vendor triumphantly. Yasmine glanced at Tara, who was cowering close to her, eyes pleading. *No money, no passport. Where should we go from here. I've had enough of navigating through Aram's pseudo-help.*

'Quick,' Yasmine grabbed hold of Tara's hand. 'We need to get away.' Tara hesitated so Yasmine added, 'He has no intention of helping us. He's just out for the money.' She nudged Tara, willing her to move quickly.

Tara glanced in the direction of the tea cart. Aram was in a queue, chatting to a man in front of him.

Yasmine pulled her friend even closer and said, 'If you stay with him, he will hand you over to the police in Iraq or in Iran and you know what that means.'

Tara's eyes widened and she clutched Yasmine's hand. They strolled towards the asphalt road they had come from, trying to look as inconspicuous as possible.

Then Yasmine looked back at Aram. He was getting closer to the tea cart. Soon, he would be turning around to walk back to where he had left them. Yasmine started to run, pulling Tara along with her. Luckily, she wore her trainers. Yasmine remembered seeing a hiking trail on her Google map.

Tara stopped running suddenly. 'Yasmine, we can't run all the way down the mo...mountain,' she panted. 'And we can't take the hiking route as there's a small problem.'

'You mean the darkness?'

'No, black triangle signs with sk...skull and bones.' Tara started shivering again.

Yasmine racked her brain, trying to remember where she had seen that sign previously. *Of course. Landmines.* She had seen those signs in the Amna Sur red museum where landmines from the 1980's were displayed in glass cabinets.

'Shit. We'll have to stay on the paved road then.' There was no turning back.

Tara explained that recent heavy rains had dislodged landmines, carrying explosives away on the current and depositing them in areas that had already been cleared.

Geez. Bones, barbed wire, landmines and wolves, together with Uncle Aram would be a deathly combination. We can't just walk into neighbouring Iran so the only way forward is to face Auntie Dilly and Uncle Jamal, even if they are furious.

Tara tugged at Yasmine's sleeve and said, 'Yasmine, the landmines were planted three de…decades ago during the Iraq-Iran war and thirteen thousand people have been vi…victims of them.'

Yasmine felt beads of sweat trickling down her face. She didn't need reminding about the dangers of these mines. And where was Google Maps when you needed it? Mines would not be marked on it.

As they walked briskly along the asphalt road, Yasmine ducked into the dark trees whenever car lights approached them. She stifled the scream that was emerging from her throat. *If someone had told me that I would be dodging landmines and wolves and a crazy uncle with a poor Iranian sex worker a few months ago, I would have thought they were crazy.*

Tara stood still. 'I want to join the MAG.'

Yasmine turned around to look at her. Tara's eyes were gleaming in the dark.

'What do you mean?'

'It's the Mines Advisory Group. They train ci… civilians to defuse explosives, not only the landmines, but also IEDs.'

'What's an IED?' Yasmine asked curtly. This wasn't the time to discuss explosives, when they needed to escape Aram quickly, but then she had never heard of IEDs.

'IEDs are improvised explosive de…devices, Yasmine.' Tara hesitated. 'They could be toys, rice sacks, sink taps or games co…consoles.'

'Shit! Do you mean explosives can take on any shape or form?'

'When ISIS left in 2014, they left behind IEDs, not only ou…outside houses but inside them.'

'You mean houses were booby-trapped?' *What a dystopian world.* Not to be safe in your own house? Yasmine tried to steady her breathing.

Tara looked at her shoes and said, 'Yes, I saw some children who lost their legs when picking up a toy or stumbling on tripwire.'

'Geez, Tara. That sounds awful. But you'd be doing a really dangerous job if you apply.'

'Not more dangerous than the one I j…joined servicing men.'

Tara's voice was barely audible. Yasmine winced but couldn't make out Tara's expression as she was still looking at her shoes, most probably ashamed of her current job.

'I know my new job will arm me with a metal de… detector and tools but that would be more than I have now to pro…protect myself.'

That much is true. Yasmine held Tara's hand gently.

Tara looked up and faced her as she added, 'From 2014, five thousand Yazidis were killed by ISIS and seven thousand Yazidi women were enslaved and sold for sex by ISIS fighters.'

Yasmine nodded. She could sense the analogy Tara was alluding to.

'I can't hold a gun, but I can hold a detector and clean mined areas.'

Yasmine took a deep breath. Everything she had heard and seen on TV a decade ago concerning ISIS and sex trade was taking shape in a vivid way here in her mother's country of origin.

What a contrast to the first time she had caught sight of the dignified, mountainous region of Sulaymaniyah a few days ago, the huge letters of the city spelled out on the Goizha Mountain, alongside a red, white, green and yellow flag in the shape of Iraqi Kurdistan. Discovering the heritage of her mother would be exciting, or so she thought.

'I don't want to die here.' Tara interrupted her reverie. She started to cry. 'Yasmine, I didn't tell you the whole tru…truth.' She wiped her nose on her sleeve and continued, 'I went to the MAG and asked to join them, but when they heard I didn't have a passport, or maybe for another reason, they didn't want to take me on as a te…team member.'

Tara leapt forward and clung to her whilst crying.

Not even able to get a job facing the perils of death. Yasmine shook her head and cradled Tara who would have been thrilled to do the dangerous demining of the borders between Iran and Iraq if they had accepted her services.

She will either die here on the Iranian border or on her way to another country. The journey to Iran and Britain would be equally dangerous. *What a farce.*

Yasmine shook Tara and said, louder than she had intended to, 'Stop it. You have options, but you can't go back to Aram.' She thought of what her mother had said. 'He's dangerous.'

Tara stood rooted to the paving and looked back in the direction of the tea cart. Yasmine followed her gaze and said, 'Don't even think about it. He just wanted to sell you.'

'I want to escape, Yasmine.' She started sobbing uncontrollably. Yasmine took her in her arms. *Why have we formed such an unusual bond?* She tapped Tara's back, waiting for her to stop crying.

'Will you help me escape?' Tara blew her nose in the tissue Yasmine offered her.

'I can help you with money, Tara, but I don't have any connections.'

The only knowledge she had of people smuggling was from TV and newspaper articles in England. Yasmine had even tried asking ChatGPT about the possibilities of people smuggling, only to be told that it was an illegal matter. She had quickly closed her laptop afterwards, wondering if anyone could trace her browsing history on AI later on. She felt her hands tremble.

'I'll try to ask my friends about transport to Europe,' Tara said hopefully. *But she doesn't have any friends except the sex workers and they are just as desperate to survive.*

'Is a smuggler's boat better or a lorry?' Tara peered at her wide-eyed.

Shit, they are both dangerous. How naïve she is.

'Where would you like to go?'

'England.' Tara's answer came swiftly.

'The smugglers want more money for that country.'

'But they understand me better there. I've heard you have protection and organisations to help you as a refugee.'

'It's not quite that easy,' Yasmine said, remembering the young mixed-race transwoman who had been injured after an assault in Soho. She couldn't bear to witness that behaviour again.

Tara had started walking quickly and said softly, 'Your part of the world is very kind.' She smiled at Yasmine. 'I heard about the Ge…Geneva Convention and the Court of Hu…Human Rights.'

The naivety of this girl was astonishing. Yasmine felt her stomach churn. Up to a million people had been wiped out during ethnic cleansing in Rwanda and yet Britain had intended to send asylum seekers to that country.

She was too tired to explain more of the situation, feeling blisters forming on her toes. *And how on earth am I going to tell Dilly and Jamal about Tara turning up in their lives again?* But there was no other place she could turn to. She wiped her forehead. She would be lucky if she didn't end up with a stomach ulcer.

21

It was pitch-black when Yasmine rang the doorbell. She looked at the small garden. *If only I could sit on the family swing and go to sleep.* The pomegranate tree in the corner of the garden appeared ominous in the moonlight, casting a shadow on the swing in the garden.

She yearned to inhale the fragrant cut grass in her mother's back garden, far away in London, have a picnic on their patio and blend into their oh-so-predictable lives. She almost chortled. Just a few weeks ago, she had longed to escape her formulaic future. Now, she longed for it.

She glanced at Tara who wouldn't let go of her arm. After wiping her muddy hands, Yasmine pushed Tara to the side of the door. Better not let Dilly see her first, that is if they opened the door. It was two o'clock in the morning. They had managed to hitch-hike their way home after waving down a taxi that already had a couple sitting in it and was deemed safe to travel with.

The light in the bedroom upstairs went on. Yasmine could hear her auntie moving down the creaky stairway.

Or was it her uncle? She hoped it would be her auntie. The footsteps sounded more light-footed.

The heavy steel door opened slowly. Her uncle peered out and squinted. 'Yasmine. *Stachferallah*! Where have you been? We were out of our minds with worry.'

She waited for him to let her in, almost stepping into the doorway. Tara was still in the shadow of a fig tree. Jamal reluctantly opened the door wider. Yasmine could see Dilly standing behind him with her hand held up in front of her mouth.

'Yasmine,' Dilly started crying, 'I phoned your friend to see why you were late. She said you hadn't even arrived at her house. I didn't know whether to phone your mother yet and—' The door was wide open now. Dilly pushed past Jamal and leapt towards Yasmine, embracing her tightly and ruffling her entangled hair. *Ah, Dilly can't help loving me. I'm the daughter she never had.* Yasmine clung to her aunt.

Dilly stopped crying when she saw the movement next to the fig tree. 'Who's that?' She jumped back towards Jamal. He pulled her into the house.

'It's only me. Tara,' a faint voice responded. She didn't come closer to them but stood next to the fig tree as if frozen.

'She's not coming into the house,' Jamal boomed, glaring at Yasmine. 'And neither are you.'

Yasmine started to sob. She felt the tears trickling down her face and wiped them with her sleeve. They were the only people she could trust in this country. What would she do if they refused to let her in?

'I've got nowhere else to go,' she stuttered. 'It won't happen again—'

'I've heard that before,' her uncle barked.

Tara took a step backwards and said, 'It's all my fault. I pho...phoned Yasmine to meet me on the Azmar Mountains be...because I was in trouble. It wasn't planned. I just panicked.' She started to sob.

Jamal scowled at her with a disgusted expression on his face. 'You want to get Yasmine into your kind of business.'

Tara shook her head, sobbing violently. 'I don't even want this job.' She flung herself at Yasmine and kissed her cheek. 'I'll get out of your life, Yasmine. I don't want you to be pu...punished because of me.'

'No, Tara,' Yasmine cried, holding her hand. 'Why should you pay for the sins of the men who were supposed to protect you?'

They clung to each other, crying inconsolably. Yasmine glanced at her uncle through blurry eyes. His raging expression had changed to a confused one as he held his wife back from the doorway.

Dilly managed to push past Jamal and screamed, 'Yasmine *can* stay. My sister would kill me if anything happened to her.' She had tears in her eyes. 'I promised to look after her and keep her from harm's way.' She pushed Tara aside and try to pull her niece back into the house.

'No, please don't throw Tara out,' Yasmine cried.

Jamal said sternly, '*Kalb, ebn-al-kalb,* dog, son of a dog, she was never part of this house.' He reverted to the Arabic language whenever he was furious. He folded his arms. 'Now, Tara, leave us alone.'

Tara looked at the ground, broke herself free from Yasmine and hobbled towards the gate. Yasmine tried to tear herself away from her auntie but Jamal stepped forward and held her back. She was too weak to fight. She almost collapsed as she watched Tara close the gate behind her.

She vowed to find her again but didn't say this aloud. Her auntie had already taken her into the house.

22

The next morning, Yasmine would have sped down the stairs quickly to avoid her uncle, but the blisters on her feet were still hurting. Plasters didn't help. She hadn't slept well but she knew that she needed to FaceTime her mother sooner or later. She didn't want to be sent home yet. Her hands were clammy. If she were banished, Tara would face imminent death.

She needed to convince her mother. Of all people, she should understand. If a doctor didn't understand that Tara had special needs, who would?

Downstairs, her uncle and auntie were waiting for her. They told her that they had already spoken to her mother. Damn. Yasmine took a deep breath. Now, she would have to work extra hard to soften her mother. Dilly nodded at Yasmine to go to the laptop on the kitchen table. She still wasn't talking to her. Yasmine glanced at her uncle who avoided eye contact and shuffled towards the corridor.

She sat down at the kitchen table, pushed the pepper and salt aside and peered at the laptop screen. It was two o'clock in the afternoon, British time. Her mother was on a break. She watched her sign some prescriptions that had been propelled out of the printer.

Yasmine scrutinised her expression. Her mother looked tired as she pushed the pile of prescriptions neatly into the cardboard box on her desktop. She wore the woolly red cardigan Yasmine had given her for Christmas the previous year. Her mother tucked a strand of hair that had fallen into her face neatly behind her ear and squinted as she looked up at the screen. The dark circles underneath her eyes had increased.

'You're there already?' She sat up in her swivel chair. 'For goodness' sake, Yasmine, why didn't you say you were ready to talk?'

Yasmine wasn't ready at all, but she had to bite the bullet. She looked at the ceramic bowl on the table, laden with fresh apples and oranges, and was surprised she didn't feel hungry.

'Um, I don't know what Auntie Dilly has told you?' Yasmine said cautiously.

'You and Tara are like a pair of separatists,' her mother snapped back. Her cup of tea almost fell from the table as she waved her hand towards the screen.

Yasmine had never seen her mother lose her temper like this. 'Mum, I know you're angry, but we can't let Tara die!' She wrung her hands in front of the screen.

'She's not going to die, Yasmine,' her mother replied sternly, moving her cup of tea somewhere safe.

'But she's not going to live either, Mum.' Yasmine looked down at the tiles on the kitchen floor. They were cracked and chipped, just the way she felt right now. Maybe she should let her tears flow... But that wouldn't change her mother's stance on Tara. So she said, 'There are checkpoints everywhere, Mum. Not only between cities but between people.' How often had they been stopped by soldiers loyal to their tribes between Erbil and Sulaymaniyah. Officials near Erbil were loyal to the KDP party and other ones near Sulaymaniyah were loyal to the PUK party. And not only that – moral checkpoints everywhere she went. She let her gaze wander to a lizard opposite side of their street.

'There's so much suspicion around anyone who's different. You know how that feels.' She let the last sentence dangle before she continued. 'Tara isn't an alien. She's a human being. She has a heart and soul.' She tried holding back her tears as she spoke but felt one trickling down her cheeks.

Her mother came closer to the screen. 'Yasmine, I understand you belong to the woke generation, but this is a serious matter. You can't change a society so quickly. Your uncle and auntie need to stay safe.'

'But Mum, this isn't wokery, it's decency.' Her leg muscles were tightening. 'I *can* handle this alone. I just need to get some money to help Tara escape.' She thumped the table, making her glass of water spill onto the wooden table. 'You used to tell me we need to bridge gaps and avoid cancel culture.'

Why am I pleading with my mother? The woman is a feminist but doesn't have the courage to announce it.

Her mother put her head in her hands. She picked it up again, looking frail and wan. Finally, she said, 'Maybe I can send you the money. But I need to know how much is involved and think about the legality of it.'

Yasmine clapped her hands, feeling triumphant.

Her mother continued, 'But I want this all to end. I need more time to think about the matter.' She straightened her posture. 'And I don't want my career to end by being complicit to people smuggling.'

'I understand, Mum. You won't hear her name again and I won't tell Dilly or Jamal.'

Yasmine felt elated but knew she would worry about Tara, day and night, until she finally arrived safely in another country. Her heart was fluttering, not with fear, but in hope. She wouldn't tell her uncle and auntie about what she had tried to negotiate with her mother. She would give her mother time to think about the money. That would stay their secret. She didn't want her mother implicated in any criminal acts. She was a doctor, for God's sake. Her motto was 'First do no harm' and that meant saving lives, including Tara's. Yasmine walked upstairs to her bedroom, feeling a spring in her step, even though the blisters in her feet bothered her.

23

The following night, Yasmine slept like a baby. Hope lingered in the air. Her mother might help her as long as she wasn't implicated in any dodgy affairs. That was what she had implied. Yasmine got out of her bed, changed into her white jeans and white top, then went to the adjoining bathroom to get ready for breakfast. Was that freshly baked flatbread she could smell? She needed some ground coffee, dreamed of red peppers and mashed chickpeas. Her hunger had come back.

When she arrived downstairs, she caught sight of a pan that was bubbling on the stove. She peered inside. Wax. A mixture of lemon, sugar and water was waiting to be used on hairy skin. Yasmine winced as she thought of her auntie pulling sticky strips off the hair on her legs. Dilly had gone upstairs to get the strips she had bought.

This is my chance to leave. Yasmine could feel the hair on her legs rise as if in fear of the ensuing torture. Should she taste the mixture? No, better not. Their maid Halima would be ringing the doorbell soon. Aha. *Auntie could try the mixture on the maid's legs.*

Yasmine was relieved her mother had never forced her to use this way of removing hair on her legs. She shuddered when she remembered that her auntie would use this method to remove her *pubic* hair. Dilly had started this in her teens and had made sure that there wasn't any visible hair on her wedding day.

Yasmine left a note for her auntie, explaining that she needed to meet up with a friend from the University of Sulaymaniyah to help her fill in an application form for a Master's at Imperial College in London. She crept out of the house and walked briskly to the taxi standing opposite their house. Hair on her legs was not one of her priorities at present, despite the stubble. She would shave them off later on. But for now, someone else was on her mind. Hawar was the son of their neighbour and they occasionally used his taxi services as he could be trusted. She had texted him to wait outside and luckily, he was around to do so.

'To Serchinar please,' she said to Hawar, after they had exchanged some small talk about the beautiful partridge that they shared in their gardens. She told him she was meeting a friend. He looked at her suspiciously but did as he was told when he saw the twenty dollar note in her hand.

Fifteen minutes later she was standing at the edge of the street where she had first encountered Tara or rather more, where Tara had flung herself into her arms. She decided to walk up and down the street, keeping an eye out for her. Motorists were blasting their horns for no apparent reason. A man in a Chevrolet catcalled her. She began to feel uneasy.

It's time to blend in. Perhaps put a headscarf on. No, she preferred her hat with a wide brim. Yasmine glanced around her. She spotted a shoeshine boy furiously polishing a burly man's pair of shoes. *Shall I ask him if he's seen Tara?* As far as she knew, Tara was the name she went by. But Yasmine wasn't sure if she belonged to a madam in any one of the houses used as a brothel or if she worked in a hotel, maybe even in the back of a car. She had been embarrassed to ask about these practicalities.

Yasmine shuddered, hoping that Tara would have been tested for gonorrhoea and syphilis. Her mother had told her that these infections were increasing. Where did the women go if they were ill? It would be difficult for Tara to approach a doctor for fear of stigmatization.

She tried turning her thoughts to the Sarchinar resort about five kilometres from the city of Sulaymaniyah. Small trees, squawking ducks, a lake and fountains made up this peaceful resort. Golden and green leaves padded the ground. Children played in the park, oblivious to the fact that only a few streets away, sex workers were busy servicing men.

Yasmine decided to approach the shoeshine boy who had stopped working for a few moments. He mopped his forehead with the back of his hand and squinted as she stepped in front of him. She wore sandals so he must have wondered why she was standing there expectantly. The boy had been at the scene where Tara had almost been assaulted by one of her punters a few weeks ago. Maybe he could help her.

'*Roj bash,* hello.' She knew he would recognise her as a tourist. The locals always did, even when she tried her best to blend in. Maybe it was her gait or the way she looked around her cautiously. She had tried everything to look like the locals, but somehow everyone realised she was a tourist.

The boy, who was about twelve years old, welcomed her and raised his eyebrows waiting for her to speak again.

'*Choni?*' she said, asking him how he was.

'*Baschim, spass,*' he answered, thanking her and telling her that he was well. This was small talk but she needed to gain his trust first before getting to her concerns.

She switched to English as he had advertisements in English on his small chair and shoe box. 'I see you watch English films,' she said looking at the photo of Audrey Hepburn. 'She's a great actress. And pretty,' she added, watching the boy blush.

'Yes, I liked her film *Breakfast at Tiffany*,' he said shyly.

Yasmine laughed. Old films were still en vogue in this part of the world. 'You must see lots of people walking up and down the street?'

The boy nodded, watching her warily.

'Remember the lady who was assaulted here two weeks ago?' The boy shook his head and started to sort out his brushes in the shoe box, averting his gaze.

Yasmine took out the twenty dollar note she had in her handbag. 'Look, if you can tell me where she is, I'll give you twenty dollars, then you won't have to work for a few days.'

He looked up again and his face lit up as he said, 'I tell you.' He hesitated. 'But you no tell anyone else.'

Yasmine nodded and said, 'Tara is my friend. I'm only trying to help her move away. Where is she?'

The boy frowned and answered her slowly. 'She leave with man yesterday.'

'What man? Can you describe him to me?'

'Same man who always talk to her,' the boy answered without any trace of sympathy.

'Oh shit,' she exclaimed. *Aram is closer than I thought.* 'When did they leave this area?'

'Yesterday, Miss. Why? Is she in trouble?'

Yasmine nodded and said, 'She's in big trouble. So I need to find her, to rescue her.'

The boy looked up fearfully and said, 'She always gave me cigarettes and coffee. She talk to me.' He glanced at Yasmine, trying to gauge her response to his affiliation to a woman who was in an industry totally different to his and maybe liaising with a people smuggler.

Yasmine felt a surge of irritation and guilt. *I need my mum's help.* She chose one of the bridges joining two large promenades in Sarchinar to FaceTime her mother, without her auntie and uncle being present. A couple passed by smiling at each other but they didn't hold hands. She remembered that public displays of affection were frowned upon and discouraged. The young man with the set jaw and biceps looked at his love interest longingly and pointed at a small boat on the other side of the lake.

Where's Harry right now? She had tentatively started texting him again and he had replied, most probably intrigued by her recent adventures.

Yasmine felt a pang of envy as she watched the young couple amble towards the boat. She looked at her watch. Harry would be in the gym working out today. He always loved the cross-trainer the best. She would phone him after her mother. *Is he becoming an on-off boyfriend? Stop thinking about him.* She took her mobile out of her handbag and dialled her mother's number.

'Hello Mum. I thought you'd like to see how calm the lake is in Sarchinar.'

Her mother blinked at her, uncomprehending. 'Yes, I can see it is. Where's Dilly?' she asked, her tone guarded.

'She's busy cooking at home.' *All women are busy cooking at home at this time of the day,* Yasmine thought, almost giggling. The previous day, Dilly had cooked *yaprach*, delicious rice-filled vine leaves. Today it would be biriyani, mixed vegetable rice. No doubt, tomorrow it will be *kubba*, round-shaped rice with minced meat inside. How young people in Kurdistan didn't put weight on, she didn't know. They must have a lot of self-discipline.

'How's the atmosphere at home now that Tara has left?' Her mother looked relieved.

'Well, it's fine at home with Dilly and Uncle, but I'm very upset. I don't know where Tara has gone and whether she's alive.' She glanced at the young couple in the boat. *Does Tara not have the same rights to love and life? Are women either saints or whores, no space in between?*

'Darling, I don't think the situation for Tara would be much better in Britain.'

Yasmine blinked at the screen. 'Why not?'

'Because hatred and fear towards this community exists here, too.'

'But why? Trolls and bullies don't even know what these women have been through.' She raised her voice involuntarily, 'She hasn't killed anyone.'

Her mother looked worried. 'I know, but there's

no future for her here. Anyway, how would she get to Britain?'

'By boat, Mum. Maybe someone could help her if she had the money.'

Her mother looked horrified.

'I don't mean Uncle Aram. Maybe someone else, once you're able to send me the money.'

'Stop talking about smugglers, Yasmine. I've made my mind up.' Her mother whispered. 'I can't give you money to help people smugglers, especially not for Aram. How can you expect me to risk my GMC registration for a girl I don't know? I could go to prison.'

Yasmine put her head in her hands. A scream was building up in her throat.

Her mother continued, 'Rwanda received an extra fifteen million pounds to accept migrants arriving in the UK on small boats. The journey doesn't end for migrants by entering Britain. They will just be sent elsewhere.'

Yasmine picked up her head. She could feel her mother's eyes boring into her.

'Okay, Mum. But you of all people should know how it feels to be vilified if you're different in any way.'

Her mother winced, shook her head briskly and turned towards the door of her consulting room, saying, 'Just a second.' She glanced back at the computer screen and whispered, 'I don't want to hear any more about this matter.'

Yasmine didn't nod but waved goodbye without smiling. *Everyone had a right to live and to have a voice.*

She glanced at the shoeshine boy across the road again. *He might have more information if given the right amount of money.* Yasmine felt her heart fluttering with hope. But now she had to return home. She looked up at the unfathomable sky. It was just as incomprehensible as the mysteries she had encountered in her mother's country.

24

Back home in Dilly's spare bedroom, Yasmine took her laptop, threw the teddy bear with the lopsided smile away and sat on her bed. Harry's face would be appearing in a few minutes. He had reluctantly agreed to FaceTime her today.

However, it was Tara who was constantly on her mind, peril pulling her forwards like a magnet.

'Oh, hi Harry.' She came closer to the screen. He was usually clean-shaven and now when he grinned at her, she saw stubble on his chin. *Is he too busy to shave?*

'I was wrong to doubt our relationship and was just too anxious about my upcoming trip to Iraq. I miss you.' She felt her cheeks go red.

'You haven't had time to miss me,' he replied, cocking his head.

'Well, I've been busy trying to sort Tara out, you know the girl I texted you about a few days ago.' She smiled at him. The blue sweater complemented his blue eyes.

'Yasmine, I thought you'd be more busy rehearsing Kurdish lullabies and songs to sooth yourself?' He laughed, then moved his lips, pretending to sing.

'I don't know why you thought that,' she said in mock reproof, wondering if he was making fun of her. 'Mum's heritage is not all shiny and sweet. Listen, Tara has disappeared.' She hoped Harry wouldn't be sick of hearing about Tara as she had been texting him about her problems.

He moved his laptop further away. 'Maybe she's found a means to get out of the country.'

'I doubt it. She doesn't have any money. I'm worried though – even if she does get the money, it's dangerous crossing the channel.'

Harry listened carefully. She liked that about him. They had only been together on and off for a year and had had so much fun together. They both loved music; Glastonbury had been such an adventure that summer, even though their tent had blown away. She realised though she knew nothing about his political views. They hadn't talked about their philosophies. Was their relationship superficial? They certainly had a lot to talk about when she returned to England.

Harry had started speaking again and she tried to focus. 'If Tara can't come illegally,' he said, 'then she'll have to try and come legally.'

'How can she do that?' Yasmine asked slowly. Harry's father was a barrister. He would have some information on such cases.

'It's difficult. My dad told me that legal refugees must have a job paying at least £38,700. I expect Tara doesn't earn that much.'

Yasmine scratched her neck and asked, 'Are you teasing me – or her?'

'Not at all,' he said, level-headed. 'However, some good news is that workers who earn less will still be allowed to come, to avoid a crisis in hospitals or homes.'

'Ah, I see. We need skilled workers, especially for the ailing NHS,' she replied, noticing the sarcasm in her own voice. 'But I don't even know what job Tara had before she had to walk the streets.'

They both kept quiet for a few seconds. What was she doing, trying to resist the social constraints imposed on them? Tara's current job would hardly be acknowledged, and what had led to it would be classified as unfortunate.

Harry was waiting for her to continue talking. She had been far too engrossed by Tara, who belonged to the margin of any society. There was very little time left for Harry and his needs. In fact, she didn't even know what he wanted from life. All she knew was that he would be starting his master's soon.

'Harry, do you think I should be heading home soon?' *He should be asking me that*, she thought annoyed with herself for asking.

'You've only been in the country for two weeks.' He hesitated. 'What do you think?' He looked at her cautiously.

Is that a red stain on his sweater? She came closer to the computer screen and scrutinised the stain. Was it lipstick? Harry didn't have any sisters. *I'm getting paranoid about everything.* Her pulse quickened.

'Harry, is that lipstick on your sweater?' She had to ask, even though she hated revealing how vulnerable she felt.

'Where? Oh that,' he laughed. 'I just had some strawberries.' He blushed.

Yasmine was about to ask why he'd have a strawberry stain on his shoulder, when she saw her auntie's name flash up on the screen. She grimaced. 'Oh, I need to go now. Auntie Dilly is calling me. I'll phone you another time.'

He laughed. 'Okay. I expect she thinks you've disappeared again.'

She blew him a kiss and accepted her auntie's call with a feeling of dread. Further questioning of the shoeshine boy would have to wait for another time.

25

Dilly was humming to a melancholic Kurdish folklore song Yasmine hadn't heard previously. A solemn flute was to be heard in the background. *Hmm, it needs a bit of upbeat rap.* Yasmine tapped the side of the table to try a new rhythm out, happy that Dilly had forgotten about Tara for the time-being.

'How about visiting your grandmother?' Dilly asked cheerfully.

'My grandmother? Um… Where does she live?'

'Not too far from here. It's a small village and she's a simple woman, kind-hearted and usually visiting sick children and trying out her herbal remedies on them.'

'Oh well, then yes. I haven't heard too much about her from Mum except that Granddad died early and she was grieving a lot. I'd love to visit the villages surrounding Sulaymaniyah.'

This city was a multitude of neighbourhoods and emotional paths much of which she had yet to discover. *Maybe my grandmother will explain a bit more about Aram's childhood.*

Liberalisation and debauchery lay so close together in Sulaymaniyah. She knew this must be the same in many big cities, she just hadn't expected it here. The district of Sarchinar and meeting Tara had already taught her a lot about the hidden parts of her mother's home city: nightclubs, brothels and street workers.

Her mother had only told her stories about the historical atrocities of Kurdish people and the beautiful areas in the country such as the Azmar, Goizha and Qaiwan mountains in the northeast of Sulaymaniyah. She'd talked about picnics near waterfalls and meeting up with her friends. She had also proudly spoken about the great poets, scholars and singers such as Piramerd the poet and the Ottoman-Kurdish prince Ibrahim Pasha Baban, who named Sulaymaniyah after his father Sulaiman Pasha. The prince focused on the importance of this town having Jewish residents. So, Qaradagh had a thriving Jewish community. *Inclusivity in those days was better than now.* Yasmine sighed when she thought about all the wars that were waged since then. Most of the Jewish population had left for Israel in the 1950s.

She couldn't wait to escape honking cars, street vendors, fortune-tellers and dust in the city. It would be soothing in a village for a while. However, she had heard from Dilly that her grandmother was also some kind of a fortune-teller – she could 'read' coffee grounds by interpreting patterns in them. *I'm not going to ask her to read her coffee grounds. What a load of rubbish.* She would drink tea instead.

Dilly and Yasmine sat in the kitchen which was the hub of the house. Dilly was busy preparing dolma, kibbe, biriyani and other laborious meals for Jamal. *Thank goodness Harry doesn't insist on having warm meals three times a day.* Yasmine watched her auntie bring a large pot of unsalted water to a boil. She then plunged the vine leaves into the water and let them cook for a minute or two, before turning around to say, 'Before we go to visit Aisha, you need to know how to prepare for the reading.'

'What reading?' Yasmine asked, worried as she couldn't read in Arabic or Kurdish. She already felt inadequate and self-conscious in the country and didn't want to add anything to her list of inefficient skills.

Dilly glanced up from shredding lettuce at the table. She started to laugh when she saw Yasmine's frightened face. 'I don't mean reading a book. I mean coffee reading.'

Yasmine smiled, relieved.

Dilly continued to explain the process. 'First you need to prepare a strong, velvety coffee, then serve it in small cups with a solid white inside. Don't worry, we will be doing that. Then,' she touched Yasmine gently, 'you have to drink the coffee with intent and think about your questions while doing so.'

Yasmine stifled a giggle, looking at how earnest her auntie looked. Tara's whereabouts caused Yasmine more anxiety than her grandmother's coffee readings. What other superstitions did she have?

'You need to place your cup upside down on its saucer.' She took a saucer from the cupboard nearby to demonstrate this. 'Then when it's cooled, Aisha can read the patterns formed by the grounds.' Dilly suddenly thumped the table to emphasise the importance and finality of this procedure.

'That sounds um … lovely, Auntie.' Yasmine jumped away from the table and her auntie. Dilly looked at her warily, so she quickly added, 'Do you think Nana Aisha can teach me how to do it myself? I'd love to go back to Britain with new skills.'

Dilly narrowed her eyes and pushed the saucer aside. 'You're teasing me now.' She grabbed hold of both Yasmine's shoulders and pretended to shake her. After a few mock-punches, they ended up hugging each other. Yasmine was relieved to do something light-hearted for a few moments instead of worrying about whether Tara was alive.

Tara's punters oscillated between contempt and desire for women and she had told Yasmine that some of them started beating her after their urges were satisfied. *Geez, the trials poor Tara has endured are immeasurable.*

Yep, a trip to the nearby village would be like balsam on her inner wounds. *If no new injuries arise.*

26

Her neighbour's son Hawar took Yasmine to Nana Aisha's house which was next to a cemetery. Yasmine shuddered. It had been raining so the mud stuck to her black shoes as she walked into the house with the white-washed walls of dried clay.

Auntie Dilly had been looking forward to the rain that morning as they didn't often experience it, and the gardens needed water. Yasmine inhaled the scent of wet mud. It was more earthy than the sludge in her local park in London. For a moment, she missed the grey skies in England. But then, she had willingly gone on this adventure and she would brave any difficult situation that came her way.

Dilly waved goodbye to their driver and thanked him many times as was the custom in Kurdistan, then carried the large pot of dolma she had cooked into her mother's house. Yasmine peered at her grandmother's house. The courtyard looked bare and there were no swings as Dilly sadly had no children. There was a darkness inside the house that baffled Yasmine. The walls were plain white with no adornments except for the familiar 'evil eyes' that greeted her. Yasmine felt a chill in her spine.

She looked up at the large blue eye on the amulet hung up on the hook next to the entrance. Her mother had had some of these talismans given to her as presents from relatives. These repellents were supposed to indicate spiritual protection against the evil eye and to ward off variations of evil intentions. Yasmine shuddered. *Why such a huge evil eye? Where would the danger come from? Nana Aisha was far away from big-town crime.*

Hopefully, this superstition was harmless as long as no one started pointing their finger at anyone who looked demonic. She suppressed a giggle. The evil eye was not as laden with constraints like religion. You either believed in them or not, and no one would judge you for not believing in them, contrary to religion.

Why am I so drawn to people with imperfections? Others would call them misfits. People whose behaviours set them apart from others, a motley collection of nonconformists, eccentrics, weirdos.

Some people thought her mother belonged to this uncomfortably conspicuous collection of people. With all her prudence of appearing traditionalist and conformist due to her ethnicity, her mother was still at danger of being ostracised because of her family setup. *Is my mum the reason I'm drawn to people on the margins of society?* She was jolted out of her reverie when the front door was slowly opened. Surely, this woman would be welcomed into the traditional society with open arms!

'*Roj bash, choni?*' Nana Aisha looked at her suspiciously and asked her how she was in Kurdish, then reverted back to pidgin English. So, this was the grandmother she had never met, standing in front of her with a toothless smile and a blue tattoo on her chin. She was much smaller than herself, but Yasmine had the odd feeling that Aisha was the towering person. There was no resemblance to her mother. The cold eyes were penetrating and soulless.

Aisha took them to a small sitting room where they were told to sit on the cushions on the unvarnished wooden floor. Yasmine glanced at the corner of the room. *Are those specks of blood? Where did they come from?* Nana should have removed the stains but then she was old and may have not noticed them. Aisha sat on a chair near the table as her arthritis was playing up. Her maid, Tula, served plates of vegetable rice, aubergines and chicken. Yasmin loved the bunker, the crusty bottom of rice in the pot. It had turned light brown and was deliciously crispy. A *feast as usual.*

Afterwards, Yasmine was just about to get up when her grandmother stood up and commanded her to eat more.

'You too thin. In England no good food, only fish and chips,' she said, wrinkling her face. 'How old you are?'

Yasmine told her that she was twenty-one years old and Aisha snapped, 'Too late!'

'Too late for what?' Yasmine asked, perturbed. Did she mean marriage?

Dilly smiled at Aisha. She appeared to obey anything her mother said, even sitting on the hard floor when her hips must surely ache. *What a strange relationship.* Yasmine remembered her rebellious banters with her own mother.

Aisha looked her up and down. The kindness in her eyes when offering her the delicacies had vanished. Dilly got up from the floor slowly, saying that her knees were not what they used to be. Arthritis was settling in and she wanted to sit at the table with her mother next time they came. Aisha nodded methodically but didn't appear happy with her daughter wanting to sit with her at the table.

Yasmine peered at her grandmother curiously. Her movements lacked Dilly's boisterous emotions and this wasn't only because of her age. Nana's eyes looked hollow. Aisha hugged Dilly as she said goodbye and promised to pick Yasmine up the following day. Yasmine frowned at the thought of Dilly leaving her alone, even if only for a day. Her grandmother's house appeared dark.

'I hope you'll be okay, Yasmine,' Dilly said, hugging her. 'I need to get dinner ready for Jamal. He can't cook like me.' She winked at Yasmine, who couldn't relate. Harry cooked for her whenever they celebrated an anniversary or birthday.

As soon as Dilly had left, Aisha said some visitors would be arriving to see her soon but that they would have some personal issues to discuss. Hmm. *Nana doesn't want me to see her friends.* Yasmine looked out of the window of the sitting room. The courtyard was still empty. There was a pungent smell of burnt metal coming through the window. It was mixed with the smell of mould, dust and something sterile like alcohol. Yasmine held her breath for a while but ended up gasping for air.

'That's okay, Nana Aisha,' Yasmine said, trying hard to regain her composure. 'I've got a book to read.'

She had bought a book from the bazaar in Erbil and intended on underlining important passages on how to learn to write in Latin Kurdish. She thought it should be relatively easy as they used the same alphabet. The washing up had been done, and Aisha said they would go to visit the local grocery after her visitors had left. She then shuffled upstairs, holding on to the banister.

After a few minutes, just as Yasmine was getting settled on the old sofa in the sitting room, she glanced up and saw her grandmother limping past with a razor blade in her hand. *Surely, she didn't need to shave her legs at this stage of her life.* The pressures and standards of beauty didn't need to be adhered to so stringently at that age, one would think. She shook her head involuntarily and turned back to reading her book.

Understanding a new language opened gateways to new thinking and new experiences. Kurds used the Latin alphabet as well as the Arabic one. The Latin version was more familiar to Yasmine.

As she read, she wondered whether she would ever belong to this country of oxymorons and different expectations of beauty and virtues, where perceived vices had to be hidden amidst ideals of strict principles.

Her eyelids felt heavy after reading about how to write in Latin Kurdish for an hour. It was time to read something more exciting. She tossed her book to the side and picked up her mother's favourite – *Orlando* by Virginia Woolf. She had read it previously. The book covered three centuries of lust and transition, featuring characters drawn from the English aristocracy. *Hmm, what would gender critical feminists think of it today?*

Writers like Virginia Woolf were like secret agents, switching their countries, timelines and genders when writing from various points of view, penetrating barriers and not shying away from transgressions. *What a joyful way to travel.*

Yasmine's romp through the British history of Virginia Woolf's era was rudely interrupted when a high-pitched scream from upstairs made her jolt, drop the book and race upstairs, taking two steps at a time. She pricked up her ears. The visitors, a middle-aged woman and a girl aged about ten, had arrived a few minutes before and gone straight upstairs to her grandmother's bedroom, peering curiously at Yasmine's book as they walked past her room.

The girl had looked frightened but Yasmine had kept herself busy with her book. Nana Aisha had told her to keep away from her visitors. Were they the cause of all the screams?

Yasmine hesitated outside her grandmother's door. She heard another piercing cry. Maybe the girl who was visiting with her mother had screamed about a lizard that had sauntered across the floor. These lizards could be scary. She had yelled too, the first time she had encountered one on the curtain.

But there it was again – a shrill cry that was so visceral as to make Yasmine's blood curdle. She flung open her grandmother's bedroom door. Whatever was taking place in that room wasn't caused by an escaping lizard. She stopped at the doorway, frozen by a scene that would stay with her for the rest of her life.

The girl in the room was being pinned down by the middle-aged woman. Her legs were wide open on the bed and blood was running down her thighs. Grandma Aisha stood in front of her, wielding a razor blade in her hand. She looked triumphant. The girl had tears streaming down her face. Yasmine gasped as her grandmother and the 'auntie' of the girl turned around to glare at her reproachfully. *Oh God. Please no.*

'Stop it, Nana Aisha,' Yasmine screamed, almost as loudly as the girl who had blood running down her genitals. The girl's relative shouted for her to get out and asked her grandmother who the meddling woman at the door was.

Her grandmother ignored the woman and growled at Yasmine, saying, 'I want to put ashes on the girl's wound to be clean.'

'But Nana,' Yasmine responded, 'you caused the wound.' She realised that her grandmother wouldn't budge and ran towards the girl, kicking the razor blade out of her grandmother's hand. Her grandmother was feeble and stumbled to the ground, crying out loud as she fell.

The pan of grey ashes she held in her other hand fell to the floor and scattered onto her grandmother's face, sprinkling dark shades around her eyes. She yelled in pain and said something to the girl's auntie. The young victim sat up on the bed to cover her genitals.

The girl started sobbing as her auntie hurried to gather some of the ashes on the floor. Yasmine didn't have a clue as to what the ashes were supposed to be useful for. The auntie yelled at Yasmine who could only understand one word – *khatana.*

Yasmine stiffened for a moment. Dilly had told her

about female genital mutilation – otherwise known as *khatana, a euphemism for circumcision* in Kurdish – but had assured her that her family were not party to this procedure. *Shit. I'm in the thick of it now.*

Yasmine ran to the adjoining bathroom and grabbed a towel and disinfectant she spotted nearby. *What idiots. At least they could have used a disinfectant after using a non-sterile razor blade. Ashes are no use.* She ran back to the bedroom where her grandmother was still on the floor and couldn't get up despite the help from the auntie. Yasmine kissed the girl on the head and held her in her arms till she stopped sobbing uncontrollably, then she showed her the disinfectant. But the girl shook her head, pushing it away. She started to cry again.

The auntie started pulling Yasmine away from the girl. 'Now, look what you've done,' she said glaring at Yasmine.

'What *I've* done?' she asked disbelievingly.

'Yes. Your grandmother is lying on the floor. Maybe she's broken a bone…'

Yasmine glanced at her grandmother, who looked as grey as the ashes she had wanted to apply on the girl's wounds. She hesitated, but then offered her a hand to pull her up. Her grandmother pushed it away, crying out in agony.

Shit. What if she's broken her hip or pelvis? She had to think quickly. There was no other option but to phone Dilly. *How many other calamities am I going to impose on Dilly? Wait a minute. It was Dilly's idea to come to Nana Aisha's in the first place. She has to carry a fraction of the responsibility.* Geez, her brain was frayed.

She dialled Dilly's phone number and waited for her auntie to answer. Her heart was throbbing. The razor blade had caused her thumb to bleed a bit. It was nothing compared to the girl's mutilated genitals though. She glanced at the girl who limped towards her auntie and was wiping her tears with her sleeve.

'Auntie Dilly,' Yasmine sobbed when her call was answered, 'you didn't tell me about Nana's job!'

'What? You phoned me to ask me that? And what's all that crying in the background?'

Yasmine felt like tearing her hair out. Her stomach was in knots again and she felt like fainting or better still, vanishing into thin air. Did Dilly really not know what heinous job her mother was carrying out?

She glanced at the evil eye hung up on the wall behind the young victim's head. It had not warded off depravity from her. Yasmine's legs began to wobble, her shoulders drooped and she tasted salty tears on her lips. She started taking deep breaths trying to stop hyperventilating or fainting. She would survive this crime, but what about the girl?

27

Yasmine sat in her bedroom in Dilly's house, alone once again. She had come to her mother's homeland, hoping to find old memories of her mother and beautiful mountains bristling with snow, yet the canvas in her mind's eye was filling up with darkening shadows and shrill screams.

Her grandmother had been taken to hospital with a broken hip and the treatment there was partly being paid for by Auntie Dilly and Uncle Jamal. She heard her auntie shuffling around the sitting-room downstairs. Uncle Jamal was pacing up and down. They were arguing but she couldn't hear what they were saying; she didn't speak the language except for small talk or when they were speaking slowly.

They were probably discussing what to do with her now that she had caused so many problems. She was curled up in bed, feeling like a foetus, not ready to emerge into the real world.

These issues were present long before I came here. It isn't my fault girls are being mutilated by my grandmother.

She covered herself with the bedsheets. It wasn't cold but she needed a blanket.

If only she could become invisible or turn back time. This journey had become an odyssey. Yasmine shivered despite the blanket. And what about the girl who had been mutilated? What protective covering had she been given? Just ashes on her wound. As if ashes could cleanse her injury. It was horrific.

'Yasmine,' she heard her auntie call, 'come downstairs. Your mother is on the phone.' Dilly's voice sounded shrill and tense.

'I'm coming,' she replied, trying not to sound like a wayward teenager. She had never felt like this with her mother.

She slowly put her blanket aside, feeling as though she was discarding a coat of armour, then went downstairs, past the oil lamp that reminded her of Ali Baba and the forty thieves in the corridor. When she opened the door of the sitting-room, she heard Dilly talking to her mother in a cold voice. They were speaking quickly in Kurdish but Yasmine understood the words, *Nana Aisha.*

'Hello Mum,' Yasmine said carefully, waiting for her to start speaking.

'Hello Yasmine.' Her mother sounded irritable. No wonder. It was a Monday, which meant that she had a heavy workload, and now she was confronted with her daughter's misdemeanours, yet again.

Yasmine pursed her lips. Why did she feel as if she was the perpetrator of some terrible injustice? She wasn't the convict, just the witness to a crime. She had merely walked in on a terrible event. She couldn't fathom how much pain the girl had felt whilst being mutilated by her very own grandmother. Where was she now? And where would she be in a few years when she would be pregnant? Yasmine shuddered.

She turned to face her mother on the screen which almost blinded her. The glare of the laptop had never disturbed her so much previously. Was she going to suffer from post-traumatic stress disorder, an ailment her mother had often encountered in her patients and spoken about. This could last for years. Oh God. She hadn't deserved this.

'How could you push Nana to the ground?' her mother asked, raising her voice in a way Yasmine hadn't heard before. Even when she had failed an important exam and came home drunk, her mother had never shouted at her like today.

'I don't know what Dilly told you, Mum.' Yasmine felt her cheeks redden. 'I merely walked in on a girl being tortured, so I pushed Nana away from her.' She waited for a response.

'What do you mean *tortured*?' Her mother scrunched her face. 'A neighbour brought her niece in to see Nana for some advice on her periods—'

'No!' Yasmine screamed at the laptop. 'She came in with her niece to be mutilated.' She saw her mother's eyes widen. Silence ensued for a few moments.

'Tell me more,' her mother demanded, looking at her intently.

'I heard screaming upstairs in Nana's house, so I ran as quickly as I could and opened the bedroom door.'

Her mother came closer to the computer screen. 'Go on.'

'A young girl lay on a sheet with blood streaming down her thighs.' Yasmine started to cry, then wiped her eyes and added, 'I pushed Nana away from her and ... she fell over. It was an accident.'

Her mother looked horrified. '*Khatana,*' she said quietly. 'Circumcision.'

She heaved a sigh of relief. Her mother was beginning to understand the true state of affairs, the torture Yasmine had only read about in newspapers. She waited for her mother to digest the seriousness of the matter. Yasmine added, 'Nana was going to put ashes on the girl's wounds. I don't know where she got that from.'

Her mother cleared her throat and picked up a glass of water on her desk. 'They get the ashes from a flat-surfaced oven used to bake traditional bread. Maybe the auntie brought them with her.'

'It was terrible, Mum. Why ashes?' She was glad her mother had stopped raising her voice. This wasn't something the reception staff in the practice should be hearing.

'Because they think it cleanses the wound,' her mother replied. 'It could have been worse.' She covered her face in her hands. 'Sometimes they use cooking oil or the spice Sumac to cover the wound.'

Yasmine stopped wiping her eyes and scrutinised her mother warily.

'Did you know about Nana's *job*?' She felt her eyes well up again.

'Of course not, Yasmine! I left decades ago.'

'Then how do you know about this khatana so well?' Yasmine felt her anger overcome her fear.

'Darling, I was told by my friends that this circumcision is still practised in some villages.' She pointed at some papers on her desk and added, 'I received some information from NHS England that doctors should declare such incidents if they found out about them.' She looked at her daughter sadly and continued, 'Also to warn any woman sending their daughters to certain countries that it is prohibited even if the circumcision is done in another country.'

Yasmine shook her head and said, 'Mum, you didn't tell me it was prevalent so close to where I would be living.' She crossed her legs involuntarily and flinched.

'How would I know Nana would do such a procedure? I haven't been in the country for years,' her mother stammered.

'Why do they do this?' Yasmine asked, boldened by her mother's defence.

Her mother took a deep breath and replied, 'Some religious leaders say it's to cleanse a girl, to regulate female desire.' She hesitated. 'And prevent women from committing adultery.' She sounded flat.

'Have you ever encountered a patient after an FGM procedure, Mum?'

Her mother looked at her, wiping her eyes with a tissue lying on her desktop. 'Yes. A young woman I saw had undergone type two FGM whereby her clitoris had been removed and the labia minora, with a partial cutting of her labia majora.'

'Shit. What about the Children Act and safeguarding you're leading in the practice?'

'Sweetheart, this was done abroad.' She wiped her

forehead with the same tissue and added, 'The most severe form is known as type three which involves the greatest removal of tissue and sewing up of the vaginal entrance.'

'What!' Yasmine lashed out at the cup of water on the table. 'How do they go through childbirth?'

'An opening can be made in the scar tissue for childbirth, but tissue can't be restored.'

'What about sexual function, Mum?' She had always been open about sexual pleasures with her mother.

'Well, in type two where the body of the clitoris is removed, the neurovascular bundle can't be preserved, even by skilful surgery so poor sexual function is the complication. This was the case with my patient.' She closed her eyes for a moment.

Yasmine shook her head disbelievingly. Silence expanded into their rooms. Yasmine could still hear the screams of the young girl who had undergone FGM by her grandmother.

'Mum, the razor blade wasn't even sterilised. She might have used it on another girl.'

Her mother took a deep breath and said, 'A patient of ours who was circumcised in Somalia was not only disfigured after the procedure, but also had a chronic fistula and Hepatitis B, a chronic inflammation of the liver that can lead to cancer.'

Yasmine didn't understand what these complications could lead to. She blurted out, 'How is she now? She must be traumatised.'

Her mother replied, 'She's pregnant and she has a special midwife assigned to her. She received counselling and is looking forward to the baby.' There was a brief smile on her lips.

Yasmine looked at her mother perplexed. 'Where does FGM originate?'

Her mother looked away for a moment, then said, 'Some scholars say it started in Ancient Egypt and Sudan or Rome, implemented on female slaves to prevent pregnancy and sexual relations.'

Yasmine ran her hand through her entangled hair. *Thank goodness, it didn't originate in Sulaymaniyah.*

'What can we do about the girl I couldn't help?' She started sobbing again. How many girls would she fail? First the transwoman in Soho, then the child who had been circumcised, then her grandmother with the broken hip and poor, homeless Tara. No. God forbid. She wouldn't allow Tara to be hurt.

Her mother had started speaking again. 'Yasmine, you can't do anything if there's no complaint.' She waited for her to stop sobbing and added gently, 'It's not your fault.'

Yasmine continued crying.

'It's not your fault,' her mother repeated. Yasmine picked up her head, grateful for her mother's soothing words.

'What about Nana?' Yasmine blew her nose. 'Dilly told me she's broken her hip. That's my fault.' She started to cry again. She alone was the perpetrator of her grandmother's injury. She covered her eyes with her hands, blocking out the images that were trying to thrust themselves upon her.

'Darling, don't beat yourself up; it was an accident. I'll speak to Dilly after this call and we'll think about the next steps afterwards.'

The next steps? Would Dilly insist on her being sent back to London? What had she done? Merely witnessed an awful crime. Goddammit. When would this nightmare of a journey end?

28

Dilly was sitting on a sofa in her favourite corner, near one of her numerous oil lamps which was softly lit. Her face was covered by her hands, but Yasmine could see her groomed eyebrows. She had let the grey ones grow through. Jamal was sitting next to her, cradling her while she cried. His prayer beads, which he usually loved to stroke, lay discarded on the floor. Yasmine stood watching them at the doorway, hesitating whether to enter the room or not. She took a deep breath. She couldn't hide anymore.

'Auntie, I'm so sorry about Nana's broken hip. I didn't mean to hurt her.'

Well, actually I did, preferring her injury to the innocent girl's wounds. She waited for Dilly to pick up her head. Jamal had already looked up and frowned at her, but he didn't tell her to go away. Surely he would want an explanation as to what had happened the previous day.

Dilly sniffled, blew her nose and slowly turned to look at her. Her red-rimmed eyes and black blouse and shawl gave her the appearance of a mythical creature. Yasmine slowly ventured forward, keeping her eyes on her auntie. As she reached her, she gently touched her sleeve and gauged her reaction.

Dilly kept still, then said, 'My mother is now in hospital, awaiting surgery.' She gulped. 'We don't know if she'll make it.'

She started to cry again. Between the sobs, Yasmine heard her say, 'She's old and she can't recover as quickly as a younger person.' She sniffled into her tissue again.

Yasmine drew back and replied, 'I'm sorry she fell and can't recover so quickly.' She folded her hands. 'But what about the girl who was mutilated?' She emphasised the final word and continued, 'The girl won't be able to recover at all.' *No solace for that poor child. Her whole life will change after that heinous procedure.* She added, 'Did you know the job your mother was doing?'

Am I being too forceful with her questions? Might Dilly throw me out of the house? But Yasmine needed to expose these crimes. She wasn't going to keep quiet about such wicked procedures.

Dilly responded swiftly, 'I had no idea about her job, but those women came to her voluntarily.'

Yasmine cringed. 'The girl I saw wasn't there voluntarily, Auntie. She was dragged along.'

Dilly started ruffling her hair and clutched Jamal, exclaiming, 'I don't know what got into Nana. She never did such procedures when we were little.'

'I would have killed her if she had,' Jamal retorted, picking up his prayer beads and stroked them aggressively, as if he wished he could give Nana a wallop.

Yasmine didn't know whether to stifle a laugh or a cry

that was emerging in her throat. *What if her own mother had been circumcised? She wouldn't have told her. But surely Sam would have found out. Shit.* She didn't want to ponder on intimacy. A circumcised mother, whatever next? No, her mother definitely hadn't known about her own mother's deeds, otherwise she would have warned Yasmine, just as she would have warned any of her young female patients going to such parts of the world.

'May I visit Nana in the hospital?' Yasmine asked meekly, hoping the answer would be *no*.

'I don't think that's a good idea,' Dilly replied. 'Nana Aisha is furious – she says there isn't any substitute to do her job now."

Yasmine looked at her auntie disbelievingly. *Bullshit answer.* Thank goodness, now that Nana couldn't do her job, no one else could. But this wasn't a global solution. How many other so-called midwives were continuing to do Nana's job? What else could Yasmine do? She could hardly trip up all these women. Now that she had seen part of the procedure for herself, there was no doubt that it was cruel and had to be stopped, but how? You didn't need to be a feminist to propagate an end to khatana, she thought, feeling sick.

Yasmine turned to look at Jamal who was still hugging his wife. He glanced at her and said, 'Yasmine, I know you hurt your grandmother, but I realise it was an accident.' He softened his tone and added, 'And you're right in refusing to turn a blind eye to this disgusting procedure.'

Yasmine heaved a sigh of relief. She didn't want to be banished from the house for trying to stop a crime being committed. *Did she want to stay at all?* She hadn't tracked

Tara down and had failed to help her till now. She may even have been slain by a punter already. What else would she fail? Her heart sank. A few failures in a short space of time, within two weeks to be exact.

Suddenly, the image of her Uncle Aram on the Azmar mountain imposed itself on her. Where was he? She had run away from him, but he might still be in the city. She shivered. At least she felt safe with her auntie and uncle; Uncle Aram would dare not appear at their house, but he could chase her elsewhere! *Wasn't he behind my stalker in the bazaar near the citadel in Erbil?*

She had dreamt of meeting him again and had refused to listen to her mother. *About what exactly?* Her mother hadn't even told her why he had left – or rather escaped. Her stomach churned as it so often did here. She needed to stay in Sulaymaniyah a bit longer. So many other riddles would be waiting to be unearthed and it seemed she was the only person willing to call them out.

29

The following day, Yasmine sat in her bedroom, eying the oil lamps on her cupboard. There were so many in the house. What was this obsession of her auntie's? If they had no electricity, the generator would kick in. She was worried about the inhalation of toxic fumes. But then these oil lamps were brighter than candles, cheaper than electricity and would withstand power outages. Hmm, just like during the Victorian era. Their presence had a soothing effect on her and she definitely needed that now.

However, she suddenly thought of the film *Gaslight* where a husband manipulated his wife into thinking she was going crazy by slyly changing the intensity of the gas lights in their home when she was left alone. *Is this what Aram is doing to me in an attempt to make me believe I can't trust my maturity or my memory?* She shuddered.

She thought of London, so far away from Sulaymaniyah and its contradictions. Her mother would be returning home after a hard day's work and Sam would have cooked a warm meal. No one else would be in the house, now that

Yasmine had left. She tried to conjure up her childhood, trying to make sense of why recent dramas had held her up instead of propelling her forward.

Her mother had told her that she had thrown tantrums as a toddler and that it had been difficult to contain them. Sam had laughed, saying that they occurred much less when *she* was with her. She drew a deep breath. Had she been drawn to dramatic events after the tantrum milestones?

She had overheard Sam talking to her mother when Uncle Aram had left, saying that she wanted to kill him. But *why?* No one had mentioned him after that. The silence made her more curious. Her mother was certainly a master of self-control and secrecy, whereas Yasmine stepped out of one drama, only to drop into another one. Surrounded by love from her mother. But drawn to Aram, her uncle, the villain. Perhaps not everything was his fault. She tried to sum up what she already knew. Maybe she could join the dots later on.

Her father had been killed in a car accident when she was aged seven. He was the driver; Aram had been with him. Yasmine had been told that the other car's female driver had died immediately after the collision. How tragic. But then, if her father hadn't died, her mother would never have met Sam at the counselling sessions. Sam, her mother's soulmate, a social worker, lover and second mother to Yasmine.

Whereas her father had demanded submissiveness from her mother, Sam had given her mother the freedom to live and evolve. Her mother had explained this to Yasmine with gleaming eyes. There were no highs and lows in their relationship, just loving, lingering glances, affectionate hugs and smiles. Sam kept the house running while Mum was working.

They never argued in front of her and made sure she attended dance and music classes as well as all the other celebrations of her school friends. But somewhere along the line, family stories had been omitted. It was this withholding of family secrets that had intrigued Yasmine. She'd known she'd join the dots one day.

There was a knock on her door. She quickly sat on the chair next to her bed and waited for Jamal to come in. His knock was always strong and assertive, while Dilly's was weaker. Dilly suffered from fibromyalgia which meant that her muscles were painful. Her mother had told her that there was no cure for this other than painkillers and possible psychotherapy. Yasmine stood up to let Jamal in as he didn't enter the room after she called him to come in. He was cautious after the incident with Nana.

'Hi, Uncle Jamal. Come in. I'm not busy or anything.'

Jamal entered slowly, and she detected a mixture of compassion and fear in his eyes.

'I wanted to check in on you, Yasmine. Your experiences here in the country have not always been pleasant and welcoming for you.'

Yasmine didn't dare to nod and waited for him to continue.

'I think your mother should have told you more about the drawbacks of living here, not only the electricity failing every now and again.'

Yasmine nodded this time and said, 'I've been camping in Britain, so I know about the lack of electricity, Uncle.' He frowned and waited for her to continue.

'I'm sorry, Uncle. I know I keep stepping into terrible events, but it's not due to my mother omitting to mention these matters. I'm old enough to inform myself about them.'

'Hmm, I think you should know more about these issues before going back home.' He looked out of her window and continued, 'I belong to the Anti-Narcotic forces here.'

Yasmine raised an eyebrow. 'I didn't know that.'

'I don't mention it for security reasons. Anyway, a few months ago, we arrested one of the largest drug-trafficking networks in Duhok, a city nearby.' He waited, gauging her reaction to this news, but she kept quiet. 'What I mean to say is that these narcotics derange our young people… and old ones of course.' He took a deep breath and said proudly, 'We seized over 236 kilograms of Captagon and around thirty-six kilograms of opium.'

'Uncle, we have drug problems in Britain too—'

'Yes, but you also have rehabilitation centres to combat the addiction.' He looked at her sadly. 'Ninety percent of our drug users are young men. The wars they've been through lead to their feelings of helplessness…and they turn to drugs.'

No wonder they wanted to dissociate themselves from the harsh realities of war and a torn society. Yasmine frowned. Her uncle continued speaking, or rather more explaining the situation in large parts of his city.

'Yasmine, you need to know that the Ministry of Finance is providing financial rewards to those who turn in illegal narcotics and the drug lords.'

'You don't need to worry about me. I don't take drugs,'

Yasmine remonstrated, feeling her cheeks burn. That one trial of ganga at uni didn't count. It tasted terrible.

'I didn't mean that, but your Uncle Aram may do.'

'I don't want to see him again, Uncle Jamal,' she responded with alacrity. Hopefully, he would never find her here or in London. But then, she would never find out why he had left Britain in such a hurry. She felt like tearing her hair out. And how could she forget Tara? Where was she?

There was a solution to this – the shoeshine boy. She got up slowly, tapped her uncle on the shoulder and said, 'Uncle, I think we need to go out and celebrate the fact that Nana's operation was successful and that she has forgiven me. Auntie Dilly told me the good news.'

She felt slightly sick while saying this. But her uncle smiled for the first time since entering the room. And she wanted to move forwards with her investigations. She hadn't finished with this city yet, or with her dodgy relatives, to which Aram belonged. How many more relatives were lurking in the background?

She smiled back at her uncle. It was good that he couldn't read her thoughts. She hadn't come to her mother's country to seek out glamour and warm-heartedness. She had also come to share the stories of torture and tears during the wars. But most of all, to face untold stories.

She left the room, linking arms with her uncle until they reached the stairs. The aroma of lavender soap on his neck was soothing.

Auntie Dilly could be heard speaking to Nana Aisha on loudspeaker. *Nana needed that jolt.* Yasmine was shocked at her insensitivity. But then, she had lost all track of cultural sensitivities here in this country. Before tackling the shoeshine boy again, she needed to speak to Sam. Was there any other avenue out of this feeling that she was lost in a limbo?

30

It was time to phone Sam, her mother's practical-minded partner, the one she told some of her secrets, not excluding the more embarrassing ones. She giggled when she remembered how Sam had picked her up from a party at two in the morning. Admittedly, Yasmine had drunk a few more vodkas than was advisable, but she knew that Sam could sneak out of their house and rescue her without waking her mother up.

'Hi Sam,' she said, peering at the computer screen. 'I need to speak to someone who is just as clueless as I am as to what is actually happening here on the other side of the world.'

Sam cackled. 'Honey, I think your adventures are making you a professional.'

'A professional offender, Sam?'

Sam giggled again. *Will she soften up and tell me more about my dad's death or why Uncle Aram disappeared so many years ago?*

'I'm not sure Mum would understand why I'm stumbling upon so many awful events here, Sam,' she hesitated. 'I mean, I do miss her a lot. I remember at this time of the year, we would go window-shopping at Selfridges and walk to Carnaby Street for the Christmas lights. With you, of course.' Sam nodded, listening carefully as Yasmine continued, 'I needed to come here – I was hoping to spread my wings and find my roots. But all that's happening, is that people I meet on the way,' she gulped, 'are being hurt.' She waited for Sam to say something, anything to soothe her.

'Darling, you'll be okay. Remember that Kurdistan is at the crossroads of Iran, Turkey and Syria so problems will arise, such as tribal laws and—'

'Hustling, trafficking, people smuggling,' Yasmine added. 'And FGM.' She felt a tightness in her chest and tried to stop herself from rocking in her wobbly chair, a mixture of fatigue, horror and despair overcoming her.

'Yasmine, when you left for Iraq, you were yearning for a vibrant entry into an almost ancient society. Surely, you knew that you couldn't change a culture so quickly?'

Yasmine frowned and said, 'I love the people, but the FGM has to stop. That girl I saw crying could have been me – or Mum.' She felt like crying and closed her eyes for a moment. Then she opened her eyes wide and said, 'I don't even know if Mum's been done.'

Sam laughed and said wryly, 'I don't think you need to worry about that.'

Yasmine heaved a sigh of relief although she felt her cheeks redden. She waited for Sam to start speaking again.

'You know, you can do something, Yasmine. You can initiate awareness of FGM in Britain so families travelling back will be hesitant about the procedure. You could also join other campaigns and educate people about sex trafficking and people smuggling.'

Yasmine looked out of the window. The clouds floating above the houses were so pure, so innocent. She wished she could drift away with them, even if only for a few minutes. She brought her dreams back to the present moment.

'I suppose so. I can also try and shed light on these atrocious procedures by writing about them.' She looked out of the window again and could see the serene garden full of yellow jasmine flowers. She could almost smell the sweet fragrance, contrary to the beads of sweat oozing out of her pores. 'But I'm worried. Not only will some people hate me for calling them out about sex trafficking, but they might also want to kill me.' Her eyes widened.

'What do you mean?' asked Sam in alarm.

'Well, the sex industry brings in a lot of money for the pimps. *Was Uncle Aram a pimp, too?* 'What if they came after me? I took Tara away from the streets. Now, I don't even know where she is!'

'First of all, Yasmine, protect yourself. Keep safe at all times.' Sam came closer to the screen and added, 'You said your Uncle Jamal is an honest and kind man. Stay with him when going out.' She giggled. 'I saw his photo and he looks like a muscular man. He could get a second job as a bodyguard.'

Yasmine smiled. It was true Jamal was a generous and kind man. He would be the only person able to help her find Tara. He didn't seem to like Nana Aisha either, so maybe they could both deter her from causing further harm to young girls. But she had to talk to him separately as her auntie might take Nana Aisha's side even though she was torturing girls. After all, Nana Aisha was Dilly's mother.

Yasmine was surprised that her mother hadn't known about Nana Aisha's heinous procedures. *What would her colleagues in the practice say or do if they found out that the mother of one of their colleagues was torturing young girls? They would feel disgusted to say the least.*

Yasmine winced. Her mother was nowhere near retirement age yet. *Now, she herself would be forced to keep this secret.* She would never tell her friends about her grandmother's job. And she'd have to think about whether she would tell Harry about this matter. He had always thought she was a proud feminist. What would he think about her family if he knew they were propagating FGM? But then, it wasn't all her family. It was just her grandmother. She could tell Harry that her grandmother was demented. She almost felt like laughing. *Am I losing my mind?*

How could a demented woman like her grandmother manage to convince her entourage that she was the right person to do this horrible procedure? She had started as a midwife, helping baby girls enter life and ended by crippling them when reaching puberty – and even before then.

Her thoughts came back to Sam. She was beginning to look more worried. She had asked a question and waited for Yasmine to answer.

'Um, sorry, Sam. My thoughts got waylaid. What did you just ask me?'

'I wanted to know whether Nana Aisha was out of the hospital?'

'She's staying there for another week, I think, but I was told that her condition was stable.'

'Thank goodness for that.' Sam heaved a sigh of relief. 'Your mother can't take more time off. She's already taken a few days off for Christmas.'

'Nana Aisha isn't going to die – not yet.' Yasmine felt some Schadenfreude when she thought of her Nana's pain. *This matter with the tortured girl and Nana has made me insensitive.*

'Sam, I think Uncle Jamal is my favourite uncle. He told me his team seized a large quantity of crystal narcotic substances and other drugs recently. And the Iraqi security forces busted two dangerous drug trafficking networks.' She smiled at Sam. It was such a relief to talk about success stories and not just torture and destruction.

Sam smiled back and took a sip of her tea. 'We all have our virtues and flaws, honey. Be careful whom you trust.'

At that moment, there was a knock on Yasmine's door. She almost jumped off the bed. 'Okay, Sam. I have to go now. I'll phone another time.'

For the time being, Yasmine wasn't sure who she could trust. But at least she could trust some people more than others. Uncle Jamal would be one of them.

31

Yasmine opened the door and smiled at Jamal. She would need him at her side when venturing further from the house. Hopefully, Aram wasn't a sniper but he knew his way around the city better than her and could easily arrange a kidnapping. Maybe he had already dealt with Tara. She shuddered.

'Yasmine, you've been through a lot,' Jamal said gently. 'Would you like to go out for a drive and a chat in a café?'

'That would be lovely. Is Auntie Dilly coming?' Yasmine stiffened, regretting her question. She needed to speak to Jamal alone.

'Um, no. She told me she wanted to have a nap.'

What a relief. Dilly's fibromyalgia meant that she was often tired and needed frequent naps. Her muscle aches occurred sporadically and mostly when she was stressed, like at the present moment.

Her uncle closed the door and said he would wait downstairs. Yasmine ambled to the cupboard opposite her bed. She would choose her dark brown cardigan for that day. *Hopefully this will camouflage me when I go out.* She was hiding from shapeless dark forces and shadows, not only Uncle Aram. There were still many pieces missing from the childhood stories her mother had told her.

She put her earrings on. One of them fell on the ground. Damn, these were her favourite silver, heart-shaped ones. She quickly bent down to retrieve it. Thank goodness she didn't suffer from the elusive fibromyalgia like Auntie Dilly and was able to bend down without any problems.

As she bent down, her foot slipped and the earring was pushed underneath the cupboard. *Shit.* These earrings were a present from Harry. She rushed to her dressing-table and grabbed hold of her comb. This would do the trick.

As she bent down again to try and retrieve the earring, she heard a scratching sound that came from behind the comb. She stopped pushing the comb further ahead and went to the dressing table again to get her small mirror attached to the blush.

Surely, a lizard wouldn't be hiding underneath the cupboard. That would be disgusting. And frogs were only to be seen in the garden. She checked this spare room every day since she had seen a lizard climb the curtain in the sitting room downstairs. The frogs in the garden didn't disturb her that much as they were more frightened of her than she was of them.

Right, time to find out what the object underneath the cupboard was. She put the mirror on the floor and peered at the reflection from underneath the cupboard. It was a small box with Sellotape around it. That made her more curious.

She retrieved the lost earring and pushed the comb further to the left side thereby shoving the box out. There it was – a hidden box with a pink ribbon lacing it. And why hide it underneath the cupboard in the spare room? Anyway, there was no turning back now. She needed to see the contents.

There was still time until she had to go downstairs to meet Uncle Jamal. The scissors on the dressing table were excellent for cutting the Sellotape and she opened the box quickly, expecting jewellery. Nothing glittered in the box.

She should stop snooping. If the box was sealed by Sellotape, there would be a reason for it. Did her auntie have secrets too? Just like her mother. She stared at the contents of the metal box. A few letters stared at her. They looked gilded, most probably written many years ago. She unfolded the top letter and peered at a very familiar handwriting, confused. Sam's.

She glanced at the recipient of the letter. It was Auntie Dilly. She scanned the letter, glancing at the door. There were no footsteps to be heard. She still had the opportunity to stop. But she didn't.

The letter read,

Dear Dilly,

I heard from your sister Sozanne that you were very upset about the disappearance of your brother Aram. You blame your sister for this. I think you need to know about the circumstances that led to Aram's disappearance. As you know, Sozanne's English husband, Dylan, and Aram were involved in a car accident. Aram was driving, erratically to be precise. Dylan, Yasmine's father, had just finished a night shift in the hospital, so he let Aram drive. We didn't know till that moment that Aram had been taking drugs...

Yasmine's skin crawled. But she needed to continue reading. A puzzle was slowly being solved. Aram had been taking drugs and he had been the one driving on that fatal night her father had died. Her head was spinning in all directions.

When their car crashed into a tree, Dylan was killed but Aram only sustained a knee injury. The car hit a young woman in a car on the opposite side of the road and killed her instantly. What Aram did afterwards was unforgivable. He pushed Dylan's body to the driver's seat and blamed him for the accident, telling the police that he shouldn't have been driving after a tiring night shift in the hospital.

Yasmine's stomach was churning but she continued to read the letter. She felt as though she was in a trance.

Sam and I believed Aram's story and felt sorry for his injury. He suffered from a limp.

Yasmine frowned. Now she knew why Aram limped occasionally. She continued reading Sam's letter.

However, forensics at the crime scene soon found out that Dylan was not the driver and police came

to Dylan's home looking for Aram, who was the only
other person in the car.

Yasmine's mind was racing by now. All this time, she had thought her father had died in a car accident and that Aram had tried to help him. She felt the rage rise in her and hoped she didn't have a fraction of Aram's DNA. She shook her head disbelievingly. Why was all this hidden from her? There must be more to this terrible story. And only one person could answer her – Aram.

The letter had one last paragraph.

The police came to the house looking for Aram. But
he had fled the country before the police could find
him and we don't know where he is, presumably
back home in Iraq. Please don't blame your sister
Sozanne for keeping a distance from the family. She
needed to grieve for her husband and felt responsible
for not warning her husband Dylan about her
brother Aram and his drug usage.

Yasmine wondered what more her mother knew about Aram. She needed to speak to her but first she needed to find Aram. She felt like she was juggling objects and waiting for them to crash down on her.

Dilly, I know you don't approve of Sozanne and my
relationship, but I have been a big support for her
after these tragic events and most importantly, we
love each other. I hope you accept us one day. Your
sister Sozanne loves you very much.

Best wishes
Sam

Yasmine felt her cheeks heat up. How dare Dilly disapprove of her mother's relationship? What morals? Aram, the criminal, was allowed to kill her father and run away like a coward! She would track him down and then—

There was a shout from downstairs. 'Yasmine, are you ready?' Jamal's voice boomed.

Yes, and how she was ready. She clenched her fists. She would deal with all of her family and smash the cycle of secrets.

32

Yasmine went downstairs, heat flushing through her body. There had been no mention of Jamal in the letter she had read. But Dilly had been implicated as a judgemental sister to her mother. *How dare she ghost my mum for so many years?*

'Good morning, Yasmine,' Dilly said in a quiet voice. 'Did you sleep well?' She looked concerned.

How could Yasmine sleep well when everything she had known about her parents had turned out to be a pretence, or to be more honest, lies. What she now knew was that Uncle Aram had killed her father by recklessly driving the car whilst under influence of drugs, framed her father and fled the scene. Worse was the fact that a young, innocent woman had been killed too.

Yasmine's jaw felt tight. Oh God. When would she be released from this torture? She glared at her auntie. 'Dilly, how could you hide the fact that your brother Aram was responsible for the death of my father?' She raised her voice and stepped closer to her auntie.

Dilly blinked a few times and touched her eye as if

she was trying to remove a foreign body from it. 'I... I didn't know about this matter until he escaped from the country.' She glanced at Jamal who stood at the doorway, looking puzzled.

'You mean your brother Aram killed Sozanne's husband?' Jamal ruffled his thinning hair, dropping his soothing prayer beads. He didn't pick them up and waited for his wife to answer him.

'No, no, that's not the full story,' Dilly faltered. 'He had a collision with another driver and hit a tree.' She took a deep breath, then continued, 'Sozanne's husband died but it was an accident, Jamal.'

Yasmine felt her cheeks reddening even more and said, 'As if it wasn't enough killing two innocent people, he also blamed the death of the other driver on my father.' She raised her voice again. 'Although Aram was the one who had been driving.'

Yasmine didn't know where to direct her anger, at Aram for the crime, her mother or Sam for hiding this fact or Auntie Dilly for continuing the pretence and lies.

Yasmine could see that Uncle Jamal was having difficulty digesting all this news. So, was he an outsider in this dysfunctional family? Why hadn't he been told about Aram? She glanced at Dilly who was looking at her anxiously.

'Dilly,' she omitted the word 'auntie' this time. 'Why did you deem it necessary to keep away from my mother for so many years?' She shook her head and looked at the ground. 'Mum lost her husband and you; her sister ghosted her afterwards. Why?'

She felt rage rising up in her when she remembered

hearing how her mother had had to take sleeping pills and anti-anxiety tablets whilst simultaneously having to go to work, taking only a week of compassionate leave after the death of her husband.

Dilly stared at her and said, 'Well, this other woman didn't keep away from her, did she?'

Yasmine stepped closer to her auntie. 'So, that's it. You were jealous—'

'Ha, why would I be jealous of a woman who stole your mother from your father?' Dilly flung her arms in the air, glaring at Yasmine.

'My mother would never have managed to get through the grief of losing my father if it wasn't for Sam's love!' She realised that she had raised her voice a tad too much and gulped before adding quietly, 'Anyway, she met Sam when she went for counselling. That was *after* my father was killed.'

Dilly looked horrified, 'You mean Sam was her counsellor?'

'No, they met in the waiting room.' Why, oh why, was her auntie so obsessed about how they had met? 'Anyway, Dilly, what has that got to do with you?'

Jamal moved towards his wife and said, 'I think we should stop this conversation here at the doorway and go into the sitting room.'

Dilly ignored him and said, 'Your mother could have come back to look after Nana instead of flying around on holidays with Sam.'

'My mother had a job to do in Britain,' Yasmine screamed. She felt her stomach churn. 'And a life to live. She also had to take care of me.' Didn't her mother have the right to a family? What a bigot her auntie had turned out to be. Jamal looked ashen. He was the outsider in this psychodrama. 'Anyway, Dilly, what have you done for Nana? You didn't even know that she was responsible for mutilating young girls.'

'That's enough, Yasmine.' Dilly glared at her. 'Your grandmother acquired these principles in the village she lives in.'

'And what about the principles my mother believes in? Love and companionship. Aren't those better principles than Nana's?'

She wanted to hurt Dilly more but she still lived under her roof. There was a deathly silence in the corridor. The two women stood still, glowering at each other.

Yasmine felt like slicing the dysfunctional family into pieces. For a moment, she felt she was Don Quixote, the delusional knight who set out to fight wrongs.

The sides of her mouth curled up wryly as she envisaged herself calling out Uncle Aram, and not only giving him a piece of her mind, but also letting him feel her revenge.

'Jamal,' her auntie screeched, 'you deal with her. I've had enough. My muscles are aching and I need to rest. There's no consideration for my chronic condition.'

She wobbled out of the room, muttering something in Kurdish on her way. Jamal and Yasmine stared at each other, waiting to see who would move away first. Jamal stayed at her side. That was a welcome beginning. Yasmine felt her muscles relax. Then he picked up his prayer beads and followed his wife to their bedroom. Jamal would need soothing now.

33

Yasmine had to admit that she was lucky to leave Dilly's house in one piece after the showdown that day. The revelations about the relationship between the sisters had been explosive. *All the pretences about not knowing what had happened after the car accident. How absurd.*

But this house was also Uncle Jamal's abode and Yasmine had detected some sympathy there. He was not an immediate part of the family, just an in law, and maybe he felt just that. He spent an hour in the bedroom with his wife discussing the revelations. Yasmine heard their raised voices and could feel his indignation about Dilly not divulging in any of the family's secrets. *Hmm. These sisters have more in common than they know.*

Dilly finally apologised to Jamal about her secrecy. Yasmine crouched on the stairs, listening to their argument. *Geez, my mothers in London never raise their voices like my uncle and auntie.* When Jamal came out of their bedroom, Yasmine ran over from where she was crouching on the stairway and apologised for her outburst.

He accepted it, although he told her that she should reach out to his wife too. Unbelievable. He was willing to forgive his wife for her secrecy about Nana Aisha and Aram's criminality.

She glanced at him sideways. His dusty suit made him look older, less distinguished. That was what she liked about him. He was humble and level-headed. But one of the best parts of his character was that he was naïve or, you may say, simple. She would use that to move forward with her plans.

'Shall we go for a drive and switch off, Yasmine?'

She squeezed his hand and nodded, relieved to leave the house. At her request, they drove to Sarchinar, one of her favourite places with lakes, trees, bridges – and the shoeshine boy. She was pulled towards the area where she had first met Tara like a magnet.

Yasmine looked at her uncle shrewdly. 'Uncle, your shoes look a bit dusty today…'

'Really? I can't see them while driving. It's difficult enough concentrating on the traffic, Yasmine.' He beeped his horn, shaking his head and said, 'People seem to be throwing themselves on the roads.' He hesitated, then asked, 'Is it better in Britain?'

Yasmine laughed and replied, 'It certainly is, Uncle. I've got my driving licence but wouldn't like to drive here.'

The nightmarish image of the car accident in London thrust itself on her. *My father and an innocent woman were killed.* Driving there had been more dangerous, and all because of Uncle Aram. She would know what to do with him. Was she seeking revenge like Hamlet for his father's death? How redeeming it would be if Aram were punished for hurting, killing women and framing her father. Adrenaline was flowing through her body, waiting for an outlet.

Admiration could turn into disgust and hatred. Uncle Jamal glanced at her, so she quickly forced herself to smile. She could learn to keep secrets too. *Is that going to be my new motto, keeping riddles in the family?* That wouldn't be difficult as she couldn't think of anyone she could confide in.

She suddenly thought of Sam. Maybe she could make another phone call to her, to convey her ideas about how she would end her trip here in Iraq. It was difficult to pinpoint her emotions. She realised that she felt murderous but hopefully, this wouldn't turn into action.

She cleared her throat, trying to dispel any criminal inclinations out of her heated body. She had better start thinking about something more pleasant. Yes, Tara who needed rescuing, not punishing. Okay, back to the shoeshine boy.

'Uncle, don't you feel sorry for women who are forced into the sex industry?'

Jamal's puffy cheeks reddened slightly. 'There are other ways they could earn money, Yasmine,' he answered curtly.

'Yes, but what if there weren't any other ways and you would otherwise die of hunger?'

Jamal took a deep breath and said, 'I feel sorry for anyone who has to go down that route.'

She smiled inwardly, realising the imaginary road she was going down to was thorny for her uncle. He was concentrating on the noisy road ahead of him. A woman in an *abaya* had dropped a tray with aubergines on the road.

'*Stachferallah,*' her uncle exclaimed, throwing his arms in the air, adding, 'That abaya is too long. No wonder she tripped.' He waited for her to pick up her aubergines and tapped on his steering wheel impatiently, adding, 'What use are traffic lights if no one uses them?'

Yasmine took the opportunity to press on about the issue with Tara. She said slowly, 'Often, women have been abused by others, not only strangers, but also by their own family.' She paused. 'So, trading their body for freedom is just an extension of abuse. How would you feel if your daughter were used like that?'

Jamal fidgeted in his seat and replied, 'I would hate it and I would kill the perpetrator.' He put his foot down on the accelerator. Yasmine kept quiet until he slowed down. At last, he said, 'I know we're a source for trafficking, forced labour, begging, organ trafficking and sexual exploitation in this area, but we have licensed shelters for trafficking survivors and it was criminalised a few years ago.'

'Does that help the women, Uncle Jamal?'

'Hmm. We need more law enforcement and anti-trafficking police units. They need to be trained and educated.' He glanced at her shyly and added, 'We didn't have children. Unfortunately.' He kept quiet and didn't elaborate on why they could never have children. Eventually, he said, 'But of course, I feel sorry for these women who have no other option but to sell their bodies.' He shook his head and looked the other way.

Auntie Dilly had told Yasmine that Jamal and she

had never had anyone else before marrying. Yasmine had been surprised. There was no way she would marry the first person she met. But then, she had been brought up differently, far away from this country and its age-old familial codes.

Jamal whooped with delight when the woman on the road had picked up all her aubergines and left the road. He put the car into gear again and started driving past vendors of tomatoes, aubergines, peppers and other vegetables she couldn't see properly, as they were driving faster than usual.

Motorists blasted their horns. She was getting used to the noise and people dodging fast cars. Side streets and alleyways were littered with plastic bottles. Yasmine felt like getting out of the car and picking them up. Was there no recycling here?

And yet, she was beginning to love the city with its glimmering lights seen best from the Azmar mountains, silk fabrics sold in the bazaars, fresh fruit, and flowers that blossomed in the parks and gardens with copious amounts of sunlight bringing them to life.

The chaotic narrative of Sulaymaniyah's traffic and the warmth of the well-preserved parks and flowery gardens formed another one of its oxymorons like the deafening silence of beauty.

It was the majestic mountains that Yasmine was drawn to. Edelgard, a Swiss friend of hers who had been to these Kurdish mountains had encouraged Yasmine to hurry up and find them.

And now to the patriarchal codes. I am finally the matador fighting a bull. At last. She would not only search for Aram, but she would also hunt him down. The pursued would become the hunter. She folded a tissue neatly on her lap. Her uncle was sweating despite the aircon. Could he guess what she had in mind? It would be better for him if he didn't have a clue as to her plans.

'I'll have to fill the car up with petrol, Yasmine. The price of one litre of super has risen from a thousand dinars to 1250 dinars.'

It sounded like a lot of money to Yasmine, but then 100,000 Iraqi dinars were merely seventy-five US dollars although it sounded like much more. She glanced at her uncle, who was looking stressed.

'The price of regular petrol hasn't been changed, but most drivers opt not to use it due to its poor quality that they say damages car engines, especially during the summer heat.' He sighed.

Yasmine shook her head. She had seen the copious oilfields burning brightly on her way to Sulaymaniyah. Who was profiting from these resources if not its inhabitants?

The car slowed down as they finally came to their destination – Sarchinar, a beautiful garden with lakes and peaceful chatter. But as she had found out, also, a playground for Babylonian sins.

Yasmine and Jamal walked along the bridge and stopped to look at the ducks floating towards the other end of the lake. How she missed the birdsong in her local park in London, the herons walking on ice in winter and the cormorants spreading and drying their wings on the lake's edge. But there was no way she would go back until she found Tara. She would deal with Uncle Aram afterwards. Her facial muscles twitched in anticipation of sweet retribution. She braced herself to look at her reflection in the lake. She could make out the silhouette. At least that hadn't changed during her stay in this city. It was time to make a move forward.

'Uncle, let's go and get your shoes polished,' she smiled at him, hoping it appeared genuine.

'You really sound worried about my shoes today,' he grinned. 'Why?'

'I'd like to go to the bazaar later on.'

He laughed. 'You don't need to have shiny shoes for that.'

'Well, I need to get some henna. My hair is getting dry here.'

Jamal looked at her curiously and said, 'What about getting the vintage cassettes you were looking for? You remember the ones by Bakhtiyar Salih and Merziyeh Feriqi?'

'Oh yes, and we can get some *nok* at a restaurant there.' She loved the chickpea stew.

Jamal read a message that came in on his phone. 'Dilly has gone out with her friends,' he said, sounding relieved.

Dilly was fuming when we left. It's better not to return home so quickly.

'Right, let's get my shoes polished.' Jamal spotted the shoeshine boy and they walked across the bridge to join him. He had just finished polishing the shoes of a young man in a brown suit.

Yasmine wondered where the parents of the shoeshine boy lived. Did the boy still live at home? As they waited their turn, the shoeshine boy looked up, a flicker of recognition passing his face. Yasmine smiled at him, hoping he wouldn't mention Tara, the woman he often saw across the street, waiting for clients to service. Jamal would be furious to hear that name again.

Jamal spoke to the boy in Kurdish and the boy started rubbing his shoes vigorously, looking up at Jamal now and again. Yasmine peered at his box of chemicals. It was covered in photos of film stars and singers in bright colours.

She tried to catch the boy's eye but he averted his gaze and concentrated on his job. Jamal chatted to him about the lake and the ducks. Yasmine recognised these words. *I really must start those Kurdish classes again.*

After a few minutes, the job was finished to Jamal's complete satisfaction. He took a few dinars out of his pocket and gave it to the boy who looked as if he had expected more of a recognition of his service. *You'll get a proper reward soon.* Yasmine smiled wryly as Jamal nodded at the boy. They walked back towards the bridge. At the middle of the bridge, they stopped again to revel at the peaceful waters.

Suddenly Yasmine tugged at Jamal's sleeve and said, 'Oh, sorry, Uncle, I need to give that shoeshine boy some money. What's his name?'

'Why's that, Yasmine? He didn't polish *your* shoes.' Jamal raised his eyebrows.

'I promised my mother to do some *kher*, Uncle.' This much was true. She had indeed promised her mother to do something charitable. And this boy – her uncle told her that his name was Haval – had been orphaned as a toddler.

Jamal beamed at her. 'Your mother would be proud of you and Haval will be grateful.'

Yasmine smiled and said, 'I'll be back in a minute.' She rushed away before he could change his mind. Luckily, Haval was free. He looked up warily. His T-shirt and jeans were partially ripped. He would be amenable to some extra cash.

'Hello Haval, I forgot to give you something.'

He opened his mouth but didn't say anything.

She took twenty dollars from her handbag and looked at him directly. 'Do you know where Tara is?'

He kept quiet, surreptitiously eying the twenty dollar note in her hand. She took out another twenty dollar note. *Right, that means I won't have enough money for the henna but who cares?*

'Don't worry, Haval. I'm Tara's friend.'

He nodded and thrust his hand forward to grab the money. She held the note tightly and waited for him to reply.

'Tara moved away from this street. She was afraid of that man.'

'Yes, of course. I can imagine that she was afraid of Aram.' She lowered her voice. 'I'm going to help her escape.' She let that sentence dangle in the air. It would please Haval to know that his friend Tara would get some help. 'Tell Tara that I'd like to meet up with her in the Azadi Park tomorrow at noon.'

Haval looked up at her puzzled and said, 'How do you know I'll help you?'

'You look honest, Haval. And Tara will bring you back a present after my meeting up with her.' She patted his shoulder and added, 'You won't be disappointed.'

'Okay, *kuhskekum, my sister,* I will tell her to be in the park at noon tomorrow.' A faint smile passed his lips. He added, 'But don't forget my other present.'

Yasmine smiled broadly, happy that he had called her *sister.* Suddenly, she frowned. 'And remember not to tell Aram about our meeting. It must stay a secret. Do you understand?' She tugged at his sleeve.

'Yes, of course. I don't like him either.' His mouth formed a straight line. 'He forces me to polish his shoes and never gives me a reward.'

That's not his only vice, Yasmine thought, walking back briskly to join her uncle on the bridge. She waved at Haval, marvelling at his gullibility.

34

Azadi Park, the lung of Sulaymaniyah city, used to be a military base during the despicable Baath reign of Saddam Hussain. But after the uprising in 1991, it was converted into a tourism attraction with several beautiful gardens, which was one of the reasons Yasmine had decided to visit it.

She entered the park, looking around her cautiously. Yasmine had told the shoeshine boy Haval where Tara could find her here. And hopefully, he hadn't told Aram about their secret meeting otherwise they would both be in danger.

Aram didn't have any scruples. She should have confided in her mother or Sam about this meeting. *What if something happened to me?* But then they had also kept secrets. *Geez. I'm contributing towards the web of lies and secrets in the family.* She walked around the park, kicking some brown leaves out of the way.

Yasmine quickened her pace. The park was a welcome rest from the hustle and bustle of the bazaar she had strolled through before coming here.

She came to a halt when she saw a white sculpture of a boy on the edge of the lake. He was lying downwards on his stomach with his arms at his side. *Oh. This has to be the sculpture of Aram Kurdi.* She remembered seeing the ghastly photos of a three-year-old Syrian boy of Kurdish heritage who drowned in the Mediterranean Sea along with his mother and brother.

The boy had tried to escape the civil war in Syria and ISIS. His body had been washed ashore in Bodrum and was found in the belly-down position the sculpture imitated. She shook her head disbelievingly – Aram, the innocent boy fleeing persecution and war, and Aram, her criminal uncle, persecuting her family.

The irony of this white sculpture was that children, not much older than the perished toddler, were playing near the sculpture and their parents were taking photos of them jumping up and down on the sculpture. Would this be a deterrent for the people smugglers? She doubted it. With all the wars and climate change, asylum seekers were bound to look for a better life, even if it meant staring death in the face to get to their destiny.

Yasmine decided to leave the sculpture and move towards the other end of the lake. She sat on a bench to gather her thoughts, when she heard someone cough next to her. It was a forced cough. She looked up and saw a woman nearby, wearing a black headscarf and a mouth mask. She also wore a black abaya. Yasmine narrowed her eyes, trying to see the woman's face more clearly.

She stood up. 'Tara?'

The woman came closer and whispered, 'Yes, it's me.'

'You look more conspicuous in that get up!' Most of

the other people were dressed liberally. But then, Tara was most probably worried about Aram finding her. Thank goodness, he wasn't around.

Tara sat down next to her and waited for Yasmine to speak.

'I'm glad you're alive,' Yasmine said, restraining herself from clutching Tara's abaya. 'You still need help Tara.' *Surely Tara would realise that she needed liberating.*

'Umm, Yasmine, I'm very grateful for your help,' she said slowly, 'but why are you helping me?'

There was a mixed expression of puzzlement and fear in her eyes. An image of her mother and Sam embracing each other crept into Yasmine's mind. Her mother, who had left this country decades ago, had married an Englishman despite her family's protests. *She was just as rebellious as me when she was younger.* But her marriage had been destroyed by her Uncle Aram's jealousy and carelessness, not only after the fatal car accident.

'Well, Tara,' she said eventually, thinking she had better answer her question, I can understand that you're confused about why I'm helping you.' She paused. 'Let's just say that I care for your safety because I have an unconventional family myself.' *No need to mention that I might be out for revenge.*

'Not traditional?' Tara asked, looking concerned. 'Your mother m…married out of her religion?'

Yasmine nodded. How far should she trust this woman? It was as if she already belonged to her family. *Hmm, unity through differences.*

'I have two mothers,' she replied, gauging Tara's reaction.

'Ahh… Your mother and your Amma who breastfed you?'

Yasmine almost laughed and shook her head.

Tara shifted her position. 'Your father has two wives?'

Yasmine smiled at the thought. That would have meant that her father was a bigamist. This certainly wasn't the case. But she liked this game. Tara should try and guess why she had two mothers, two caring mothers to be precise, each different in their own ways, each seen to be transgressive by the society they lived in. In her opinion, they were unique.

Tara cocked her head, trying to read Yasmine's expression. Yasmine stayed dead pan, waiting for another guess of Tara's as to why she had two mothers.

'Your mother had someone else to c…carry you in their tummy? Then when you were born, your mother and the woman who carried you till birth lived together in one house?' Tara looked at Yasmine triumphantly.

Yasmine let out a hoot of laughter, realising that Tara was thinking of IVF and surrogate carriers, a genetic mother and a birth mother. Tara was getting restless despite her curiosity. It would be better to explain a bit more about her family before she ran away.

'After my father died, my mother met a lovely lady at her counselling sessions.' She hesitated. 'And they loved each other. I mean, they became lovers.' She trailed off, watching Tara closely.

Tara tilted her head again. It was her usual ritual whenever she wasn't sure about something. Yasmine watched her curiously. She was usually very open about her mothers and their unconventional relationship. But

Tara was a Kurdish Iranian and she wasn't sure how she would react to this, considering where she had grown up. Surely she would have secretly seen foreign films about these relationships.

There was a flicker of recognition on Tara's face. 'Yes, I know about such matters.' She smiled. 'One mother was a man.' She peered at Yasmine questioningly, 'Then she made herself a wo…woman.'

Yasmine pursed her lips, feeling irritated. Time to spill the truth.

'My two mothers are women who love each other.' She said bluntly, wondering if Tara had ever been in love.

'Ah,' Tara nodded slowly, 'I heard about this before. It's okay for me.' She suddenly had a curious expression on her face and asked, 'Are you like your mother?'

Yasmine shook her head and replied, 'Don't worry. I'm not coming on to you. I have a boyfriend.' Annoying that she had to defend herself for something that was natural.

Tara looked at her dreamily and said, 'So romantic, your mother,' then added, 'but forbidden and dangerous.'

'Not forbidden in Britain where they live, but yes, it can be dangerous and attacks happen in some places,' Yasmine said flatly.

'That is sad. I get attacked sometimes.' Tara looked at the horizon, no doubt she was remembering various attacks by misogynistic men who hated women even when they accepted their sexual services.

'Tara, have you ever had any romantic feelings?' They were close enough to share some experiences.

Tara looked into the distance and replied, 'I don't have any sexual ur…urges.'

Yasmine took her hand and squeezed it. *So, being asexual, Tara is on the LGBTQIA+ spectrum.*

Tara looked at her directly and said, 'I have never had any urges, even before I ended up in my job.'

Should I be sad or happy for her?

Tara added, 'But friend...friendship means a lot to me.' She hesitated and added, 'Your friendship.'

Yasmine pulled Tara towards her and embraced her tightly. Her hair was so soft, even when entangled. She tried undoing some knots in her hair, then decided it was just a part of her persona. She sighed. Tara's melancholy reminded her of what one of her favourite authors, Virginia Woolf, had written before dying – '*As a woman, I have no country, as a woman, I want no country, as a woman, my country is the whole world.*'

Will Tara be free if she transcends into another world?

They sat in silence for a few moments. The air was cool. Yasmine turned her thoughts to events that had taken place in this park the previous year. She had read about it in a Kurdish news channel article. The pavements of Azadi Park had been painted in rainbow colours to promote equality and peaceful coexistence on the International Day Against Homophobia, Biphobia and Transphobia.

However, the colourful murals became a hot topic on social media and locals began claiming that the paintings were made to support the LGBTQ+ community. The team of friends who had initiated the colourful murals had spoken to the park authorities and their colourful murals had been approved, although the authorities didn't know that the rainbow colours were used to stimulate acceptance and understanding of this community.

A Kurdish page with thousands of followers called on the city to be aware of a campaign to corrupt the morals of the Kurdish community. The rainbow murals were erased. But how could the officials erase the love behind this community?

Yasmine remembered the look she had seen in her mother's eyes when she touched Sam lightly to pass the salt on their dining table. It was one of many gestures Yasmine encountered whilst growing up in their unconventional household. *What would happen to them here?* She had heard of arrests and violence towards these communities. A few days ago, the Iraqi parliament had passed a law, criminalising all same-sex practices and sex reassignment surgeries. Anyone who engaged in consensual gay relations would be imprisoned for a period of no less than ten years and no longer than fifteen years. Yasmine frowned. The amendment to the law dictated that promoting homosexuality in any way would also be punishable by no less than seven years in jail and a fine of ten to fifteen million dinars. Where was free speech? Her mothers would be put into notorious jails here in Iraq. Geez. Hopefully, this law wouldn't be ratified in the Kurdish areas.

She glanced at Tara who was gazing at the lake, most probably transported to faraway seas and countries. She too, was in a precarious situation and prone to violence and non-acceptance according to the anti-prostitution law. *And what about the men who pushed her into it?*

She moved an inch closer to her and said, 'Tara, do you want to go somewhere else?'

'I like it here near the lake, in Az…Azadi Park,' Tara replied in a croaky voice. 'I come here many times a week.'

'I don't mean to leave Azadi Park now. I mean to leave the country permanently, but without Aram's help. To follow your dreams?'

Tara looked at her with misty eyes. Yasmine detected a tear threatening to tumble down her cheek.

'I know you still love this country, but you're in danger, not only from your … um … clients, but also from my Uncle Aram. He despises you.' *He hated her too. She most probably reminded him of her mother.* 'Remember the slogan *Zin, Zhian, Azadi*? A young Kurdish woman in Iran was killed because her headscarf was allegedly loose!'

Tara frowned and nodded. 'I wasn't in Iran when th… this happened.'

'I know. But you could have been there and the intelligence agency would have killed you.'

Tara watched her, horrified by the thought.

'You can trust me. I will try and help you, Tara.'

Tara got up to hug her. *How the heck was she going to fulfil her promise to save her?*

Out of the corner of her eye she could see someone cycling towards them, maybe a father cycling with his child close behind him. Azadi park was a family park and Yasmine had seen many parents cycling with their children. These wide pavements were ideal for cycling.

Yasmine turned to check Tara wasn't in the way of the cyclist. A flicker of recognition and fear crossed Tara's face, a fraction too long. Yasmine swerved around to scrutinise the cyclist. He wore ripped jeans and a woollen black cardigan. His receding brown hair and black-and-white peppered goatee beard were a stark contrast to the colourful bicycle he was riding. Yasmine's eyes widened as he came closer and stopped an inch away from Tara and herself. *It couldn't be...*

'We seem to be bumping into each other quite a lot.' Aram grinned at her as he stopped close to their bench, his eyes gleaming with triumph.

Yasmine glanced at Tara. She looked resigned. *Did she know Aram would be cycling here? Had she given away their destination today?* The traitor. She felt her blood curdling. Was there anyone she could trust?

She gulped before asking, 'Did you betray me, Tara?'

'I had no c...choice,' she stammered. 'Aram said he'd kill me otherwise.' She winced and averted her gaze.

Yasmine's heart skipped a beat. Shit. She took a deep breath and looked at Aram directly. 'You appear to have a habit of killing people.' Her blood was boiling.

'What do you mean?' He tilted his head and raised an eyebrow, waiting for an explanation.

'I found something out yesterday,' she said. 'Something I'd never even dreamed could be true.' She felt Tara stiffen beside her.

He looked at her, a hint of wariness in his eyes. 'What?'

'You killed my father,' she responded bluntly.

Tara turned towards Aram and shrieked, 'You killed her father?'

Aram shook his head. 'She's lying Tara. Don't trust her. She's just as deceitful and weak as her mother.'

Yasmine stared at him, trying to control her laboured breathing. 'As useless as you, huh? You have to exploit women because you can't hold *down* a relationship or keep *up* an erection.'

Do women's lives have no value? Tara had been bought

and sold and there would be no escape for her. Yasmine had invested so much time and energy in saving her, trying to get her out of the country, giving her the chance of a better future, only for bloody Uncle Aram to snatch it away? No, no, no. Yasmine had been taught to fight back.

Aram's face distorted with rage and hatred. He threw down his bicycle and hurled himself forward, slapping Yasmine across the cheek.

'You bitch,' he roared.

She felt the sting of his hand. Her head snapped back as she reeled in shock and pain. This couldn't be happening. Not now when they were so close to leaving the country. Aram loomed over them both, his reeking tobacco breath churning Yasmine's stomach. Tara whimpered, pushing herself back onto the bench. She wasn't going to be any help.

A young man walked past them but barely glanced in their direction. He must have thought that a husband was disciplining his wife. Did women's lives have no value? Tara had been bought and sold and there would be no escape for her. Yasmine had invested so much time and energy in saving her, trying to get her out of the country, giving her the chance of a better future. Uncle Aram was not going to snatch it away. She glared at him.

White-hot rage swept over her body as she leaped towards him. She brought her knee up hard, slamming it into his crotch. She followed it with a shove in his chest which sent him sprawling on his back, moaning and clutching his balls.

Tara hadn't moved and was staring at her wide-eyed. Aram was struggling to get up, using his right hand to grab hold of the bench.

'Quick, Tara. Run.'

They both had trainers on and were a couple of decades younger than Aram.

Tara glanced at Aram, then at Yasmine and didn't hesitate any longer. She took Yasmine's hand and pointed to a direction at the south of the park.

'There are a few gates here, but that one over there is the quickest route to get out.'

They started to run in the direction of the gate. Yasmine felt her pulse quicken and the sweat trickling down her face. She turned back to glance at Aram. *Oh no.* He had got back on his bike. But that wasn't all. She saw something in his hand. Something that glinted.

'Faster, Tara! He may have a knife,' she shouted, looking around to see if there was anything that could help her. A blue coloured bin was lined up at the same side of the paving she was running on, but it was stuck to the ground.

Not far away she spotted a table covered by a white tablecloth laden with fruit juice drinks, white and pink roses and what looked like baklava. This was either for a graduation ceremony or for a wedding. She tried to breathe in but her breathing was shallow. There wasn't much time to think. Aram was catching up with them on his bike and she could see the glinting object clearly now. It was definitely a knife.

The beautiful and dignified Kurdish mountains in the background were no protection now. She had to help herself and Tara who was running slowly behind her. No wonder she could hardly keep up with her. She had most probably been at work, prior to coming here to join her.

As they came face-to-face with the laden table, Yasmine came to a halt and pushed the table to the floor. The fruit juices came down with a crash and the baklava was strewn on the pavement. Pink and white roses were now scattered in between the sweets.

A man shouted in the background. He was approaching them with a box, no doubt more food for the celebration which she had spoiled by attacking the table. There were no other footsteps to be heard.

Her chest felt hot and she couldn't tell if Aram was nearby or just behind her. She risked another glance behind her then felt a sharp spasm in her arm. Her heart was hammering in her ears. But the pain in her arm was excruciating.

She glanced down. Blood oozed down her arm. She stared at it, almost mesmerised by the speed with which it left her body.

Behind her she heard Aram's breath, rasping near to her. *He stabbed me!*

She stopped running, and raised her other arm up in order to show Aram that she had given up and was ready to stop this chase. He put his bike down and she could see that he was out of breath too. Standing so close to him, she could smell his cheap aftershave. He lunged at her. She was too weak to stop him. Her mother had told her to put out her arm if she was ever attacked so that her internal organs wouldn't be damaged. But her arm was already hurt. The wound was the width of the blade she had been stabbed with.

Was this how her journey was going to end? With death. She felt her tears mingle with the sweat oozing out of her pores.

'No!' She heard a roar from beside her. Tara flung herself onto Aram, knocking the knife out of his hand. He screamed in pain. She picked up the knife and dug it into his thigh. This time he howled as he put his hands on his wound to stop the bleeding.

'Come,' Tara ordered Yasmine. 'I know the way out.'

Yasmine was in no state to argue. She nodded. Aram had managed to move onto the grass and lie down, unable to shout any more. His breathing was shallow.

Tara wrapped Yasmine's wound on her arm in a scarf she kept in her handbag. 'Let's go before someone finds us.'

'But I'm wounded, Tara.'

'Then we'll go to the ho…hospital nearby.'

'No. They'll question me as to why and when I got this wound,' Yasmine protested.

'I'll say we were pla…playing with a knife and you fell. I'm your witness,' Tara said calmly.

There was no other option. Yasmine asked Tara to call a taxi to take them to the nearest hospital. Her list of injured people was getting longer: her grandmother, her uncle, Tara and now herself.

Goddammit. She was more dangerous than she had thought.

35

Tara strolled into the hospital as if nothing threatening had happened. Most probably, she was used to keeping her feelings at bay, blocking them out, especially when she had punters. Yasmine followed her quietly, dismissing this thought.

She looked at the blood oozing out of the makeshift dressing they had put on her arm. It was Tara's scarf. Damn. Her knife wound needed prompt treatment to prevent an infection and minimise the bleeding. Her mother had taught her some first aid, but this was excruciating. Thank goodness, a doctor in the emergency department triaged her without too many unpleasant questions. A gauze and a sterile bandage were used to apply more pressure on her wound.

Yasmine looked at the pink flesh of her arm while it was being cleaned. It was the width of the blade of knife. It could have been lethal. Luckily, she hadn't exhibited any signs of shock. Her pulse had been normal when she reached the hospital.

Oh God. Would she need to leave the country before

causing more harm to others and herself? Events had been leading to a crescendo of violence she couldn't stop. But if she returned to London, what would happen to Tara?

Tears welled up in her eyes. If left here, her friend would be killed after this recent encounter with Aram. She needed to leave the country. But she couldn't leave it legally. That would take too long and success couldn't be guaranteed. She would need to leave illegally which meant facing perils on the way. Also, this would cost a lot of money, at least $10,000 and where could one find someone to trust? The smuggler might take the money, never to be seen again. She took a deep breath. Would it help to phone Sam? She might be able to think of a way out of this dilemma without her becoming a criminal.

And what happened to Nana Aisha? Was she in the same hospital? That would be so ironic. Nana had been almost battered by her own granddaughter. Then her granddaughter was assaulted by her son, Aram. This was her family. And she was part of it. What a newspaper headline that would make in London. She searched her mind for some cohesive thoughts. What had made her uncle so combative? Her mother hadn't spoken much about their childhood with their parents, or maybe she had, but only to Sam.

She had to get out of this hospital as quickly as possible before Aram came looking for her, or before Dilly came to visit Nana Aisha. There shouldn't be any more chasing now, she thought, looking around her.

The doctors in Jumhuriyat Hospital were clean and tidy even though they looked tired. Their white coats didn't look creased. The doctor at the emergency department had told her that they hadn't received their monthly wages from Baghdad for a few months. How did they manage to survive? The doctor had also told her that he needed to work in his own private practice in the afternoons to earn enough money in order for his family to survive.

Yasmine held the painkillers tightly in her unwounded left arm. But she wondered if it was out of date as Tara had told her that some of them in the pharmacy had already expired. She looked at the date on the side of the medication box. The painkillers were in date. Thank goodness. She didn't feel like going to buy them from the black market. They would probably be placebos or out of date. In fact, she didn't feel safe wandering the streets now that Aram would be on the lookout for Tara and herself.

'Tara, where are you going when I leave the hospital?'

Tara averted her gaze and replied, 'To another st… street. I can't stay on the same one. Your uncle will find me there.'

Yasmine winced when she mentioned the words 'your uncle.' She didn't want anything to do with him.

'Right, listen Tara,' she said as they walked out of the hospital, 'we will stay in touch. I need time to think about how to solve your problem – and mine.'

Tara nodded. She probably didn't believe a word of what Yasmine was telling her.

'If we do make it, where would you like to go on a break?'

Would there ever be a post-escape break? Tara looked at her blankly and kept quiet.

'You remind me of a Hollywood movie.' Yasmine

smiled at her. 'Have you seen the film *Pretty Woman* with Julia Roberts?'

Tara shook her head and looked confused.

'The movie is about a wealthy businessman and an escort.' She gauged Tara's expression. It was deadpan.

'Vivian, a pretty woman, is hired to be Edward's escort for several business trips and social functions, and their relationship blossoms during her week-long stay with him.'

Tara's dimples widened and she blushed. Yasmine detected a tear in her eye. She most probably hadn't experienced love or romance, just many power imbalances with men who craved control and submission.

Come to think of it, Yasmine was aware that the film she had just mentioned romanticised sex workers by revealing Vivian's experience as glamorous and socially uplifting, enabled by a rich businessman instead of promoting the idea of self-empowerment. Issues of exploitation and sexual violence weren't addressed. *What a farce.*

Both Tara and she had a faint understanding of a similar kind of pain. The spiking. She pushed the memory aside.

'Umm, okay Tara, maybe a trip to Vienna would be a good post-escape break.'

Tara's eyes widened.

'Yes, that's the place we'll go to after you get your asylum in Britain. I'll invite you to the cosy Viennese cafés and we'll have Sacher torte, the original one.'

Tara's eyes revealed a mixed expression of hope and sorrow. She still kept quiet. *No wonder. She must think I live in a parallel universe.*

Yasmine didn't blame her.

'You know what, Tara? I'm going to take you to the Notting Hill carnival in Britain instead. You'd love it.'

Tara looked at her curiously, so Yasmine added that it was a celebration of Caribbean culture and had taken place every year since the sixties.

'Dancers in costumes, live bands and sound systems parade through west London. You can choose the wackiest dresses and parade in drag.'

Tara started laughing. No doubt she was imagining the kind of outrageous dress she would choose. Her dimples stretched across her face. How appealing she looked when there was hope for a better future!

Suddenly, Tara took her hand and said, 'I'd love to d…dance with whirling dervishes, Yasmine.'

'What?' Yasmine let out a hoot of laughter. Wasn't this what she had wished for when leaving London? And now her friend expressed the same wish. Were they both becoming Sufi followers?

'Okay, if we ever make it to London together, we can join the whirling dervishes and dance spontaneously and passionately with them.'

Tara closed her eyes, a smile on her face.

Yasmine chuckled and said, 'But first we need to find some turbans and swishing coats.'

Tara started to twirl, her long auburn hair following her path. Yasmine smiled and joined the performance by whirling slowly alongside her friend. Music wasn't a sacrilege. Why had the Taliban forbidden it? Whilst dancing she felt she was undergoing a metamorphosis of herself, something deeper and more compassionate than ever before, defying codes of honour and family rituals.

Yasmine heard the gentle swishing of Tara's skirt. She took a deep breath, never having felt so connected to anyone till then. True friendship was a blessing, an epiphany. It was the transformation and sharing of souls. But that also put her in danger of heartache if the love ended.

She stopped dancing and watched Tara slow down. When she stopped whirling, they looked at each other and clasped hands. Yasmine felt at a loss for words. She waited for Tara to speak first.

'God isn't only co…confined to mosques, synagogues or churches,' Tara said in a low voice, looking at Yasmine gently.

Yasmine had never seen her that pensive. She would never have thought that she would learn so much from someone on the margins of society. For a moment, the divine flow of love and friendship overtook her anxiety and doubts. She embraced her friend and nodded, wondering if she would ever see her again, suddenly aware of human limitations. If friendship created pain, then that was better than allowing the heart to shrink.

They exchanged their phone numbers again. Yasmine watched Tara walk towards a side street until she disappeared into an alley nearby. She sobbed quietly for a while, then she called Sam, not her mother who was at work at this time of the day.

36

'Thank goodness, you can speak to me, Sam.' Yasmine peered anxiously at her other mother on her WhatsApp. She was clad in her green gardening overalls and had a small pot plant in her right hand. From far away, Yasmine couldn't make out what plant it was, maybe a cactus.

'I'm on my way home to Auntie Dilly and Uncle Jamal now.' She tried to sound cheerful but winced when she stopped to sit on a bench outside the hospital and accidentally jolted her wounded arm.

'What's wrong, kitten?'

Yasmine couldn't contain herself anymore. She missed these endearments, the strolls in the parks, darling on-off Harry and her mother. She felt tears escaping from her eyes.

'Yasmine, you're sobbing.' Sam put down her pot plant and sat down on the bench in the garden, giving Yasmine her full attention.

'I ... I'm in trouble, Sam.'

'What kind of trouble?' Sam pushed back some

straying strands of hair with her muddy hand and waited for Yasmine to explain her situation. Yasmine couldn't hold back her tears. She snatched a tissue from her handbag and wiped her eyes.

'Darling, you are beginning to look like a racoon.'

Yasmine sniffed into her tissue, then a staccato-like sob and half-laugh emerged from her throat. 'Oh Sam, I miss your jokes…'

'That wasn't a joke, Yasmine. Better wear less mascara next time, especially if you're tearful … anyway, racoons are intelligent animals.'

Yasmine smiled. She was tired and heartbroken. Her journey had started off with her restlessness and a whiff of adventure. She had been so excited to explore her mother's heritage. And now, she was drained but nonetheless wiser. Or was she? She had met lovely relatives who showered her with small gifts of jewellery and food, and the mountains were gorgeous. But she kept stumbling upon traditional values and tripping over them.

'I keep hurting people, Sam.' She didn't mention her own wound. 'Nana is in hospital and Tara is still in danger. I don't know whether I'll ever meet her again.' She wiped her tears. 'And Aram is on the lookout for both of us.' Suddenly she felt breathless. 'Mum didn't tell me much about him.'

'Well, you were so engrossed in happy memories, she didn't want to disappoint you.'

'But I had illusions about him. He isn't like I remember him as a child, playing hide and seek and…' She giggled suddenly. 'And now, we're still playing hide and seek but in a much more dangerous way.'

'You're a work in progress Yasmine.' Sam winked at her. 'You don't need to figure everything out straight away. You're still very young.' She smiled at her.

'What shall I do now Sam?'

'What would you like to do?'

Yasmine wiped her forehead and said, 'I'd like to make a difference. Hearing that young girl scream in pain at the FGM procedure was shocking and heart wrenching.'

Sam looked thoughtful. 'You could become an advocate for women's rights and raise awareness about the harmful effects of FGM, supporting survivors on their journey to recovery.'

Yasmine nodded, encouraging Sam to elaborate on her ideas.

'When I used to work as a social worker, I remember organisations such as the NSPCC, the Havens and others used to do a great job of helping victims and raising awareness of these crimes.'

'That sounds just right for me. Do you think they would take me on as a helper?'

Sam nodded, then said kindly, 'There's something else you want to ask me, isn't there?'

Yasmine hesitated. 'I need to help someone here but that will cost me…'

'You're talking about Tara, aren't you?'

Yasmine nodded. As if she didn't have enough unsettling connections to her family. Now, she was confronted by her desire to rescue someone she had met three weeks ago. What an earth had propelled her towards this girl? She was an outcast, a person on the margins of society, rejected and ostracised. Was this how her mother had felt with her family? They were both regarded as freaks by some people, an aberration, at most an oddity.

'I must help Tara. She can't continue here. She can only survive in exile.' *Just like Mum,* she almost said, but she kept quiet. 'Sam, I don't ask for much—'

Sam laughed, 'Um… Except when you need a new laptop.'

'Okay. Stop Sam. I didn't get the laptop.'

'That's because you took Harry's old one.'

Yasmine nodded, feeling irritated.

Sam looked at Yasmine thoughtfully and said, 'Hmm. You've got a savings account, Yasmine. Would you like to use it?'

Yasmine frowned. She had hoped to use this money for a flat share with a friend. But when she weighed up her options, there weren't many. Where else would she get enough to rescue Tara?

Her mother would never agree to pay Tara for an escape route. Besides the fact that this would be illegal and damage her reputation as a doctor. She would be struck off by the GMC. And Sam was a retired social worker. She also wouldn't like her reputation smeared with a campaign about collaborating with people smugglers. Oh God. Was she deranged thinking of enabling such a criminal activity? People smuggling would come with a prison sentence. But then, she wouldn't be the one arranging such an activity. Who would?

'Sam, I need the money. I can't tell you what for and how I'm going to use it. But I can tell you that it's for a good cause.'

Sam hesitated and watched her carefully.

'And it's my money, Sam. You are the co-signatory. And mum wouldn't find out.'

Sam pursed her lips. 'I don't keep secrets from your mother.'

Yasmine was beginning to get desperate. Harry didn't have any savings and her mother was flush but would never agree to pay out for a girl she didn't know and had never met, not to mention the stigma attached to this poor Tara.

'Listen, honey, you're dabbling in murky waters. You can't think straight for some reason.' Sam swiped a fly away from her face. 'I'll tell your mother that you want to come home soon but forget the other issues until you return. There are plenty of good deeds you can do here.'

'But I know this girl. I can do good things here. And she'll appreciate it.' Yasmine felt like sobbing again. She turned away from the screen for a moment.

'You know you may do more harm than good,' said Sam gently. 'Even if Tara managed to get enough money to escape somewhere else, how do you know she'd survive? She may die on the way, in a lorry or on a boat crossing the channel.'

Yasmine thought of the cold water on the channel. So many immigrants had perished in its waters. No one would cry for Tara if this happened. Even her family had disowned her. She felt like tearing her hair out. Was there no way Tara could earn enough money to escape? Certainly not with her current job. That was only tormenting her. And what about Uncle Aram? Sooner or later, he would find her. That would be the end.

Yasmine put her face in her hands, thanked Sam

for listening and ended the call. It was time to plan her journey back to London. A fugitive tear escaped her while she imagined Tara alone in the country, a girl of ill repute in a part of society where men needed her services and yet pushed her away.

37

Tara had disappeared and wasn't answering Yasmine's phone calls. She wasn't in the Serchinar area anymore and even Haval, the shoeshine boy didn't know where she could be found. She hadn't been working in a brothel, so there was no way she could be found. *There's no use in fooling myself anymore. Tara has disconnected herself from me and Uncle Aram. And who can blame her? Will Aram find her? Oh God, no.* Yasmine's skin prickled with fear.

She couldn't change anything now. She straightened her position in the back seat of her uncle's Cadillac. They were driving to her farewell party in a restaurant half an hour away from her auntie's house. Yes, it had finally arrived – her last day in Iraq. Had she really only been in the country for three weeks?

Her auntie had chosen some close relatives to attend the gathering, that is, all but her grandmother who was still in hospital. *Thank goodness she needed further care to stabilise her heart condition.* And of course, Uncle Aram wasn't taken into consideration as he had disappeared.

With so many relatives around, I'll be safe, Yasmine thought as they drove to the restaurant situated in a closed compound of an affluent residential area.

She thought back to the day she had entered the country. She had been calm until she had stumbled upon Aram. Had she been swimming in shallow waters till then? Air bubbles were breaking through the rivers of her mother's secrets. This country, full of poetry and melancholic songs, had displayed an underbelly of society that her mother had never spoken about.

Yasmine peered out of the window of their large Cadillac, taking in the view of the palm trees. She would miss the lush green meadows, the pomegranate tree in her auntie's garden, the waterfalls and huge mountains. And of course, her Auntie Dilly and Uncle Jamal's house where neighbours would constantly knock on the door to invite them out.

As they parked their car, Yasmine glanced in the direction of the restaurant. She loved the neon lights decorating the adjacent oak trees. The place looked full with rows of visitors chatting to each other and toddlers playing around the tables. Children seemed to be awake at all times of the evening and went to bed late, not at fixed times like in Britain.

When they walked into the restaurant, the people on the tables stood up and clapped their hands. Her name was chanted out loud. *Surely they're not all waiting for me?* Wow, she hadn't known she had so many relatives. What a secluded life her mother led in London. She had never seen so many aunties and uncles all in one place. Thank goodness, no one mentioned Uncle Aram. They most probably kept him a secret.

'Your relatives all want to say goodbye to you.' Dilly beamed at her and added, 'They would like to have seen you more, but you were so busy exploring museums that there was no time.'

Yasmine stifled a laugh that was emerging from her slowly. She nodded, glancing at the relatives she never knew she had until now. She felt like a trophy. *What a wonderful change to fighting with Aram or my grandmother,* she thought.

'Yasmine, sit next to my son, Barzan.' One of her uncles beckoned her over and added, 'He is good boy. Finished college and engineer now.' Yasmine glanced at Barzan. He looked at her shyly. *Nice blue eyes. But I'm not into good boys,* she thought, *but I'm not into bad boys either.* She didn't know what she was into after all her adventures in this country. She would embrace a bear if she could.

'Barzan your cousin. Speak good English. Need job,' one of her uncles declared proudly.

Yasmine nodded. Her cousin kept quiet and smiled obediently.

'Leave Yasmine alone, Zakariah,' Dilly giggled, pushing Yasmine in the opposite direction. 'She's leaving for London tomorrow. No time.'

Yasmine was relieved to sit next to a man who already had a ring on his finger. He introduced himself as Hawar, the husband of another cousin called Shireen.

After ordering their favourite dishes, Hawar looked directly at Yasmine. 'We Kurds are brave,' he said. 'We fought ISIS, we survived Saddam Hussain, mustard gas poisoning and the Anfal ethnic cleansing.' He exhaled slowly, as if trying to rid himself of the memories. 'But we haven't got a country. Did your mother tell you about all our ordeals?' He looked at her with a quizzical expression in his eyes.

Yasmine didn't know whether he was critical or appreciative of the fact that she had travelled so far to get acquainted with her mother's heritage. 'Yes, my mother told me so many stories,' she exaggerated, 'And I'm very proud of you all – I mean, us all.'

She felt protected, maybe because she was flying back to London the following day. Safety at last but sorrow mixed with despair in this cocktail of feelings.

'Do you and your mother celebrate Newroz in London?' Hawar asked.

She didn't like his piercing eyes. She replied, 'We celebrate the Kurdish New Year ... But we also celebrate Diwali, Hanukkah and Christmas with our neighbours. London is very multicultural.' Hawar's wife giggled, rejoicing in Yasmine's assertive answer.

Yasmine felt proud of Sam's Scottish heritage. Well, to be precise, Sam, her second mother, had never insisted on celebrating the Scottish Hogmanay in Edinburgh. She was happy having a small gathering on Newroz, the Kurdish New Year.

For the first time, Yasmine felt comfortable in the multiplicity of her ethnic identities. *Birds of a feather should not flock together*, she thought stubbornly, giggling about the cliché. It was so much easier to say this with two mothers. It had been more difficult with an English father and a Kurdish mother. The ethnic boundaries had been more stringent when her father had been alive. But she couldn't debate all this now.

Sam was right – society couldn't be changed so quickly. Some people were still not ready to accept same-sex families in any culture although the power dynamics were much more equal and subtle. She picked up her knife and fork and started to eat her kebab, picking up a naan at the same time.

Everyone else at the table was chatting about the weather in Britain and which cities they had visited. She heard the names of Bath and Bristol. They seemed to be the favourites.

Hawar finished chewing his kebab and turned to look at Yasmine again. 'Did you ever hear about a British man called Ely Sloane?'

Yasmine shook her head and waited for Hawar to explain who Sloane was.

'Sloane was a British man who pretended that he was Kurdish.'

Was Hawar trying to make out that she was British and not Kurdish?

Hawar picked up his napkin and wiped his mouth, adding, 'Sloane was born in Kensington in 1881 and was sent to Persia through Tehran, Shiraz and other cities. He learned local languages including Kurdish.'

'I'm sure he spoke better Kurdish than me,' Yasmine smiled. *Where is this story leading to?*

'Soane was in disguise and most locals in Sulaymaniyah believed he was Kurdish.'

'Erm. Wow. Why did he do that?'

'Hmm. To learn about our culture.' Hawar hesitated. 'He wrote a book *Through Mesopotamia and Kurdistan in Disguise,* full of lively camaraderie.'

Yasmine heaved a sigh of relief. The theme of betrayal ran deep with the Kurds. First in the Treaty of Lausanne which promised the Kurds autonomy but was never ratified in the contract of Sèvres, then by the neighbouring countries in later years. No wonder Hawar was wary of anyone propagating friendship and loyalty to Kurds.

She smiled. 'I will always remember the Kurds as loyal and friendly people.' *No need to mention the underbelly of society on this occasion. Kurdistan is a gorgeous but multifaceted country.*

Hawar beamed at her. 'Is England safer than Sulaymaniyah?'

'Well, it depends where you go. Brixton and some other parts of London aren't safe and we have a lot of stabbings and killings.'

Hawar looked surprised. 'But it's safer than here. We never know whether we'll be attacked by militias. Recently an Iranian drone above our airport led to the whole airport being closed for a few days. It was shot down but we don't feel safe.' He looked sadly at his wife. 'Wages from Baghdad are paid irregularly and we have so many poor people.' He frowned.

'That's why some of us try to escape to Europe,' the shy Barzan added, looking at Yasmine longingly.

If I was going to rescue someone, it would be Tara. But where is she? All the chats and games they shared, and now I might never see Tara again.

Yasmine frowned and spent the rest of the dinner speaking to Dilly, reassuring her that she would keep in touch and return soon, but not with the baby that Dilly was hoping for. In fact, Dilly was asking for twins – one to stay with her and the other one for Yasmine.

The dinner continued till midnight. Yasmine had to travel to Erbil early in the morning to catch the flight back to London as Sulaymaniyah airport was closed for a while due to the Iranian drone attacks. Yasmine planned to meet her mother and Sam in St Pancras before travelling back to their home.

She scanned her surrounding relatives. Surely there weren't any more family secrets to explore before she returned. With a heavy heart, she knew it was time to leave.

38

Yasmine took the comfortable Elizabeth Line from Heathrow to St Pancras and was relieved that her suitcase had four wheels and slid easily along the pavements. The weather in London was drizzly and cloudy as usual. She missed walking along Kurdish streets without a coat and hat.

However, it was a relief to stroll the streets without checking if her skirt was too short or her décolleté was too revealing.

She couldn't wait to stroll down Carnaby Street to view the sparkling Christmas lights, holding hands with Harry. The previous year included a universe theme with vortexes of neon.

It was soothing dreaming about Harry, but she was afraid he would be slinking into the background. Her neck muscles tensed at the image of them walking down the streets, hugging each other tightly. Freedom here, but would she enjoy it the same way as before her trip? She realised that there had been a shift in her dreamy, laissez-faire way of looking at life. It wasn't uncomplicated anymore. She could only hope that it wouldn't get worse.

She finally arrived at St Pancras, pushing past many tourists, trying to find their way in the labyrinth of London's streets. The essence of multiculturalism was what she loved. Post-colonial immigrants from Afghanistan, India, Pakistan lived side by side, even though there were some tensions.

As she walked into the station, she glanced at the Eurostar trains connecting London with several other cities in Europe, including Paris, Brussels and Amsterdam. She should book a weekend somewhere with Harry to rekindle their relationship.

She stopped pushing her suitcase and looked up at the ceiling in the station. A masterpiece of Gothic architecture. Anyway, there wasn't much time to admire it. She was supposed to meet her mother and Sam at the 'Meeting Place' statue in the station. She passed the boutiques and bookshop and went upstairs.

She walked towards the large bronze statue of a couple embracing. It was located near the station clock which indicated that it was almost three o'clock in the afternoon. This was a popular meeting point.

The statue celebrated the joining of two cultures, England and France. It was about thirty feet high and revealed a man and woman looking lovingly into each other's eyes. *I need to hold Harry's face in my hands, feel the stubble on his chin.* But first a meeting with her mothers. It would be easier to talk about her escapades in a neutral place where there would be enough distraction from the hustle and bustle of city life.

'There's our daughter!'

Yasmine turned around briskly to face Sam who was ahead of her mother by a metre or two. She revelled in the words Sam had used – *our* daughter. She almost bumped into a woman with a Bichon Frisé who started to bark at her.

'I knew I'd arrive before you two,' Yasmine said cheekily. Home at last.

Her mother ran towards her and hugged her tightly. 'How I missed you, Yasmine.' She had tears in her eyes.

Sam tapped her on the shoulders and said, 'I hope you've some nice stories to tell us, not only stabbings and chases.' She winked at Yasmine. Her mother looked taken aback. She hadn't heard about all the calamities and visit to the hospital yet. *Stay calm. No need to tell her about all the stories yet.*

She turned to look at Sam. 'Ah, Sam, you still love your jokes,' she said in mock reproof. Sam should keep schtum about all the misfortunes till Yasmine was ready to tell her mother all about them. Sam smiled wryly and kept quiet for a while.

Yasmine's mother wouldn't let go of her. Yasmine started laughing again. It was so relaxing to be back with her two mothers.

Finally, Sam took her suitcase and said, 'Right, let's decide where to go and have dinner, otherwise we'll turn into statues ourselves.'

Yasmine was relieved when her mother let go of her and Sam started pushing her suitcase.

Her mother gave her a lingering look. 'You've been eating well, I see. All that delicious Kurdish food. Yaprach, biriyani, bamya…'

'Yes mum. I had fewer black puddings, haggis and Aberdeen Angus beef burgers.' She threw a glance at Sam. Usually, Sam was the one to cook in the house as her mother was too busy working and doing her on-calls.

Yasmine added that she'd love to walk to Coal Drops Yard as it was within walking distance from where they stood, and she wanted to walk past the canal to admire the barges. The area used to be a coal distribution and storage facility before boutiques and shops were built.

It only took them ten minutes to walk to the canal. As they stopped at the small bridge to admire the barges, Sam stood next to Yasmine and said in a low voice, 'I'm glad you didn't do anything illegal with Tara. You know that if you are found guilty and convicted of assisting illegal entries into this country or harbouring any person, you're likely to receive a prison sentence of a few years.'

Yasmine yanked at her suitcase. This was the solid and unpleasant truth.

Where was Tara? Why didn't anyone feel sorry for her suffering? Her phone calls hadn't been answered. For all she knew, her phone could have been stolen or she could be dead.

After her reunion with her mothers, Yasmine knew she'd have to face Harry. Why did she use the term 'to face him'? Surely, the reunion with him would be less worrying than the one she had with her mothers. She didn't have any secrets from him. But did he keep any from her?

39

Yasmine had arranged to meet Harry after his work in Shoreditch. It was a trendy area for artists and designers. *Just the right place for a reunion.* Harry was working as a barista in a vegan café to earn some extra cash. Yasmine loved the arty vibe of this area. If she were braver, she would strive to find a canvas for some graffiti. But this would be seen as vandalism. Anyway, she was getting used to being transgressive and pushing boundaries. Hadn't she done just that with her family abroad?

Her experiences in Sulaymaniyah weighed heavy on her chest, especially the altercations with her Uncle Aram and her grandmother. Her mother hadn't spoken about them in length, but then Yasmine had only just come back home and no one wanted to spoil the peace that surrounded them. That was one of the problems in her family. Conflicts were shunned so that they solidified into grief that had to be buried somewhere unreachable and untenable. She vowed to change that rule.

She walked past the town hall and peered at the

billboard outside. An Afro-Caribbean dance event was advertised. Maybe Harry would go to that event with her. He had not been abroad much and she was surprised as her other friends had been to many continents.

They had arranged to meet at the William Shakespeare statue in Shoreditch. As she approached it, she marvelled at the likeness to photos she had seen of this famous playwright. His sitting statue was perched on a bench with a plume in his hand, writing on a scroll. She followed his gaze and saw Harry approaching her. She ran towards him, dropping the leaflet she had picked up on the Afro-Caribbean dance event.

'Harry, I thought I'd never see you again.'

He looked dapper in his blue Abercrombie hoodie and jeans. His hair seemed more blond and had grown longer. He'd also lost weight. 'Yasmine,' he said, sounding surprised, but not as elated as he used to be. 'I didn't think I'd see you again.'

The creases around his eyes had intensified. No doubt he was tired. She pulled him tightly towards her. The aftershave she had loved to smell on him was replaced by the scent of sweat mixed with coffee. She pulled away. It would be better not to overwhelm him if he was so tired.

'Um … I missed you!' She hesitated. 'Shall we walk to Spitalfields Market or Brick Lane? You look tired.'

'Yeah, of course. We can walk to Spitalfields Market and have a bite to eat there.' He looked at her curiously. 'You look great, just…'

'Just what?' She mock-punched him.

'Just older and – different.'

'Great, thanks. It's been a long three weeks in Iraq.'

She closed her eyes, conjuring up the kaleidoscope of emotions she had been through. She'd block the lingering fear out for now. She didn't want to start sweating again.

As they walked up to Spitalfields, Yasmine glanced at the silver plaque outside Amnesty International. The plaque revealed a burning candle with barbed wire twisted around it. The candle would probably represent hope and life, the barbed wire was a symbol of prison. *No, I'm not going to think of the 'red prison' in Sulaymaniyah or Evin Prison in Iran.*

She shuddered, thinking of Tara. Hopefully, she wouldn't be arrested whilst trying to escape Iraq. She stopped to look at the opening hours of the Amnesty International organisation. They were closed on weekends so they wouldn't be able to enter the offices today as it was Saturday.

'The work this organisation is doing is great,' she said, turning towards Harry who was glancing in the opposite direction. A few women were walking past them, giggling and pointing at one of the women's high-heel shoes that had snapped. 'Um, Harry, I think those women can sort out their problems themselves.' She tried not to sound too hurt.

'Oh, yes. Of course. What did you say? Amnesty International? I don't know what they do exactly. Just try and bring more immigrants in I suppose.' He looked at the plaque for a second, then turned away. 'We need more help for our own homeless people.'

Yasmine stared at him, realising that her mouth was still open.

Harry pointed at a tramp crouching in the corner of

a shop, patting his sheepdog. 'This tramp needs our help, not people abroad who already have a home and family.'

He flung a coin into the tramp's hat which lay on the ground in front of him and she realised he might as well have thrown her soul into it.

'Harry, I can't believe you're so insensitive.' She grabbed his sleeve. 'Just to inform you, Amnesty's motto is *it's better to light one candle than to curse the darkness.*'

'Well, I don't know what that means but we're only a small island and we need to protect our shores.'

Yasmine almost gasped. He had never spoken like this previously. What had happened in the three weeks she had left the country? Who was he working or hanging out with?

'Excuse me, Harry. You do know that my mother came to these shores as a child and studied in London. Her auntie brought her here, running away from Saddam Hussain.'

Harry folded his arm. 'That's different. Saddam was a dictator and she was a persecuted Kurd. Other immigrants invading our country are not running away from war. What about all the Albanians? Their country is safe.'

'And what about the LGBTQ+ community? They're killed in some places!' Yasmine raised her voice, glaring at Harry.

A man in a brown suit laughed as he watched their display of emotions. 'Watch it mate,' he said, turning towards Harry. 'She may be gay.'

Yasmine shifted her position and retorted, 'So what? Out and proud.'

Harry looked at her with a shocked expression on his

face. 'Yasmine let's go somewhere else. We're attracting too much attention here.'

'No Harry. Let's have it out here.'

Harry pursed his lips. 'Are you going to do something revolutionary?' He laughed. 'You're always so opinionated.'

Yasmine clenched her fists. 'I'm opinionated because I express my beliefs? I'm just as entitled to them as you are.'

An uncomfortable silence followed. Yasmine felt a shift in their togetherness. Had they ever been together in that sense? She had never probed his philosophies previously, just lived in their cocoon of music festivals and tents. It was time to get to know him properly, warts and all.

'My mother lives with another woman.' She looked at Harry directly. 'Would that mean she wouldn't be allowed to come to our shores? What if she had been persecuted for being herself in another country?' She felt like shaking him.

'I didn't mean that,' Harry protested. 'But she'd have to prove that she's gay.

Yasmine stamped her foot. 'That's enough Harry, you're behaving like a judge.'

'And you're pretending you're the Virgin Mary. Pure and merciful, but willing to rescue a sex worker.'

Yasmine felt her eyes well up with tears. She couldn't speak any more. Harry's eyes narrowed and he shook his head, the blond mop of hair she had adored fell into his face. His wan complexion gave him the aura of a ghost, a phantom from the past.

'You go and rescue whoever you want.' He was already turning away. 'I don't need questioning and rescuing.'

As he stormed off, Yasmine wiped her tears on her sleeve and closed her eyes for a moment. Her stomach churned but it wasn't because she was hungry. Not hungry for food anyway.

She walked back towards the tube station, trying to wipe away the tears that had strayed from her eyes. It began pouring with rain. A woman stopped to give her a tissue outside the tube station. Her kindness made Yasmine sob even more.

40

By the time Yasmine arrived back home at her mother's house, she was exhausted and her eyes were stinging. She took her key out of her rucksack and slowly crept into the house. Why was she sneaking into the house? *Shit. Heartbreak is so painful.* Her eyelids were drooping and her mouth felt dry. How had she not seen this coming? Harry had been so understanding whilst she was abroad. But then that was a long-distance relationship. Had the three weeks' distance changed everything or had there been cracks in their relationship prior to that?

'Yasmine, you're back early.' She turned around before going upstairs to her room. Her mother walked towards her and stopped suddenly. 'You've been crying, honey. What happened? Weren't you on a date with Harry?' Her mother was so understanding and liberal.

Yasmine leapt into her arms and started to sob again. 'I thought,' she stuttered, 'it would work while I was abroad…' She trailed off.

Her mother held her tightly and ruffled her hair like she used to do when she was a child. *After all the hurt*

I've caused Mum's mother, Aisha, her brother Aram and Auntie Dilly, I'm still cherished, at least by my own mother. But she felt guilty. Her mother needed to rest during the weekend. Her job was full on with lives to save. *Not like me, destroying lives. There I go again, feeling miserable and guilty.*

'Let's go to your bedroom and lie down, sweetheart.'

'I feel so weak, Mum. I'm sorry.'

'I'll help you upstairs.' Her mother's voice sounded so soothing.

'I'm keeping you away from your work.'

'It's just paperwork, sunshine.'

Yasmine hung her head. How could she be compared to the warm rays of the sun? Damn Harry.

Her mother continued, 'I can do the rest of my work later on. Sam's out shopping, getting you the aubergines you love.'

Yasmine nodded slowly. She didn't deserve all this. Her legs were as heavy as lead. They hadn't felt like that while she had been in Sulaymaniyah. All the chases she had experienced with Aram and the awful confrontation with her grandmother were nothing compared to this heartbreak. It really was as if her heart had been shattered into many pieces. And it wasn't just Harry's rejection of herself, it was also his outlook on life and his values. Her motto was *Equality, Diversity and Inclusivity*, always had been. How could he ignore it? She had been away for too long. She wiped her eyes with her sleeve and let her mother lead her to the bedroom.

They reached her bedroom and lay down. Yasmine kicked off her soaked trainers and took a deep breath.

She stared at the bare ceiling. It was white, just what she needed, no overstimulation by colourful patterns. And she didn't want to see the kilim downstairs that reminded her of a flying carpet. What was she thinking, leaving the country and expecting to rekindle her relationship to Harry again so quickly?

'You don't need to say anything yet, just close your eyes,' she heard her mother whisper into her ear. She lay down next to her, stroking her hair gently most probably guessing that she had broken up with Harry, livid on the inside, but trying to compose herself on the outside.

After a few minutes on the bed, she heard her mobile ping. She turned to look at it, lying on the bedside cabinet.

'Don't pick it up now,' her mother said.

Yasmine looked at the name on the screen. It wasn't Harry's. It was Tara's. Her eyes widened. *What the heck was she thinking, waiting for such a long time before contacting me. Is it good news or danger? Please make it good news.*

'I'll just check that it's nothing urgent,' she said to her mother before picking up her mobile.

'Hello, is that Yasmine?' The woman's voice didn't sound like Tara's.

'Yes, it's me.' She sat up in her bed, glancing at her mum who was frowning at her.

'I'm a friend of Tara's. She asked me to phone you in case something happened to her.' The voice sounded low and fearful.

'What do you mean?' Yasmine's heartbeat was racing.

'Well. We're in Boulogne, hiding in the sand dunes.'

Yasmine kept quiet for a moment. Geez. How could they hide in sand dunes?

'Tara is here with me. If you don't believe me, you can speak to her.'

Yasmine sat up in her bed, pushing the blanket aside.

'Hello Yasmine. I'm with a f...friend ... She'll explain everything. I feel cold and my voice is h...hoarse.' She hesitated. 'I want to come and stay with you in Lon... London.' She rasped into the phone, 'I don't mind wo... working as a maid.'

Oh God, oh God. This was happening quicker than she had expected. How had Tara entered the country so fast and who had given her the money to escape? She would first be put into an asylum hotel and not allowed to live with friends or relatives. Didn't she know that? She glanced at her mother who looked startled.

'Tara, you mustn't—'

She was interrupted by a crackle on the phone. 'It's me again, Tara's friend. Her voice is hoarse and she doesn't feel very well, so I'll explain what's happening.' She took a deep breath. 'We're waiting for the smugglers to give us the order to run towards the sea.'

Yasmine gasped. A storm was looming. There were warnings on social media and the news. It had been pouring with rain after she had met Harry. 'The smugglers can't do this to you.' she heard herself shout into the phone.

'They're good men,' the gullible voice continued. 'When the wind drops and it gets darker, they'll give us the sign to run towards the small boats.' Yasmine heard someone clap their hands. What naïveté! Tara's friend added, 'We can't wait to reach Dover.'

'Don't do it. People die in the English Channel,'

Yasmine cried, throwing her pillow on the floor. She grabbed her mother's arm, pulling her towards the middle of the bed.

'We can do this,' Tara's friend whispered almost inaudibly. 'The dunes are steep but we can run quickly.'

Yasmine shivered. God, how she hated slippery dunes and freezing water. 'The gendarmes have rifles,' she shrieked. 'Please don't run towards the small boats. They're not safe! Even if you do manage the crossing, the government will send you somewhere else.'

'So what do you propose?' The woman's voice was angry now. 'To stay in our makeshift camps and freeze? Or go back home to a deathly future?'

Yasmine kept quiet for a moment. Why didn't the government open up long-term policies to open safe and *legal* pathways for migrants to come to the UK? There really wasn't much choice for them.

'Give me that phone,' her mother said loudly, reaching out for the mobile phone in Yasmine's hand.

'No, Mum, I don't want you to get implicated in this.' Yasmine hid the phone behind her back. Surely, this wasn't punishable, answering a distressed phone call. Should she contact border control? But then, she didn't even know exactly where in the sand dunes in France Tara was hiding. Also, she could easily move to another area. And what about the smugglers? They were scrupulous men who could come looking for her in retribution.

Then she heard a man in the background saying, 'Run.' Her mouth felt parched. *Was that the smuggler or were the gendarmes nearby, ready to chase them away?*

She glanced at her mother, usually so calm, but now

shaking her head and reaching for the mobile again. Yasmine shook her head and held her phone away from her mother.

She could hear the howling of the wind in Boulogne, then screaming in the background. The phone crackled before it was cut off. How much bad news could she tolerate in one day? Yasmine's head was spinning as she fell back on the bed and succumbed to her exhaustion.

41

Yasmine spent the next few days clutching her phone and putting it near her head even when she was asleep, although she knew that this wasn't healthy. *Maybe Tara will phone after reaching the shores of Dover.* She scanned the news headlines on every channel and even turned to French newspapers for any scrap of information.

Her mother was back at work and Sam stayed home with her. There were always household chores to do, gardening and shopping. Yasmine stopped biting her nails when Sam was around the house, but the lack of communication from Tara was excruciating. *I have to get out of this rut.*

She scrutinised possible jobs advertised in the local newspaper. Tutoring was one option. That would make more money than working as a barista. The thought of Harry working in the vegan café imposed itself on her. She felt sick. She had always thought that she was a good judge of character, but it certainly hadn't felt that way in the past few weeks.

There was a knock on her door. Yasmine picked up her head and waited for the door to open. Sam popped into the room.

'Right, Yasmine, we need to get you out of your room now,' Sam said.

Yasmine nodded, feeling tired although it was only lunchtime. 'Let's just look at the news, then we can go for a walk.'

'Okay, I'll put the kettle on,' Sam responded chirpily, a tad too quickly.

After a few moments, Yasmine went downstairs and switched the TV on. Should she follow the BBC or Sky news channel? She decided to try the BBC first. Often, she would look at various channels, hoping to get the 'real' news somewhere in between. She was tired of fear mongering and exaggerations about the amount of immigrants travelling to Britain. Why didn't she hear more about how the NHS could be salvaged?

She propped up her cushion on the sofa so she could sit more comfortably. She would need to listen to the news carefully.

'Another boat has capsized in the English Channel,' said the news reporter.

Yasmine pricked up her ears and quickly turned up the volume on the TV. The journalist was talking about a possible drop in the number of migrants crossing the English Channel. *Tara is not a number.* Yasmine threw her slipper at the television.

The journalist continued to explain that the UK had pledged hundreds of millions of pounds worth of support to help France stop people from crossing the Channel.

Images of gendarmes appeared on the screen. They had thermal-imaging binoculars. A long white blob indicated a solid mass of bodies shuffling fast in one direction. Those were identified as being the immigrants. Yasmine grimaced. They were being portrayed like insects.

She picked up her slipper and glared at the TV. She watched the gendarmes break the outboard motor and smash some foot pumps on a dinghy. *As if policing alone could put off the illegal crossings.* She would find out who was on the dinghy that capsized in the Channel. *It mustn't be Tara.* How on earth would the police be able to identify people without their passports? They had most probably been flung into the sea. *No way Tara was in that small boat.* She closed her eyes.

Sam entered the sitting room again and Yasmine opened her eyes to see a tray with a steaming cup of tea and a few biscuits on the side of a plate. She didn't feel hungry. If only the news would show photos of the dingy or bodies if they had been found. *What a dilemma.* There would be no white cliffs of Dover for the immigrants if their boat capsized.

'I need some fresh air.' Yasmine got up brusquely and opened the door to the garden. She took deep slow breaths and stepped outside the house.

The garden had been mowed and she realised that Sam had planted a few more trees earlier on.

'Let's step into the garden together,' Sam said quickly. When they left the house and reached the middle of the garden, Sam stopped and clasped Yasmine's hand tightly. 'Take a few more deep and slow breaths, Yasmine. Feel your feet firmly grounded on the floor.'

Yasmine nodded, too tired to remonstrate. *The earth would support me. Or it would swallow me.* But it would be better than a sea engulfing her. She almost collapsed into Sam's arms.

42

Yasmine hardly slept that night. She had scrolled on her phone, trying to find out more information on the dinghy that had capsized in the Channel. After fidgeting in her bed, she decided to get up and go downstairs for a cup of tea. *The photos on a large television screen should be more revealing than on a small mobile.*

She sat down to use the TV remote control. *Please God, Tara had better not end up being washed up on the shores.* She closed her eyes, but her imagination conjured up the image of the child – Aram Kurdi – who had been washed ashore, swept away from the arms of his mother as she too had tried to escape persecution. She quickly opened her eyes to try to get rid of this gruelling image.

Putting the TV on, she chose one of the news channels and turned the volume down as she didn't want her mother to wake up. On a Tuesday, she would be very busy at the practice. Having said that, what day wasn't her mother busy at work? Yasmine flicked through various channels to find one where she thought the best facts would be provided – Sky, CNN, Al Jazeera – and finally opted for the BBC again.

It was coming close to midnight so she waited for the headlines, nestling on the sofa with a blanket to comfort her. *Did Tara have a blanket to warm her up on the dinghy?* Yasmine shuddered despite her blanket.

At last, the newsreader started shuffling her papers and read out the latest news. 'Dozens of people including two children have died trying to cross the Channel to the UK in an inflatable dinghy.'

Yasmine came closer to the TV, almost tipping her cup of tea on the table in front of her.

'Two survivors are in intensive care while police have arrested a man suspected of being linked to the drownings.'

There was hope, Yasmine clenched her fists. Two survivors, maybe Tara.

Yasmine peered at the images of the drowned people in body bags, wincing. The TV presenter explained how there had been a Cobra meeting the previous day to discuss these increasing incidents of drownings. While the Prime Minister was appalled by the tragedy, he had condemned the trafficking gangs as they were literally getting away with murder. The French president had told Britain to stop politicising the issue for domestic gain. No one spoke about the victims.

Yasmine stopped listening to the newsreader and switched channels. Maybe a different broadcaster would reveal the countries these immigrants came from. However, there was no information on this. She held her breath as the news channel continued to talk about the issue in a detached way. Geez. How could they sound so level-headed? She shook her head. Of course the journalists had been paid to be impartial.

The chief executive of the Refugee Council asked how many tragedies like this recent one had to be seen before the government changed its approach of safe routes for men, women and children in desperate need of protection. *Should she join one of these charities helping immigrants near Calais?* The image crossed her mind but she brushed it aside.

Whereas the 'jungle' had been dismantled in that region, tents were still to be seen nearby and the immigrants were surely freezing and hungry. Wars and persecution had led them there, and of course this included the plight of being persecuted due to ethnic and religious reasons or persecution due to sexual preferences.

The newsreader explained that an emergency search had been sparked in the early hours of the morning when a fishing boat sounded the alarm after spotting several people at sea off the coast of France.

Yasmine put the television off and wandered into the kitchen to look out into the garden. It was pitch black and she felt cold. She needed to be involved in nature, not humans and their tragedies. Despite the cold, she walked towards the oak tree at the back of their garden and stopped to feel the smooth edges of the leaves that grew in bunches. They were host to hundreds of insect species. Yasmine sighed. *If only humans would be as kind as trees, giving nutrients to others in need.*

The oak tree was a symbol of power, strength, endurance and wisdom. That's what Sam had told her.

How Yasmine wished to be an oak tree, spreading strength and wisdom. But all she had done till now was spread a lack of resilience and veer towards weakness and folly.

She turned around to peer at the insect hotel that Sam had built. It consisted of logs piled up on top of each other, leaves and pinecones. She smiled briefly. It offered wild bees and other pollinators a suitable shelter. In finding a home for them, they would help Mother Nature. Yasmine felt her neck muscles relax.

Mother Nature indeed. She would have a heart-to-heart with her mother when she came home from work. That was the only way forward in their dilemma about Tara. But first, she would succumb to the fatigue engulfing her. Reality was perilous. Dreams were hopeful. She climbed the stairs and entered her bedroom where she hoped she would drift off into the realms of sleep.

43

Yasmine's lips felt parched. She pushed the duvet cover away from her and got up to get herself a glass of water. She had managed to sleep for a few hours.

As she went downstairs, the doorbell rang. She looked at her watch. It was just after six in the morning. Her mother and Sam were still asleep and it was too early for the postman. She moved towards the front door and opened it slowly, peering through the gap in the door.

A tall policeman in uniform and a plain-clothes policewoman were standing outside. She could see them through the small side window in the sitting room. Their car was parked outside on her mum's driveway. Her heart started to pound. Were they coming to the house to give her information on Tara? Would the news be ominous or hopeful? She had no choice but to open the door. Her eyes started twitching.

'Miss Yasmine Brewers?' the tall policeman enquired.

'Yes,' Yasmine replied in a low voice. She tried not to sound distressed.

'May we come in please?' There was a sternness to his voice that made Yasmine's hair on her arms crawl. She nodded reluctantly and led them into the sitting room.

'Would you like something to drink?' she asked, hoping that she didn't sound naïve.

'No. Thank you. Who lives in this house with you?' The female officer said in a gentle voice.

'My mother and her partner,' Yasmine responded. 'Shall I wake them up?'

'That may be advisable,' the male officer said, introducing himself as Detective Andrews. Yasmine felt her face redden. This wasn't just about parking tickets, she presumed. The policeman declined to explain anything till her mother came downstairs.

Yasmine went upstairs as quietly as she could to knock on her mother's door. There was a grunt from Sam who never liked waking up so early. Yasmine went in, excused herself for getting them up so early and told her mother that the police officers were waiting for her downstairs. She put her hand gently on her mother's arm.

'What? Has someone died?' Her mother's voice sounded drowsy, tinged with fear. She sat up slowly, rubbing her eyes.

'No, Mum. I don't think so but they want to talk to us together. Sorry.' Why was she apologising for the stern policemen? Surely, their presence had nothing to do with her.

Both her mother and Sam put on their dressing gowns and went downstairs, Sam leading the way and Yasmine right behind her.

'Officers, what kind of time do you call this?' Sam

started, staring at both the officers. Yasmine's mother put her hand up to quieten her, then they both sat down next to each other.

'Dr Sozanne Brewers?' The male policeman asked.

'Yes, that's me.' Yasmine's mother answered, frowning. 'How can I help?'

'Well, Yasmine, your daughter, may have been involved in people smuggling. We need to ask a few questions. She lives here.'

Her mother's face was ashen, even more so without her usual make up. Yasmine almost collapsed on the sofa. *I have to keep calm.*

'I was never involved in people smuggling,' Yasmine said loudly. 'Why would you think such a thing?'

Detective Andrews looked at her directly. 'Yasmine, do you know Mr Aram Kazzaz?'

Yasmine felt the blood drain from her face.

'Intelligence tracked your phone number to Mr Aram's mobile.'

The sicko must have secretly photographed me without my knowing. But where?

'When did you last meet him?'

Yasmine pretended she was trying to remember. 'Um, in Sulaymaniyah. He's my uncle, so of course he has my phone number on his mobile.' *Why do I feel guilty?*

'Did your uncle talk to you about trafficking?'

'Of course not. I wouldn't have engaged in this procedure anyway.' Yasmine stared at the policeman.

'Where did you last meet him?' He scrutinised her. *Thank goodness he couldn't read her thoughts.*

'I met him in a museum,' she replied, sitting up in

272

her chair, trying to appear assertive. That much was true.

'Was anyone else there with you?'

Yasmine couldn't remember seeing any surveillance cameras there.

'No, we just had a look around the museum. Then he had to leave.'

'Where did he go?'

'I don't know, officer. I stayed because I was interested in the artefacts and history of my mother's heritage.'

The officer glanced at her mother. She was frowning. Sam held her hand, staring at the policeman, willing him to leave.

'Dr Brewers, do you have anything else to tell us about your brother, Aram?'

Yasmine watched her mother's expression. It was a mixture of shock and curiosity. She would have had enough time to gather her thoughts.

'I don't know any more about the recent dealings of my brother as we had a falling out a few years ago.'

'Why did you fall out?' the plain-clothes policeman asked.

'Oh, I'm sure you've already read the police records... He caused the death of my husband and fled the country.'

The policeman nodded. Her mother rubbed her temples and added, 'We also had a difference of opinion about my lifestyle.' She held Sam's hand tightly and gave her a lingering look.

'I see,' the policewoman said, nodding compassionately and looking from one woman to the other.

The plainclothes man stared at them. A few moments of silence ensued.

The shrill tone of the landline made Yasmine jump. She looked at her mother's phone warily. Who could be phoning them at this time of the day? It was still dark outside. Where was Aram? Surely, that couldn't be him on the phone. She held her breath.

'Don't you want to answer your phone?' The policeman asked, watching her mother curiously.

'Um, it might be one of the locum doctors for today, calling in sick.'

'Well, that would be problematic, Dr Brewers. Wouldn't you agree?' The policeman said with a tinge of irony in his voice.

'Well, yes. They're supposed to phone the practice manager.' Her mother looked worried as she turned her gaze towards the phone.

The answer machine went on. Yasmine held her breath. Oh God, please don't let Aram speak on the answer machine. He would be capable of anything with all that hatred in his heart.

Yasmine heaved a sigh of relief. It was the cleaner on the answer machine, explaining that she had the flu and couldn't come to clean that day. *I have to shake off that feeling of guilt and fear.* She eyed her mother anxiously. How much more would she have to endure?

The policeman started probing again in his matter-of-fact voice. 'Dr Brewer, did you know that your brother Aram opened a business in Birmingham?'

'No, I didn't,' her mother answered laconically. She clenched her fist, the way she did when she was nervous.

Yasmine tried breathing more slowly. Aram must have opened the business under someone else's name as he was wanted by the police. With his English passport, it wouldn't have been too difficult for the crook to enter the country and keep a low profile. The quick breaths were making Yasmine feel dizzy.

'We have objections to him opening a garage as a wanted man,' the policeman said with a wry smile. 'However, he used someone else's name and spent the money he earned as a smuggler to finance his business.'

Yasmine gulped, fearing the policeman would hear her gasp. She held on to the soft cushion next to her.

'You do realise that two immigrants died on the boat that capsized in the English Channel a few days ago?' Detective Andrews said, raising his voice and glaring at Yasmine's mother.

'Yes, officer. We watch the headlines,' Sam answered, almost snarling at the policeman.

'Detective, we despise these smugglers, whoever they are and wherever they live,' her mother said calmly, 'but we don't have more information on them.' Her mother's voice sounded genuine. She really wouldn't know anything else about the smugglers, even if Aram belonged to them. Yasmine frowned. Aram hated Tara and would never have helped her cross the channel. It must have been his accomplice who enabled Tara's channel crossing. But where had Tara got the money for this?

'Where is Uncle Aram now?' Yasmine tried to sound inconspicuous.

'We don't know.' The policeman looked at her

suspiciously and added, 'If found and proven guilty, he'll end up in prison, especially as we have been looking for him since the fatal car accident in which he was involved. This would be classified as manslaughter.'

Yasmine felt her stomach churn. *At least I'll be safe if he ends up in prison.* When would this nightmare end? And how would her mother react when the policemen left the house? She shuddered but was happy that the policemen were closing in on Aram after so many years in hiding. He should burn in hell.

44

Cold air blasted the corridor when the two plain clothes officers left the house. Yasmine felt as if a ghost had been let into their cosy sitting room, the nebulous apparition of her uncle. She walked back into the dining room and faced her mother and Sam. She watched her mother wringing her hands underneath the table while Sam brought in two cups of tea.

'Yasmine, would you like a cuppa too?' Sam said in a shrill voice.

Yasmine shook her head and sat down opposite them. She looked out of the window at the rear end of the house. *The lies in this house are shifting into my weakened body and soul.* She clasped her hands.

'Yasmine, it's time to tell us what exactly happened between Aram and you.' Sam folded her arms and looked at her directly.

'Pardon me? So now I'm the one who's apparently keeping secrets?' Yasmine exclaimed.

Her mother fidgeted in her chair, touched her cup of tea but then decided not to take a sip.

'Yes, Yasmine,' Sam continued, 'those policemen were very intimidating. Your mother hasn't done anything wrong. She doesn't deserve this havoc in the house.'

'It's you two who have been keeping secrets,' Yasmine heard herself say loudly, realising that her voice was a mixture of aggression and accusations. *Damn. No one told me how vicious my uncle could be.*

Her mother stared at her, frowning. Sam raised her voice and said, 'Your mother was trying to protect you. We didn't want you to go looking for trouble.'

Her mother added softly, 'You wanted to discover your heritage.'

'Yes, Mum, but I also wanted to explore my family. We don't have any family here.' She almost thumped the table. *We're all talking past each other,* she thought irritated. Would they ever be able to move in one direction? She stepped towards her mother and said, 'You don't need to hide your struggles, your past. I can cope with them. I'm not a child anymore.' She looked at her mother, feeling her tears well up, but her mother was averting her gaze. 'How many other mysteries do I need to find out for myself?' She glared at Sam. She had been complicit in these untold skeletons in the closet, but she wasn't to blame for the recent happenings too.

Sam stood up, her face red. 'So now, you're blaming us for your liaison with Aram. The criminal you decided to befriend.'

'You never told me he was a criminal. You waited until I found out for myself.'

Her mother looked up and said, 'We knew about the car accident, not about the people smuggling out of Iraq,' her mother said, almost croaking.

Sam looked at Yasmine as if waiting for an explanation. *These family silences are excruciating.*

'Listen, Mum, I don't know what he was involved in. All I know is that he's capable of anything.'

Her mother looked at her curiously. 'How do you know that?'

This wasn't the time to tell her about the various chases she'd experienced with Aram. She tried weighing up what events she should share with them and which ones she should hide. *Geez.* Now she was the one honing secrets. When would this cycle end? She felt the urge to make a pledge with herself. But this was a precarious situation.

The more she told her mother about trying to get Aram to help Tara escape Iraq, the more she would be implicated in his possible crimes. And her mother wasn't old enough to retire yet. She still needed a few more years for this to happen. Besides that, if the police thought she was complicit in people smuggling, she would be arrested. And that would be the end of belonging to the General Medical Council and the Royal College of GPs. All their friends would turn away from them and Sam would be furious, to say the least.

Yasmine was silent for a few moments. She turned to look at Sam. 'What did you say?'

'I asked how you knew that Aram was capable of anything, including people smuggling.'

'Well, I just meant that the police officers were sure he had paid for his mechanics' business with money he earned via people smuggling.' She detested using the word *earned.* It would mean money obtained for labour, not dollars used for putting people's lives in peril.

'Hmm.' Sam was still watching her suspiciously. 'We'll find out more soon. Those detectives looked intelligent enough to find out who belonged to Aram's criminal team.'

Yasmine nodded. Admittedly, she had asked Aram for help but she hadn't agreed to him pursuing the job of smuggling innocent people in boats. She had merely asked him for advice. *How could I have known that he was the ringleader of a big criminal gang?* Maybe he wasn't. Wishful thinking.

The police would have to do further investigations. What else did Aram have on his mobile? Her photo wasn't enough to implicate her but her phone number could easily be tracked. As his niece, she would have been on it. Most uncles had photos of their nieces somewhere on their phones.

She realised that she was trying to talk herself out of these intrusive thoughts. No wonder. Who would have thought that she would be suspected of people smuggling? A scream was mounting in her throat. Sam continued to watch her curiously. Yasmine gulped and said that she needed a glass of water. All this in the early hours of the morning was a bit too much for them. At least she didn't have to go to work. Her mother would be preparing her porridge soon.

'You know,' her mother was lost in thought, 'Aram was placid as a child. It was only later on in his teens that our father started reprimanding him.'

'What?' Yasmine stayed at the table. 'Why?'

'He kept telling Aram to go hunting with him, wanting to teach him how to shoot guinea fowl, amongst other things.'

'Well, wasn't that normal in that part of the world?' Yasmine asked, surprised.

'No, most men in the city bought food from the shops. And their fathers didn't teach them how to shoot cats for fun.'

Yasmine winced. Their cat Bobby came in and out of their cat flap without fearing for his life. If Aram came to their house, would Bobby be in danger too? She suppressed a faint giggle that was mounting in her throat. *Geez, I'm going mad.*

'Our father was a domineering man. He decided where to go on breaks, what to buy in shops and who was allowed to visit our house.'

Yasmine frowned.

Her mother added, 'Aram is trying to replicate the same controlling relationship he had with his father.'

Sam stood up. 'That's no excuse, Sozi. He's a misogynistic bastard.'

Her mother flinched and kept quiet.

'He belongs in prison,' Sam added, pursing her lips.

45

The following day, Yasmine paced around the house, periodically looking out of the windows outside the sitting room. She turned to look at Sam. 'There's no suspicious car out there.'

'And why should there be?' Sam asked, walking towards Yasmine after putting the vacuum cleaner in a corner of the sitting room.

'Well, the police were here yesterday looking for information on Aram, weren't they?' Yasmine answered, rubbing her neck. It felt itchy as if an inflammation was coming on. Her eczema had been irritating recently. No wonder with all the stress and worry going on.

'Listen, Yasmine, now that your mother's left for work, why don't we have an honest chat about what happened with your Uncle Aram?'

Yasmine looked at her with widened eyes and said, 'Let's just recap what the policemen told us and then maybe we can move forward.'

Sam nodded and said the policewoman had told her that the smuggler gang had made one and a half million

Euros from the boat journeys even if all the dinghies didn't reach Britain. They had found out that a journey to cross the channel would cost a person one thousand five hundred Euros.

'Where would they get that amount of cash?' Sam asked, looking exasperated. 'The policewoman said they found the keys to the garage where dinghies and boat engines were kept – in Aram's pocket. He even had videos of migrants on his phone. He was arrested in England and is now in custody.'

'Maybe we could find out if he had Tara's photo on his phone.' She hoped she didn't sound too desperate.

'We need to tread carefully otherwise we'll be in trouble.' Sam held up her arms in despair. 'Aram's garage, under his accomplice's name, was being observed for a year even though he lived in Iraq. Who knows whether we're under scrutiny too.'

'Listening devices and trackers may have already been planted in our car.' Yasmine's voice was shrill.

'Your mother doesn't deserve this, Yasmine.' Sam said massaging her temple. 'What have you done to us?'

Yasmine ignored her, frowning. *What if listening devices had been planted around their house discreetly while one of the officers had interrogated them recently?* She looked at the ceiling, half expecting to see cameras. Then she looked all around the room. Sam followed her gaze and whispered for her to put the radio on.

Yasmine walked towards their radio and put it on, increasing the volume. *Geez. She felt as if she were in a film, a dystopian one.*

'Sam, I may have tried to get some information from

Aram.' Yasmine peered at her, gauging Sam's willingness to listen. 'But I didn't tell him to smuggle Tara to Britain.'

Sam stared at her. 'Isn't that the same thing?'

'No, it's not. I didn't expect him to be a people smuggler. I thought he may know someone who could help Tara, but not a gang.'

Sam shook her head. Yasmine could tell from her expression that she was disapproving of her dealings with her uncle. *I'm not going to take the blame for what Aram did.* She scrunched her face, suddenly stamping her foot on the soft kilim in the house. Sam widened her eyes. The wrinkles around her eyes deepened. How she had aged.

'Oh, Sam, what are we going to do now?' Yasmine said, tears welling up in her eyes. She couldn't see the following expression on Sam's face as her tears began to tumble on to her face.

'We?' Sam asked, moving towards her.

'Yes, *we*. I can't do this on my own. I need support. I need to find out if Tara is alive or not.'

Sam moved towards her and took her in her arms. She squeezed her gently, saying, 'Okay, honey. I haven't seen you this distressed since you broke up with that terrible boyfriend of yours. What was his name? Harry? The one who thought that we were being overrun by *insects.*'

Yasmine stopped crying, confused. 'What insects?'

'Immigrants. That's his fear. He forgot that his father came from Poland. Totally disconnected from his heritage.' She picked up some fluff on the carpet. 'And all the fearmongering going on in the country to distract us from other problems.' Sam's cheeks had reddened.

Yasmine nodded, clinging on to her again.

'Instead of sorting out the crumbling NHS, we're told that immigrants are our downfall,' Sam flung her arms in the direction of the television, 'rather than a lack of organisational skills which would help overcome our problems.'

'Sam, if we could at least save one person, that would be fantastic. Tara would be so grateful.'

Sam looked thoughtful for a few moments. 'Why is she so important to you?'

Yasmine took a deep breath. 'Aram has destroyed many lives. I don't want him to destroy Tara's life too.'

She glanced at the ceiling. There was a scratching noise coming from it. Were squirrels or mice looking for tunnels to pass through? She turned her thoughts back to Tara. 'Sam, I feel responsible for Tara, as if she belonged to our family. She was hurt by *my* uncle.' Sam didn't look convinced, so Yasmine continued to explain herself. 'I want to reach out to others who need our help.' She grabbed hold of Sam's hand and added, 'The other is us. We are one.' Yasmine folded her arms defiantly. 'We need to start by finding out if Tara is alive, then give her a purpose in life. After all the abuse she's had to endure, I think she deserves a second chance in life.'

Sam listened cautiously. 'Okay, honey. I was once the person who needed a second chance in life. I'm proud of you, trying to reach out to others in less favourable circumstances than you.' She smiled. 'The apple doesn't fall far from the tree.'

'Thank you. Let's keep this to ourselves. If Mum finds out, she may be implicated.'

Sam laughed and said, 'So, it's okay if I'm implicated, but your mother should be spared?'

Yasmine grinned, saying that her mother was the breadwinner and if she stopped work, they would all suffer as they didn't earn enough money to support them all.

Sam smiled wryly and said, 'you could start tutoring or work as a barista. Let's begin by finding out if Tara is still alive. Don't worry.' She let out a laugh. 'This action is legal.'

Yasmine agreed but was surprised how easy it had been to convince Sam about the urgency of their proposed activity. The following day, they would need to look into how a missing person could be found.

46

Sam proposed looking through the national register of deaths, or turning to a detailed paper register that was held at the British Library. But Yasmine reminded her that they didn't know under what name Tara was entering the UK. If she died trying to come into the country, would she be on British records or French ones? Also, these records wouldn't be available yet. Tara might have even chosen a different nationality. Yasmine's throat felt tight. Should she be googling and searching news sites?

'There must be a phone number we can call in Kent,' she said hopefully.

'Well, I suppose if she came via Dover, she would have arrived in Kent,' Sam replied, frowning.

'She'll be so anxious and I'm not sure she knows what to say in order to claim asylum.' Yasmine started picking at the tablecloth in the dining room.

'She'll have a meeting with an immigration officer before the Home Office decides whether her claim can be considered in the UK,' Sam said. 'If she gives any false information, she'll get up to two years in prison or have to leave the country.'

Yasmine waved away this possibility. Her muscles tightened.

'If Tara wants to claim asylum, she needs to prove that she's being persecuted because of her race, religion, nationality, political opinion or gender identity and sexual orientation, Yasmine.'

'It's most of those matters,' Yasmine almost shouted. 'I want to help her.'

'She needs to show evidence of persecution,' Sam said bluntly.

'Hmm, just a thought, how can someone prove they're gay?' Yasmine asked gingerly.

'Indeed. They ask some ridiculous questions.'

Yasmine waited for an elaboration of the possible questions but Sam kept quiet, then said, 'And it would take months to decide about the application. While waiting for a decision, asylum seekers aren't allowed to work.'

Yasmine felt somewhat relieved. Tara would definitely not want to work in her current job once settled in Britain. She'd rather die than do that, she had told Yasmine.

Sam looked as if she was weighing up their options. She told Yasmine that the Border Force would have intercepted Tara's dinghy and taken her to the Port of Dover.

'Tara will be exhausted and hungry, I'm sure of that,' Yasmine turned to look at Sam directly, well aware that she was beginning to bargain with her. She added, 'If we can't get through to the phone number of Border Control, we need to drive up to Kent and find out for ourselves.'

'And what will we tell your mother? That we're on an exciting road trip while we're being watched by detectives?' Sam slapped her thigh, almost laughing at her own explanation.

Yasmine had to admit that she had a point there. Her mother would definitely be suspicious if they decided to drive up to Kent, which was where all asylum seekers were taken after leaving the dinghies. Anyway, they still didn't know if Tara was alive. Yasmine shuddered. They were going around in circles and she was entering a maelstrom of anxiety which she couldn't shake off. She closed her eyes.

Time was crucial. What she definitely didn't want was to frame her mother as a suspect in a case of people smuggling. She would rather leave Tara for a while than implicate her mother.

'Right, we need to make our minds up, Yasmine. I propose we wait for a day or two until we make our move.' She scratched her head. 'Maybe we could Google a few facts or use AI to gather information on the dinghies that arrived in the UK recently.'

Yasmine spilled her cup of tea. They weren't moving forward as quickly as she had hoped and they needed to move fast because Aram might not stay in custody for too long. If there was no sufficient evidence against him, he would be released. He had legal aid and he was astute enough to talk himself out of the predicament he found himself in. Hadn't he done just that till now and thrived on it?

This wasn't the first time he had escaped the police. He had killed her father under the influence of drugs and was still at large. Yasmine clenched her fists till it hurt. She wasn't going to allow him to kill Tara. Aram would want revenge. He hated his sister Sozanne and herself. He felt betrayed by them. How far would his revenge go? She shivered.

Maybe he thought his sister should have saved him from his father's torture and bullying. These thoughts didn't cross his mind fleetingly, they enraged him. She realised that he would soon not only be after Tara but also after her mother and herself. In his eyes, they were traitors. She covered her face with her hands, trying to blot out the image of bloodshed that would occur if Aram found them.'

As if reading her thoughts, Sam said, 'Finding keys for a garage full of dinghies would be enough evidence to keep someone in custody if the police find Aram, especially as he's already wanted for manslaughter.'

Knots started to snarl in Yasmine's stomach. She nodded, aware of the importance of acting quickly to save their lives. There was the danger of Tara self-harming if her case for asylum led nowhere. She might even contemplate suicide. Her own mother might be killed and Aram certainly hated Yasmine. She had escaped him twice but that would not extend to a third time.

She looked out of the window, feeling anxious. Yasmine didn't even know what kind of car she would have to look out for. The plainclothes officer and policewoman had left in an Audi, but they could come back in a different car.

A Mercedes approached the opposite side of her street. Yasmine's heart started to pound. Two men sat in the car, looking around them slowly. Yasmine stayed glued to the window, hidden from view, not daring to move.

Was there more evidence? Would Aram implicate her to save himself? He was the root of all problems.

He had to disappear.

47

Yasmine scoured the headlines in all the newspapers she could find in her local newspaper shop. *Immigrants heading towards our shores*, one newspaper headlined. Sam was right, the article might as well have written *insects*. The tone was derogatory. Grainy photos of men and women in life jackets with two children appeared on the photos. They had life jackets on. Yasmine couldn't detect anyone who looked remotely like Tara.

She bought one of the newspapers which portrayed the immigrants as less dangerous than the other ones. She shook her head. These people, including Tara, were escaping danger only to be seen as vermin and taking away jobs from local people even though they weren't allowed to work as asylum seekers.

The newspapers gave the impression that the migrants were coming over to accost the girls in England and commit crimes. She took a deep breath. Her Uncle Aram had lived in this country and had acquired a British passport. Aram was the one the newspapers had to be wary of, not the immigrants coming from abroad, escaping persecution of any sort.

In the broadsheet that Yasmine held in her hand outside the tube station near her local park, she quickly read that two dinghies had left Calais for Dover. The people smugglers, of which there were two, had jumped into the safer boat that was larger. Apparently, the night was rough and waves rose up, rocking the dinghy hard and swaying from all sides.

The smaller boat quickly started soaking up seawater and the immigrants had started to scream. The bigger boat stopped for a moment, according to the people inside it, but the smugglers had warned them not to save the immigrants in the smaller, capsizing boat as it would thereby overcrowd the bigger boat, risking their deaths, too.

Yasmine gulped back her tears and decided to read the rest of the article on a bench in the park. It was difficult trying to hold back her tears. She almost choked as she ran towards the park.

When she sat down opposite the lake that herons, geese, coots and swans frequented, she let her gaze travel towards the far end of it. The heron that had built a nest before she travelled to Iraq had three chicks peeping out of it. The clucking of the hungry heron chicks made her smile briefly. They would soon spread their wings and fly out into the exciting world. Just like herself a few weeks ago. And where had that led to? She didn't know whether to laugh or cry.

She spotted an orange-chested kingfisher chirping softly whilst trying to feed on freshwater fish in the lake.

Hadn't I compared Tara to a red-breasted robin, puffing herself up when she was excited to see me? How she yearned to take her in her arms and comfort her. Tara had confided in her that she was asexual. Not everyone needed sex to be happy. But Yasmine would give her friendship and warmth, if only she could find her.

Some pale brown Egyptian geese with dark brown eyepatches were huddled on the grass. *They can easily transgress boundaries, unlike humans.* She fidgeted on the bench, waiting a few moments before she continued reading the harrowing details of the immigrant journey the previous week.

Yasmine peered at the newspaper. The writing was blurred. She realised that her tears had fallen onto it, mixing with the black ink. She quickly started wiping the page she was looking at. Then it got smudged. *What an idiot.* She squinted, trying to make out the words that were left without smudges.

A fisher boat's searchlights tore through the darkness and one of the immigrants who went by the name of Tara...

Yasmine stopped reading. This couldn't be true. Was it her Tara who had spoken to the guard picking them up in the sea?

She started to wring her hands, took a deep breath, then looked at the newspaper article again. One of the surviving immigrants, going by the name of Tara, had explained that their dinghy had also been filling up with water and that they had tried emptying it with their bare hands. The men had used their clothes to empty the vessel. *It must have been freezing.* Yasmine shuddered.

She put the newspaper down for a few minutes, then

continued to read it after focusing on the kingfisher plunging into the lake. A smuggler had told everyone to turn off their mobiles as the GPS sent signals. However, one of the immigrants had left their mobile on. This was how the fisher boat had received their signal and approached them in the stormy weather.

This rescue had come too late for the smaller boat that had capsized into the channel. Those people had tried swimming towards the larger dinghy but the smuggler on board had already moved their dinghy away, afraid that it would capsize too.

Yasmine covered her face with her hands. Callous smugglers. *This experience must have been harrowing. What state would Tara be in now?* She started taking deep breaths again as her mother had taught her to tackle anxieties.

A cyclist peddled past with a Scottie chasing after her. The dog had been covered with a cloth to keep away the cold wind. How much worse the wind would have been aboard the dinghy in the freezing channel. Brr. Yasmine pulled up the lapels of her dark coat.

What a relief that Tara was alive, but disgusting that the smuggler, most probably an accomplice of her Uncle Aram's, was putting innocent people's lives in danger. In fact, the smuggler had caused the immigrants in the smaller boat to drown and refused them help.

Was there no legal way to enter the country? Would she have to study law to help these desperate immigrants? She would be able to represent them then, though she knew she wouldn't be able to change society's impression and prejudices. She clasped her hands tightly and squirmed on the bench.

Then she realised she could tell Tara's story. Yasmine straightened her posture quickly. Her lungs filled up with oxygen again and her heart started beating stronger. Yes, that's what she would do. She would seek out Tara, talk to her, vouch for her, be her guarantor and tell her story. Bring it on.

Then she frowned. Would Tara be in a state of shock? Surely, the whole experience would have deeply upset her. She'd need a psychotherapist if she was diagnosed with post-traumatic stress disorder which would be highly likely after her ordeals.

Yasmine realised that her mother needed to be included in this. She had a list of very good psychotherapists. She would pay for it. Or if she didn't, Yasmine had some savings… *I need to stop rambling.* She got up from the bench and walked back to the entrance.

Her mother would be home in a few hours, but she needed to tackle Sam first as she was the stricter parent, more like a bodyguard. Yasmine almost felt like chuckling for the first time in many days. Tara was alive. She felt her body expand with every thought of reunion. She needed to get to her before Aram was released from custody. What a family she belonged to. If she was quick enough, there was still hope.

Yasmine waited until her mother had sipped her cup of tea after dinner. Sam had cooked as usual, and Yasmine made sure to chop up some iceberg lettuce, avocado and tomatoes to make a salad her mother loved.

She watched her mother gaze at the sunset. Hues of orange, red and pink set the scene. Yasmine smiled. Her mother would be more relaxed as they were approaching the weekend.

'How was your day, Mum?' she asked softly, bringing over the plate of salad she had prepared.

Her mother stretched her arms, closed her eyes for a moment and said, 'Hmm, okay. I was visited by an unaccompanied minor, together with his social worker today.'

Yasmine looked at her curiously. Her mother explained that the child was fifteen years of age and had escaped war-torn Cameroon.

'His English wasn't good but he spoke French, so I managed to help out as his social worker didn't speak enough French. I explained what I intended to do, namely catch up with childhood vaccinations.'

Her mother had a faint smile on her face. Suddenly she frowned and said, 'I read his psychiatric report. It was awful.' She glanced at Yasmine. 'I'm not allowed to tell you about the details because of confidentiality, but you can imagine what he must have been through, travelling alone from so far away.'

'What did you do for him, Mum?'

'I asked for some blood tests and examined him. It's so difficult when they don't speak the language. It'll take time for him to learn.'

This is my cue, Yasmine thought as she came to sit next to her mother on their sofa. Sam was still in the kitchen clearing up.

'Mum, I was wondering if we could have an outing in Kent this weekend. You've worked so hard this week and you need to switch off.'

Her mother looked outside warily and pulled her blanket closer to her chest. 'You'd like to go there in this cold weather?'

'Um, yes. Sam loves Canterbury, especially with the Christmas decorations being displayed. We could visit the cathedral and then...'

Her mother looked in the direction of the kitchen where Sam was putting the cutlery away. 'I suppose we could. Sam has been working hard too. This house is too big and there are so many chores to do. Thank goodness, we can leave the garden in peace during the winter months.' She looked closer at Yasmine. 'And then what?'

Yasmine stroked her mother's arm. 'And then we could do a good deed...'

Her mother looked at her curiously. 'What deed?'

'Mum, I've been bursting to give you the good news.'

Her mother cocked her head and waited for the explanation.

'Tara is alive.' Yasmine jumped up and hugged her mother. 'We should visit the asylum seekers' detention centre to talk to Tara, now that we know she's okay. We could help her out with the application for asylum.' Yasmine looked out of the window and added, 'She needs help like the refugee who visited you today.'

Her mother looked at her pensively.

'Mum, Tara must be out of her mind with worry. Her English isn't that good.' She stroked her mother's arm. 'And you speak a bit of Farsi because you went to school near the Iranian Border in Sulaymaniyah. It's your secret language.'

'I knew you were after something else, not just a

weekend away at a seaside resort.' Her mother sat up and pushed the blanket away. 'You know they have translators at the detention centres, Yasmine.'

'I know, Mum. But we need to support her and more importantly warn her about Aram.' Her mother bit her lip. Yasmine realised it was an opportunity to venture forward with her plan. 'He'd kill her if he found her.' She let that fear dangle in the air. 'Tara grassed him. He's afraid she'll implicate him again.'

'He will be in custody,' her mother said curtly.

'Yes. But not for long. Even if the police found him, a trial would need to take place.' She grabbed her mother's hand. 'You don't want your brother to be in the newspapers, do you? The paparazzi would love to get hold of a story like yours.'

'What do you mean with a *story like mine?*'

Yasmine winced. She should be careful and try and paraphrase the dysfunctionality of their family. She waited for a moment to collect her thoughts and to respond in a gentler way. 'I mean, I want to protect you, Mum. You've been through such a difficult time with Aram.' Her mother looked away. 'I only found out that he killed my dad – your husband when I read some letters from Sam to auntie Dilly in Iraq.'

Her mother took a handkerchief out of her pocket and snuffled into it, trying to forget her distress about those harrowing events that had taken place so many years ago. She stood up, taking Yasmine's hand and squeezing it. 'I'm so sorry, Yasmine.' She had a tear in her eye. 'You know I couldn't tell you about those events because I wanted to protect you too.' She paused. 'I don't think

Aram deliberately killed your dad.' She hesitated. 'It was a tragic accident.'

'Yes, Mum. That might be true, but Aram framed my father, saying that he was the driver of the car. He lied.' She took her hand away from her mother. 'And he's capable of more lies and murder. We need to warn Tara. She's so young and vulnerable. She could be your daughter and she may be the next one to die because of Aram, your brother.' Yasmine tried to squeeze out a tear but she felt more furious than sad.

Her mother massaged her temples. Yasmine hoped she didn't have a migraine coming on. She picked up her mother's hand again and squeezed it. 'Please Mum.' She hesitated. 'I'm doing my Master's application soon and I don't want to be in the headlines.'

Her mother scrunched her face and turn to look at her curiously. 'Yasmine, I can see what you're trying to do here.'

'What?'

Her mother had a twinkle in her eyes. *She was softening.* Yasmine's neck muscles started to relax. 'You're trying to win me over.'

Yasmine leaned over to her mother and wrapped her arms around her, planting kisses on her cheeks. 'I've already won you over, haven't I?' She whooped just as Sam entered the sitting room with a bowl full of clementines.

'Won your mum over for what?' Sam asked, eying Yasmine suspiciously.

'We're travelling to Canterbury for an overnight stay, just like you wanted.'

'Really? When?'

'This weekend. And then we're going to visit Tara in the detention centre.'

Sam stopped walking and held onto the dining room table to steady herself. 'You do know that your uncle might be looking for us there.

Yasmine tried to reassure Sam but she felt she was talking to a brick wall.

'Count me out,' said Sam. 'Aram has caused too many deaths and caused so much destruction. You two have to be very careful.'

There was a finality to Sam's tone that silenced Yasmine. She would have to drive to Kent alone with her mother. And Aram had better not escape from custody and find them there.

48

Yasmine heaved a sigh of relief when the detention officers in Kent told her that Tara had retained her mobile number and divulged the information that she had a friend in the UK. Now all that was needed was to get to Kent before Aram reached Tara.

Yasmine ran her hand through her hair which was longer and tangled up after her journey abroad. Appearances weren't her priority now. Her throat was parched although she had drunk two glasses of water before setting out on her journey to Kent.

What else had Tara told the detention officers? Would she mention any organisation she had been affiliated to in Iraq? Or would she admit that she had been working in the oldest job in the world? *Hardly.*

Yasmine glanced at her mother who was almost speeding on their way to Kent. Her wavy hair wasn't tied back as usual but tucked behind her ears, and she kept frowning although the music in the car was her choice. It was Fairuz, the popular Lebanese singer who sang in a clear and yearning voice. *What does my mum yearn for?*

This was no time for melancholic music. Maybe they should change the music to something more cheerful. Miley Cyrus and her song *I Can Buy Myself Flowers* entered her head, making her smile for the first time that morning. No need for Harry to buy her roses. She shifted her position in the car. Her legs were getting stiff.

Her mother glanced at her as they slowed down behind a lorry. 'We're lucky that the translator isn't available today.' She took a deep breath. 'We can visit Tara before she implicates herself in any way.'

'Why might she convey something that would harm her, Mum?'

Her mother slowed down again as the lorry in front of them was turning to leave the motorway. 'Because she doesn't know how the system works.' She put her foot on the accelerator again. 'She's frightened and has just experienced the ordeal of losing friends on the dinghy that capsized.'

Yasmine felt a heaviness on her chest. She had been thinking of the *old* Tara in Sulaymaniyah, not the newly traumatised one who had just landed on the shores of Dover, almost drowning in the Channel. But then Tara's whole life had been a succession of traumas, running away from torture, only to enter a different one.

'Is Tara gay?' her mother asked.

Yasmine jolted. 'No, she isn't. Why?'

'Because that would be a reason to ask for asylum.' She laughed. 'But then she would have to prove it.'

Yasmine was surprised about the Home Office requesting evidence of being gay, but she was also relieved that her mother sounded less melancholic and more light-hearted for the time being.

'How on earth can someone prove to officers that they're gay?' Her mother scratched her head.

'Well, Mum, if you don't know, it's a lost cause.' Yasmine almost chortled.

'One of my patients told me that she was asked how she had sex with her girlfriend.'

'That's obnoxious. Was the officer having a laugh?'

Her mother sighed and shook her head and replied, 'Most gay asylum seekers from abroad suffer from internalised homophobia as well as external threats to their lives.' She hesitated. 'How would they be able to admit this to detention officers if they aren't even ready to accept it themselves?'

And *how would my mum be living if she was in another part of the world?* Yasmine glanced at her and patted her shoulder gently. 'Thanks for coming with me to meet Tara, Mum.' What a chain of events and her mother was still at her side.

'Of course, Yasmine. You were away for a few weeks and I missed you.' She glanced at the rearview mirror. 'I want to spend as much time with you as possible.' Her lips curled up in a smile.

Yasmine leaned back in her seat and started tapping her fingers to the rhythm of *Rescue* by one of her favourite singers. Tara's innocence had been stolen from her but there was hope she would regain her happiness and start living.

The rest of their journey was spent in silence and they soon arrived at the detention centre where their IDs were checked and they were led into a sparse room. *So this is the interrogation room,* thought Yasmine. She sat down on one of the wooden chairs with her mother perched next to her. The windows had bars on it, like in a cage. Her heart sank. What had she expected? Tara would be used to cages. She was imprisoned in man-made social norms wherever she went.

The door opened to reveal a middle-aged female detention officer. Tara was cowering behind her. Yasmine's heart started to flutter as she leapt up and ran towards her. She was alive. The officer restrained Yasmine, saying that she needed to be gentler as Tara had been crying and feeling weak all day. *What a remark. Tara needed even more hugs now.* Something in the detention officer's eyes made Yasmine step back, though, and she sat down on her chair again. Was the detention officer protecting Tara or making sure she didn't run away?

Tara wiped her tears with a tissue the officer gave her and sat at the other side of the table, waiting for someone else to start speaking. She wore jeans and a green pullover but no make-up. Most probably, she didn't possess make-up anymore. She looked younger and more natural with her hair tied back, although Yasmine was startled about the pallor of her skin. Tara's face looked lifeless. She tried smiling at her but Tara's eyes remained downcast.

The officer was the first person to speak. First, she looked at Yasmine's mother. 'How do you know each other?'

'Um, what did she tell you?'

The officer looked at her sternly. 'I'm the one asking questions here.'

Yasmine quickly answered to defuse the situation. 'I met her in Sulaymaniyah a few weeks ago.'

'I need to know more than that.' The officer said, pursed her lips. 'Tara says she's an Iranian Kurd. Can you confirm that?'

'Oh yes, yes,' Yasmine squealed, thinking it would make the officer more sympathetic towards Tara. She was sure to remember the demonstrations after Zina Amini was killed by the morality police because her headscarf had apparently revealed some of her hair. The irony was that Tara belonged to the other side of the morality scale. She had been misused and abused to the extent that her body had become something she had to trade in order to survive. What irony. And tragedy. Yasmine peered at the detention officer. She was writing down some sentences on her notepad.

'Did Tara belong to a political party?' asked the officer.

Yasmine pondered on this question. Even if Tara didn't belong to a political party, she was persecuted just for being herself, a Kurdish woman living in Iran under a misogynistic rule. Besides that, she had been abused by her own family.

However, she went with the version of Tara belonging to the Kurdistan Democratic Party which was outlawed in Iran. Yasmine told the officer that Tara had lost her papers proving that she had worked for this party. The officer raised an eyebrow. Had she heard this excuse previously? She glanced at Yasmine warily.

'Tara has entered the UK illegally,' the officer said curtly. 'She may be prosecuted. We asked her if she wanted a lawyer but she declined.'

Yasmine turned towards her mother with pleading eyes.

'Officer,' her mother said gently, 'most probably Tara

thought she would have to pay for a lawyer. Her English isn't as good as her Farsi. I'll ask her.'

Her mother turned towards Tara quickly and asked her in Farsi whether she wanted a lawyer. Thank goodness, her mother spoke the language, having lived in the neighbouring Sulaymaniyah. Tara's eyes gleamed at the chance of having an understandable conversation with someone who spoke her language. And of course, the detention officer didn't speak Farsi. Yasmine hoped that her mother had also told Tara to say that she had indeed belonged to the Kurdish Democratic Party. It would make matters easier for her and speed up the process. There was no way they should mention her real job: servicing men. Yasmine held her breath. Tara should play along with the reason given. Tara nodded quickly. Thank goodness the detention officer didn't speak Farsi.

Yasmine's mother smiled at the officer and told her that Tara would accept legal aid if offered.

The officer peered at Tara who was looking down at the ground. Yasmine's mother added that Tara would also accept an official translator if one became available. The officer waited for a moment, then nodded and told them that she would arrange another meeting as they had many more queries to resolve.

'Maybe we could go out to the courtyard for some fresh air, officer?' Yasmine asked, realising that her voice sounded hoarse.

Her mother added, 'It would just be for a few moments. She looks pale and needs some fresh air.' The officer hesitated but agreed when Sozanne explained that she was a doctor.

Her mother added, 'I don't want her to collapse in this room. You look like a kind officer.'

The officer's shoulders straightened at this compliment. She paused, then glanced at Tara who was sobbing again. 'All right, just for a few moments. I'll come with you.'

Yasmine almost jumped up from her chair. She felt Tara's eyes upon her as she flung her arms in the air triumphantly. But would their short outing bring them closer?

Yasmine shivered with fear. They were in the middle of nowhere, in a detention centre that looked more like a prison than a sanctuary.

49

There were no orange-red hues of sunset to greet them outside the detention centre office. Instead, greyish-black clouds descended upon them, but they were better than the neon lights and linoleum floors in the office they had just left. The drizzle outside felt cold and Yasmine edged closer to Tara in order to give her the warm gloves she had bought in London.

'Tara, please don't cry. Mum and I will help you.' She hugged her. 'But you must keep calm. Any wrong word and your application for asylum will be declined by the authorities.'

Tara listened carefully. Yasmine explained to her that temporary accommodation would be available, although the officer had told them that she may be sharing a room with Iranians who might have worked for the Iranian regime as spies.

Tara jolted and held on to Yasmine's arm, saying, 'I'll kill myself if I have to leave this country.'

Yasmine took her hand and squeezed it. 'If you leave this country, you'll be killed in Iran. Your family will hound you.' She paused. 'And if you return to Iraq, Aram or his henchmen will harass you.' It was as if Tara was taking up too much space in the world, when all she needed was somewhere quiet where she could just be herself. Yasmine's eyelids were drooping. Was she that helpless? No, No. She would fight on!

'I don't want to go to Ev...Evin prison,' Tara cried, clinging onto Yasmine as Sozanne looked on, most probably wanting to give the two women time together as they wouldn't be seeing each other again so soon. She took a step back and started to talk to the detention officer.

'Tara, don't worry,' Yasmine said, holding her hand tightly, 'We'll win this case and then we can work for any charitable organisation together.' That was wishful thinking as Tara wouldn't be allowed to work as an asylum seeker. But, hopefully, her application for asylum would succeed within a year.

Suddenly, Tara's eyes widened. She looked terrified.

Yasmine stepped closer to her and tried to smile. 'Tara, I told you not to worry. Whatever job you're offered, it's better than staying here in the detention centre.'

Her friend looked as if she was going to die in Evin prison. *She must be fixating on that ghastly jail; that's why she was looking so terrified.* But Tara's eyes appeared to be transfixed on something else in front of her. Yasmine turned around slowly to follow her gaze.

A piercing scream filled the air.

Yasmine froze.

A few metres away from where she stood, a man held a shimmering object in his hand. He was grinning at her.

She felt repulsed by his nicotine-stained teeth and glazed eyes.

It couldn't be. It shouldn't be.

She was unable to breathe.

'Let's keep the killing in the family, shall we?' Aram cried, wielding his knife. He jumped closer. 'Now who shall I take out first? My sister Sozanne, the traitor, or my oh-so-meddlesome niece Yasmine?' He laughed hysterically. 'Tara can be the last one to die.' He turned around to look at her directly and pointed at her. 'She thought she would die in Iran or Iraq. Ha! She'll die where she wanted to come to, here in Britain.'

Tara watched him, unable to move.

Aram laughed again. 'And all the detention staff and this society will say is "one asylum seeker less".'

He suddenly sprinted towards Yasmine, kicking a plastic bottle out of his way. *Shit.* How could she escape him this time? They were all standing in the corner of a small courtyard, being sentenced without a judge.

'Mum,' she screamed, putting out her arms to protect herself.

Her mother had already turned around when Aram had started speaking. She had edged towards him while he was laughing. When she saw him lunge at Yasmine, she jumped towards him, putting her rucksack in front of her.

'You bastard!' Yasmine had never heard her swear like that.

The detention officer gasped and rushed towards Tara, pushing her away from Yasmine towards a small bin located at the side of the courtyard.

'Security. Help!' The detention officer tripped and fell on top of Tara, who squealed in pain.

Yasmin's heart pounded as she watched Aram's knife rip through her mother's rucksack. How long would it take for a security officer to appear? She had never heard her uncle growl so vehemently. A vein was throbbing in his neck and the fingers of his left hand were claw-like.

He thrust his knife forward again, narrowly missing her mother's arm. The detention officer had got up from the ground and screamed for the security guard again.

Yasmine pulled a hardcover book from her bag and threw it at her uncle. It hit his head and he started to scream. *I never thought a book would save my life.* She ran to her mother's side. She couldn't die here, shouldn't be sacrificed for Tara. No, no.

Aram glanced at Yasmine, fury blinding him. He grabbed the knife from the floor and surged towards her. Yasmine screamed as the security guard appeared from behind Aram. There was a brief scuffle after which the security guard pushed her uncle to the ground. The guard tried to get out the handcuffs that were fixed to his trousers.

Tara stood up from the floor and stepped in front of Yasmine.

Aram's face reddened as he shouted, 'You traitor! You liar. I helped you get your job – is this how you repay me? Siding with disgusting sister and niece. Aargh!' He charged at Tara while the security guard fumbled with his handcuffs.

Yasmine gasped as Aram plunged his knife into Tara's tummy. She tumbled to the floor again, just as another security guard lurched forward from the doorway and jumped onto Aram's back. They both fell to the floor. This time the two security guards managed to put the handcuffs onto Aram who was screaming at the top of his voice, 'You filthy bastards! You should be raped, not given money for your services.'

The detention officer ran towards Tara, shouting to Yasmine's mother, 'You're a doctor, do something. Tara has been stabbed.'

Sozanne stumbled towards Tara and took her pullover off to compress the bleeding from the lower part of Tara's tummy. Yasmine looked on, horrified, as the blood trickled through Tara's green blouse.

'Quick, call an ambulance,' Sozanne said to the detention officer as she placed her fingers on Tara's wrist. 'Her pulse is weak. She's in shock.'

Yasmine felt her breathing quicken. Her stomach churned as if she was the one who had been stabbed. Everything around her appeared blurred and the last thing she remembered was falling to the ground as Aram's screaming filled the courtyard with a cacophony of threats and insults.

50

Yasmine slowly opened her eyes. Blurred images started to take shape. A television appeared in front of her. When had a TV been placed in her room? *This isn't my room.* She tilted her head to the right. A window revealed a sky overcast by dark clouds. She tried to concentrate on her breathing. Her chest hurt every time she took a breath.

She winced. What time of day was it? Either dusk or dawn. She glanced at her clothes. These weren't her pyjamas. It was a white hospital gown. She frowned, trying to get out of the bed but her legs felt weak and she fell back into it. The previous time she had ended up this confused was when she had finished a bottle of gin at a wedding in the Lake District.

She looked around the room again. It was bare. A bedside cabinet had a glass of water on it and a half-eaten cheese sandwich on a plate she had never seen before. She slowly moved her head to the left of the bed. A tall machine towered over her. It was a blood pressure machine. *Shit. I'm in in a hospital. But why?*

She tried to get out of her bed again. Someone needed to tell her what had happened! There was a knock on the door. She let out a cry. *Why do I feel I'm in danger?* She was in a hospital. Surely, this was the safest place to be even though she didn't know why she was there.

After a second, the door handle turned slowly. Yasmine held her breath as a woman entered the room holding a bunch of pink roses. Her pulse slowed down and her lips curled into a faint smile.

'Mum!' she cried. 'What happened? Why am I here?'

Her mother ran towards her and squeezed her gently, stroking her hair and whispering her usual endearments. 'Sweetheart, I'm so happy you're awake now.' No explanations were offered.

'You need to rest some more.' She put the roses on the table and reached out for the glass of water, putting it towards Yasmine's lips.

Yasmine pushed the glass away. 'I need you to tell me why I'm here.' She sat up in her bed and peered at her mother.

Her mother wiped her eyes. *Is she crying or taking out an annoying eyelash?* Yasmine waited for her mother to answer.

'You don't remember anything?'

'Um, we were in a car driving somewhere.' She trailed off, trying to remember what had happened when they stopped the car.

'Yes.' Her mother watched her carefully. 'Anything else?'

Yasmine tried to concentrate on her thoughts, not that there were many. 'Well, if we're in a hospital, we must have had a car accident.' She looked at her mother expectantly. She didn't look injured.

'Hmm, there were injuries, but they weren't caused by an accident.' Her mother hesitated. 'Do you remember Tara?'

Yasmine kept silent. An image of a young woman formed itself in her mind. She was in a different setting, somewhere far away surrounded by palm trees and mountains. Her mother's country. Then a different image descended on her – Tara was lying on the ground with blood trickling down her tummy. Yasmine shook her head but that hurt so she kept still, waiting for more images to clarify the events that had led up to her hospitalisation. Surely, this young woman lying on the floor needed more medical attention than herself!

'What happened to her?' She winced as she sat up in her bed and grabbed hold of her mother's arm.

'Darling, you're remembering the events now. So I think I can tell you what happened to her.' She stroked Yasmine's hair. 'She was stabbed – do you remember? She's still alive, but in a critical condition.'

Yasmine's cloud of images merged into one terrible culmination of an assault. Aram stood smirking whilst Tara lay in a pool of blood. But Aram was in handcuffs. Yasmine felt weak and felt herself slump back into her bed. Her fear was overwhelming but she could only take the events slowly.

She looked at her mother anxiously. 'Where's Tara now?'

'She's in hospital, actually in the same one as you.'

'I need to see her!' Yasmine said loudly, trying to get

out of her bed. She slumped back into it, feeling fatigued and dizzy.

'Sweetheart, I went to visit her but the nurse only let me sneak into her room that one time because I'm a doctor and she had no other family.' She hesitated. 'Do you remember that she asked for asylum before she was stabbed?'

Yasmine sighed. Everything was coming back to her slowly now that she had seen her mother. Where was the vicious man who had attacked them?

'What happened to Aram?' Her eyes widened with fear as the realisation forced itself upon her.

'Don't worry about him. He's in custody now.'

Yasmine started to sob. 'Why does he hate us so much, Mum?' she stuttered in between her sobs.

Her mother stroked her hair again and said, 'He hates himself more than he hates us.'

'He's a criminal. Don't downplay it anymore.' She glared at her mother who was looking out of the window. *She's too docile; she needs to face her demons.* And the devil was her Uncle Aram. 'Mum, we didn't have to go through all of this violence for the truth to be laid bare, did we?' Her voice sounded accusatory but she didn't care. The pain was unbearable.

Her mother frowned and covered her with the bedsheet. 'The wounds will heal in time,' she said gently.

'If you'd been more open with these family secrets, we wouldn't have to wait for them to rear their ugly heads.' *When will our nightmare end?* They couldn't go on as if aggression and violence didn't exist. For a moment, she hated her mother, covering up secrets and ugliness as if they were seeds that wouldn't be able to grow.

317

'There's a time for everything,' her mother replied, shifting her position. 'You need some more rest and the visiting times are ending soon. I'll come again tomorrow.' She looked at Yasmine gently. 'Maybe we can visit Tara then. I'll take you there.'

Yasmine nodded. *What choice do I have?* Her mother would have to take her in a wheelchair as her legs felt weak. And Tara was most probably in no position to walk over to her room. Yasmine's head felt fuzzy. She felt her mother plant a kiss on her forehead and smelt her familiar Dior perfume. Her breathing slowed down.

'I'll let you rest now. See you tomorrow and I'll bring Sam with me.'

Yasmine smiled, wondering how Sam was coping with all the assaults in the family. Yasmine would have run away long ago. Only you couldn't run away from your family – or could you?

51

The following day, Yasmine looked around her bed. She picked up the newspaper her mother had forgotten on the bedside cabinet. Or had the nurse left it there for Yasmine to read whilst recovering?

'*Asylum-seeker chaos on our shores.*' Yasmine sat up, her sleepiness dispersing. She continued reading the headlines.

'*The Home Secretary is shocked at the lack of security at the detention centre in Kent. GP Dr Sozanne Brewers embroiled in sex worker's claim for asylum.*'

Yasmine covered her mouth to stop screaming. *My mother's reputation is in tatters!*

She read one more sentence: '*Lesbian doctor (55) questioned by police about sex trafficking.*

Yasmine collapsed into her bed. Oblivion was better than the tabloids scapegoating her mother. What did her mother's same-sex relationship have to do with Tara? *If she were heterosexual, no journalist would have mentioned it. What if the paparazzi appear at my mum's house, or worse still at her practice? God forbid. What would her patients think?*

Yasmine's eyelids felt heavy. She wanted to open them but something was stopping her while she was breathing heavily. It was cold in the room. She tentatively opened one eye. The TV was in front of her, the bedside cabinet still had a glass of water on it.

She tried to sit up but groaned. Her chest was hurting her. She had to collect her thoughts! Her mother had come in to visit her. She had told her about Aram's assaults and that she had fainted during these events, thereby knocking her head on the ground. She was in hospital with concussion. Yasmine tried remembering what happened afterwards. She looked at the bedside cabinet again. There were no items on it except for the glass of water. She would like to have had some magazines to read or a newspaper. *The newspaper heading.* She gulped.

The insinuation that her mother had liaised with a sex worker and people-smugglers was preposterous. Tara wasn't a sex worker. She had only unwillingly participated in this job a few times because she had been spiked and encountered so much abuse from her family in her native country. And besides, what did this have to do with her mother?

She felt like screaming but only a guttural noise left her throat. Her Mum had always been so careful about her reputation and now it was ruined. She wasn't even out to her patients. What did her sexuality have to do with any of this? Yasmine felt rage rise in her.

The paparazzi would have a feast with her soon. She covered her eyes. No, she needed to open them. She needed to talk. Looking around her again, she saw the call-button. Great. She'd activate it and get some help. She managed to press the button, then waited for someone to come in.

A nurse entered the room, holding a small container, presumably some medicine for her.

'Are you okay, Yasmine?' Her voice was warm and clear.

Yasmine's neck muscles relaxed. 'I'm okay.' She cleared her throat. 'I want to see my mother, please.' She knew she must sound pathetic.

'Your mother isn't here, but someone else is,' the nurse said. She sounded cagey. Who was this other person? Tara? As far as she knew, Tara was in a critical condition and couldn't walk over from her ward.

'Who's here to see me?' she asked, watching the nurse closely.

The nurse shifted her position. 'Um, she says she's your other mother.'

Yasmine felt something gurgling in her throat. *It must be a laugh trying to get out.* Surely the nurse had heard of other diverse families.

'Please tell her to come in. I feel better,' she lied. 'I need to talk to her.'

The nurse nodded, then came forward to take her blood pressure. 'Okay, I'll go and find her. She was just going downstairs to the cafeteria for a moment.'

Yasmine heaved a sigh of relief. Where was her mother? She couldn't even remember what day it was. Most probably, her mother was back at work. *Business as usual.* She felt flippant. Sarcasm wasn't her usual demeanour. *Am I losing my mind?*

It wasn't long before there was another knock on the

door. Yasmine tried sitting up and looked up expectantly. 'Sam,' she croaked, 'I've missed you so much.'

Sam walked towards her, wiping a tear away. *Why is she tearful? I'm better now. No need to feel sorry for me. Or is something else going on?*

'Kitten, how are you?'

Yasmine hugged her tightly before answering. 'I'm feeling better. I don't even know why I'm still here. I know I suffered a concussion from a fall, but I want to go home now.'

Sam took a deep breath. 'The doctors say you can go home tomorrow.' She averted her gaze. It was clear there was something she wasn't saying.

'Where's Mum?' Yasmine started to wring her hands. 'Why isn't she here?'

Sam sat down on the chair next to the bed and kept quiet for a moment. Yasmine watched her expression closely, waiting for her to speak. 'Your mum had an appointment today so she couldn't come.'

Yasmine felt a shiver go down her spine. 'What appointment? Is she ill?'

Sam took her hand and squeezed it. 'She's not ill. But—'

'But what?' Yasmine tried to read Sam's expression. It was a mixture of concern and fear. *Has Aram escaped from custody?*

'Your mother had an appointment with the Medical Defence Union.'

Yasmine opened her mouth, then hesitated, an ominous feeling overcoming her. 'What for?'

'There was a newspaper article. I don't think you read it…'

Yasmine looked at her bedside cabinet. She had read the headlines somewhere but the newspaper had disappeared. 'Geez.' She raised her eyebrows. 'She's done nothing wrong.

Sam shook her head and looked at the floor. 'The detention officer was questioned after the assaults.' She hesitated, then said. 'The officer was given a verbal warning because she had allowed Tara out into the courtyard without taking a security guard with her.'

'And?'

'Well, she was very angry about her verbal warning and told the journalists that there was a rumour about Tara participating in sex work.'

'You mean, she tried to distract them from her failings?' Yasmine almost spat her words out.

Sam nodded, looking out of the window.

'But Sam, what has that got to do with mum? Everyone knows that a lot of female refugees have been raped or had to participate in sex-work in order to survive... And what has that got to do with mum's private life?' Yasmine's cheeks reddened. 'The newspaper is just trying to increase their miserable sales.' She clenched her hands.

'I know darling. But this particular newspaper is interested in sensational news.' Sam patted her on the shoulder. 'And a same-sex relationship attracts attention. That's why we tried to keep our love out of the limelight.'

'I'm so sorry,' Yasmine heard herself rasp. 'I didn't want this to happen.'

Sam picked up her head. The rims of her eyes were purple. *She hasn't had much sleep.* Yasmine wrung her hands again.

'Does this mean the end of mum's career?' Yasmine asked, biting her lip.

'I don't know,' was the shrill answer.

Yasmine started to sob. Her mother loved her profession. Where would they go from here? Who would earn the money? Sam was older than her mum and retired now on a meagre pension. She was hardly going to start work again. Yasmine had only just finished her degree and planned to take a Master's. Would she have to give up her dreams and look for a job to support them all? Her concentration had diminished since her concussion and the world looked bleak. All the positivity her mother had tried to teach her had suddenly vanished. She hid her face in her hands, trying to blot out the stark reality that faced her family.

52

asmine stood at the window. Heavy clouds sauntered through the dark sky. She caught a glimpse of the sun scurrying behind one of them. *Even the sun is trying to hide.* There were no more fluffy clouds that moved across the sky like peaceful sheep. One of the clouds was almost orange and seemed to have taken on the shape of a fox. *Am I becoming delusional?*

She moved away from the window. Her mother would be here to pick her up soon. She would have all the time she needed, now that the GMC were investigating her involvement in sex trafficking. Yasmine closed her eyes. How had all this started? She had been looking for the truth, family and heritage and had ended up with wounds and death. And the final curtain was nowhere in sight.

There was a knock on the door. Yasmine jumped away from the window and carefully walked towards the door. What state would her mother be in? She loved her job despite the exhaustion she felt in the evenings. Now, all that mattered was how to keep it.

The door opened slowly and her mother slouched

into the room. Her shoulders were hunched and her face looked gaunt. Yasmine's heart lurched.

She ran towards her mother, tears trickling down her cheeks. 'I'm so sorry, Mum, I didn't want all this to happen,' she stuttered. 'I was just looking for the rest of our family. I wanted to find out the truth.'

Her mother let her cry on her shoulders and they kept quiet for a moment or two.

'The truth can be an ordeal, Yasmine. You need to be strong enough to face it.'

Her mother led them to the bed. They both sat on it, Yasmine putting her head onto her mother's shoulder. The familiar smell of lavender soap on her mother made her sob even more. She needed to go home. Yasmine wiped her tears away with her sleeve and her mother cradled her. They sat for a while, rocking each other. Yasmine remembered how her mother had done this when she had failed her driving licence a few years ago. *If only I'd known then what failure really looked like.*

Finally, Yasmine was able to loosen her grip on her mother. Her arm muscles relaxed and she started breathing more evenly.

'Mum, are we safe now?' *Geez. I should be comforting my mother, not the other way round.*

'When is a person ever safe, sweetheart? But we have each other to comfort ourselves.'

Yasmine snuggled into her mother's arms again. 'Mum, I wouldn't know what to do without you.' She started to sob again. When her mother had visited her in hospital a few years ago, after the syringe-spiking event, she had vomited so much that she thought she would die.

What if she had died. She held on to her mother. 'Mum, I'm so grateful you're there for me.'

'Well, sweetheart. I know I've been very busy with my job and I haven't always been present in your life...' She trailed off.

'But you were there when I needed you most, Mum.' Yasmine squeezed her hand. 'When I was spiked in the club, you were there for me.'

Her mother looked deflated and stared out of the window.

Yasmine followed her gaze to the seagull perched on the windowsill. Then she sat up quickly, remembering who else was in the hospital with her.

'Mum, we can visit Tara now that I'm leaving.' Her lips curved up into a small smile.

Her mother looked up anxiously. 'Yes, I enquired about her. She's still in a critical condition, even after her surgery.' She looked at Yasmine tenderly. 'Apparently, she lost a lot of blood when Aram stabbed her. The surgeons have done their best, but Tara was in a frail condition anyway because of the channel crossing and the freezing conditions.' She paused to take in Yasmine's reaction.

Yasmine's stomach lurched. *Is she preparing me for something?* 'I want to go to her room now.' She got up and pulled her mother up from the bed.

'Tara's still in the critical care unit.' Her mother reached up to stroke her hair. 'I don't think they'll let us in.'

'I have to go there.' Yasmine pushed her mother's hand away. 'She hasn't got anyone else in this country.' She was surprised at her sudden vigour.

Her mother got up slowly and picked up Yasmine's small case next to her bed. 'We can try, then.'

Yasmine stopped suddenly. 'I'm sorry, I didn't ask about who referred you to the GMC.' She glanced at her mother who winced.

'Darling, I knew about Tara's previous job and that she had been persecuted in Iran.' Her mother covered her face with her hands. 'But you know I had nothing to do with sex trafficking.' Her mother looked away; Yasmine couldn't make out her expression. 'I don't know who referred me, Yasmine. Anyone can make an anonymous complaint.' Her voice sounded weak.

Yasmine hugged her mother again, this time to comfort her, rather than be comforted herself. 'Surely, they'll find out that you knew nothing about Tara's sex trafficking,' she said urgently. 'Anyway, Tara can tell them herself.' She tried to sound triumphant and upbeat.

'Yasmine, they also want to investigate me about the people smugglers.' Her mother didn't sound convinced about being exonerated by the GMC.

Yasmine frowned.

The machinery of the GMC appeared like a nebulous space containing bureaucrats waiting to strike off precious doctors. She had read articles about doctors who had abused patients, but her mother hadn't been cruel to anyone.

Suddenly an idea came to her. Tara needed to explain to the GMC how she had come to Britain and that her mother had nothing to do with her escape from Iraq. Her mother's job and livelihood were at stake, as well as Yasmine's guilt.

53

Yasmine and her mother stood outside the critical care unit, waiting to speak to the doctor. Yasmine shuffled her feet. The walls were white-coloured and the reception desk was littered with patient files. Was it time to do the ward round? Yasmine looked around her. How must her mother have felt working on these busy wards before training to be a GP. All this while trying to bring up her daughter? Once this nightmare ended, she would catch up on all these questions. But would the terror ever end? She was becoming more aware of her own mortality.

Yasmine watched the nurses taking medication into the bays. Not that there were many nurses. She didn't see any English ones. She spotted a nurse coming out of the critical care unit bay and stopped her to ask if they could go in and check on Tara. The nurse had an Eastern European accent, maybe Ukrainian.

'It's not visiting time.' The nurse hesitated. 'Do you belong to her family?'

'She hasn't got any family here. I'm the closest she has.' The nurse walked away. *I mustn't cry.*

Her mother tapped her on the shoulder, nudging her to keep calm. Yasmine followed her gaze. A policeman stood outside the bay where Tara was kept. He was eying them suspiciously. Geez. *Is he expecting another assault? When will all this end?* She cleared her throat and glanced at her mother. 'Mum, can you please ask if you're allowed in to see Tara?'

Her mother hesitated.

'Please, Mum. You're a doctor. Your chances of seeing her are better than mine.' She kissed her mother on the cheek and pressed her closer to her chest. Her mother sighed and glanced at the doctor who had just come in to do the ward round. She nodded, walking up to him.

'Hello, Dr Patel,' she said, looking at the badge with his name on it. 'I'm Dr Brewers. Would it be possible to visit your patient, Tara? My daughter and I live in London,' she pleaded, 'so this will be our only chance to visit her.'

Yasmine stood at her mother's side, forcing herself to smile at the doctor.

He raised his eyebrows as if trying to remember something. 'Aren't you the doctor who was involved in her asylum case?' He took a step back.

Yasmine saw her mother blush. *Oh yes, the newspaper article.*

'I wasn't involved in an asylum case. All I did was accompany my daughter to visit a friend at a detention centre.'

Yasmine winced. Her mother sounded defensive. There was nothing to be guarded about. She didn't deserve criticism or need to ward it off. She stepped closer to her mother. They were a team.

'Hmm, I saw your photo in a newspaper.' His eyes widened. 'You're being investigated by the GMC.'

Her mother coughed. 'I'm not here as a doctor to examine or treat Tara,' she said carefully, 'I'm here to inquire about her health, Dr Patel.' She clasped her hands, the way she usually did when she was trying to abate her anger.

Yasmine frowned. 'We're asking out of compassion as she has no family in this country.' She glanced at the policeman standing next to Tara's Bay. 'We have no intention of intimidating anyone.'

The doctor pursed his lips and nodded at the policeman outside the bay. 'I'll ask the policeman whether you're allowed to see the patient.' He gave Yasmine a razor-sharp smile and walked off towards a desk to write some notes.

Yasmine and her mother looked at each other horrified. *We don't look like criminals.* Yasmine had to try hard not to grind her teeth. How else could she pacify the doctor?

And why do I get the feeling that we are being treated like villains? Her mother's eyes were downcast, as if she didn't feel she belonged to the medical world anymore. Yasmine spotted a blood pressure machine that was placed in front of her. *No doubt her own blood pressure would be sky high.*

The doctor started to write in some patient charts. He wasn't in a hurry to speak to the policeman. Yasmine patted her mother on her shoulder. *It must be more painful for her.* She yearned to touch her mother's face. Once upon a time, Mum would have been welcomed with open arms in any hospital. Now, she was treated like a crook.

Her mother took a deep breath and turned towards Yasmine. 'Okay, sweetheart. I think we may need to go home. Sam will be worried. We can phone in tomorrow.'

Yasmine felt like her feet were glued to the ground. Her legs felt heavy and her throat was dry.

'You don't think they'll give me a glass of water?' she asked her mother, trying to buy time to think about the next steps. Her mother looked at her curiously. *I can't fool my own mother.* She eyed the sturdy policeman who looked more like a statue than a human with feelings.

Suddenly, a siren wailed through the sterile ward. Yasmine and her mother stared in the direction of the bay. The ward doctor dropped his files onto the desk and rushed towards the shrill sound. A nurse shouted from the bay and the policeman popped his head in, glancing to the left where the nurse was shouting from.

Yasmine felt a knot in her stomach. *Surely it isn't...*

'Is it Tara?' she screamed at the policeman who was back on guard. He looked taken aback and stood in her way when she tried running into the bay.

'I need to get in there,' she gasped. 'My friend's in danger.' *Odd that I'm thinking like this in a hospital.* Tara had been in jeopardy all her life, starting with her parents, the senior-ranking Iranian military man and her cold mother who had preferred their son. It would have been easier for her to live as a man. *Why am I seeing all this in a kaleidoscopic way? This isn't the end of Tara's life, for God's sake.*

Yasmine tried to run past the policeman again. He

blocked her way into the bay and pushed her back towards her mother. Damn. This might be her last chance to hug Tara before… She barricaded any further thoughts.

The policeman was much stronger than Yasmine. He snarled at her, saying that he would have to use his handcuffs if she continued disrupting the doctors and their work. She stepped back and clung to her mother who held her tightly as if she was afraid her daughter would try to run into the bay again.

Yasmine heard a frenzy of noises coming from the bay.

Dr Patel shouted, 'Get the defib. She's flatlining!'

She clutched her mother's hand and asked, 'Who are they resuscitating, Mum?'

Her mother shook her head, tears welling up in her eyes. Yasmine put her head on her mother's shoulder and started to cry. There was nothing they could do now.

Please God, please let her live. I'll work for any charitable cause if she survives. I'll join an NGO, anything. Please just let her live.

The cacophony of noises continued for a few minutes. *My mother's a doctor, for goodness' sake. She should be in there with the other doctors.*

Suddenly there was silence. Yasmine raised her eyes and watched Dr Patel leave the bay. His forehead revealed beads of sweat as he slouched past them.

'Is Tara … alive?' her mother asked him.

The doctor grimaced and shook his head, taking the surgical gloves off his hands.

Yasmine wailed, clinging onto her mother. Sozanne started to pat her back like she used to do when she was a child. Whenever she was ill or had fallen or someone had bullied her, her mother would plant butterfly kisses on her forehead. This time, there would be no kissing it better.

'I need to see for myself.' Yasmine gasped as she broke free from her mother's embrace. She ran towards the bay again.

The policeman pushed her back. She heard him swear as he blocked her way. She tugged at her hair and started pacing up and down the corridor, shouting. She'd failed Tara – but then who hadn't failed her? Her mother tried to clutch at her but she pushed her back, screaming as she did so.

Not allowed to help Tara during her lifetime and not allowed to see her in death. She ran back towards her mother who had started arguing with the doctor. She heard her plead with Dr Patel to let Yasmine say goodbye to her friend. Dr Patel pointed at the policeman. Yasmine realised that she would only be able to say a prayer. She pulled her mother towards her and cried.

Where was humanity?

54

fter she left hospital, Yasmine spent a few days in bed at home. The worst had happened. Tara was lifeless, killed on foreign soil instead of being rescued. *Was it my fault for putting ideas into her head that she would be safe in another country?* Yasmine didn't want to see anyone. Her mother told her that Harry had phoned, but she didn't care. He hadn't called her since their breakup. Why would he care now?

'Aargh!' she screamed, punching her pillow. *This is a nightmare.* She looked outside her window. The clouds were grey as always at this time of the year. Winter had not changed. Her bobbing robin had disappeared. She was in no mood for the approaching festive season. It was now more than two months since she had decided to enter Iraq. She had merely wanted to follow her mother's footsteps and bond with the extended family. She threw her pillow on the floor, wondering whether there was something more to her adventure. Something must have been lacking for her to enter a country in the Middle East that could turn into a cauldron, easily spilling over.

There was a light tap on the door.

She got out of the bed to pick up the pillow. 'Come in.' Her voice sounded like someone else's, more like a meek and frail woman. *What has become of me?*

Her mother came into her bedroom, but without her usual confident stride. Her wavy hair was tied back. She looked as tired as when she used to go to work on Mondays.

'Good morning sweetheart,' she said, obviously trying to sound jovial. 'Or should I say good afternoon?' Her lopsided smile was a welcome change to the dark thoughts entering Yasmine's aching head.

Yasmine sat up and tried to let her lips curl into a smile. Maybe if she did that, she'd feel better.

'Oh Mum.' She took her mother's hands into hers and looked into her brown eyes that didn't shine as brightly as they used to. She hadn't noticed the dark circles and puffiness under her eyes previously.

'I'm sorry I got up so late. I took the sleeping tablets Dr Ashraff prescribed and they knocked me out.'

'Well, I'm glad they did. You couldn't carry on with your insomnia.'

Yasmine wondered whether her mother was taking sleeping tablets too. She wouldn't blame her.

'When is your matter with the GMC going to be sorted out?'

Her mother looked out of the window. 'It's going to take time.' She took a deep breath. 'Aram has implicated me as aiding people smugglers in order to bring Tara back.' She hesitated, looking at Yasmine carefully. 'Tara isn't here to refute that.' She took Yasmine's hand and squeezed it. 'There's no evidence at all, as you know. No messages on my phone. No calls. The GMC has to take it seriously, though, so I'm suspended until they've investigated thoroughly.'

Yasmine buried her head in her mother's lap. She couldn't cry any more. Her tears seemed to have dried up.

Her mother asked, 'What attracted you to Tara in the first place?'

'She needed help.' Yasmine sniffled. 'She was going to be assaulted and no one came to help her.'

Her mother hesitated. 'Did you have flashbacks to when you were assaulted?'

Yasmine shook her head vehemently. 'I wasn't assaulted Mum. I was just spiked.'

Her mother frowned. 'That's an assault, Yasmine.'

'Whatever,' she said, getting up from her bed.

Her mother stood up and followed her to the window. They were quiet for a few moments.

'Have you got any pleasant memories of Tara you can share with me?' Her mother wiped a stain on the window.

Yasmine smiled. 'Yes, we were running down the Azmer mountains and ' She turned to face her mother. 'Did you ever run down that treacherous mountain?'

Her mother gave a quiet laugh. 'I wasn't as boisterous as you.'

Yasmine believed that. Her mother was very guarded and level-headed.

'Well, while we were running down that mountain, we tried to do the Charleston.' She chortled and held on to her mother to keep her balance.

Her mother pushed her to the middle of the room.

'Show me how to do the Charleston,' she demanded, poking her in the ribs in mock irony.

'You mean, you don't know how to do the Charleston swing? At your age?'

They both started to laugh.

'Your arms swing forward and backwards, with your right arm coming forward as the left leg steps forwards.' She demonstrated the steps for her mother. 'And then you move back as your left arm and right leg begin their forward movement.'

Her mother tried to join in but ended up kicking her slippers off. They knocked Yasmine's thigh. She yelped and mock-punched her mother. They fell back onto Yasmine's bed, laughing.

'Okay, Yasmine, where do we go from here?' her mother asked more seriously.

'The cha-cha?' Yasmine offered, grinning. *It's so good to be able to chuckle again, to release my anger and tearfulness. Don't psychotherapists say that communication is the key to all relationships?*

'Oh, stop it,' her mother said, throwing the pillow at her.

Yasmine covered herself with the duvet and was quiet for a few moments. 'Okay, Mum. I remember Tara wanted to join an FGM charity once she arrived in Britain. Her sister had been *done,* and Tara had only been able to escape because she was a fast runner.'

Her mother looked at her disbelievingly and said, 'Poor Tara had been through a lot.'

'Yes and no one cared,' Yasmine smiled, 'until I came along.' She gazed out of the window again. 'Now that we

338

both have more time on our hands, why don't we join an FGM or refugee charity?'

Her mother looked at her curiously.

Yasmine added, 'it would have been Tara's dream.' Her eyelids felt heavy. She searched her mother's face for an expression of interest.

Her mother took her hand again and said gently, 'Are you sure you would cope with the work a charity of this kind would do?'

Yasmine didn't hesitate to answer, 'Yes, I'm sure. I couldn't help the girl in Sulaymaniyah when she was assaulted with female genital mutilation.' She winced as she pictured the screaming girl escaping her grandmother. 'But I can help girls here in Britain.'

Her mother nodded slowly. 'We'll look up some charities tomorrow. I've already found a humanitarian organisation that help and treat refugees, signposting them to access healthcare. I need to get two references and a DBS. They prefer volunteers with lived experience of migration. I would be treating refugees and sex workers.'

'What do you mean, you *would* be treating these people, Mum?'

'Well, I'll have to wait till the GMC considers my case.'

Yasmine squeezed her mother's hand and asked, 'But what will we live on? I mean I can start tutoring and working as a barista but that won't bring in enough money.'

Her mother gestured towards the living-room.

Yasmine followed her gaze. 'You mean Sam?'

Her mother chuckled and said, 'Yes, she's going back

to work as a social worker, and thank goodness I'll be on my salary during the investigation.'

Yasmine laughed. 'I'm sure she has enough experience by now. But does she know about her new job?'

'Um, not exactly,' her mother said, picking up an apple. 'I just told her that now it's her turn to work.'

Yasmine took the apple off her mother. 'What was her reply?'

'Oh, just that I would have to do the cooking. That might be a problem.'

Yasmine roared with laughter as they fell into each other's arms and hugged each other. This was what family meant. All for one, and one for all, non-conventional and inclusive. She felt dizzy with relief. Now it was her turn to look for a charity. She would start researching FGM the following day. And of course, she would work as a barista and do some tutoring until she earned enough money to start her Master's. No need to hurry. Experience was the best lesson and she would learn to cherish every second of her life.

55

Yasmine opened her laptop in the café in Regent's Park and googled FGM. Her heart felt heavy and shattered as she thought about her razor-blade wielding grandmother. With all the recent problems, she hadn't found the time to phone Dilly and find out whether Nana Aisha had been discharged from hospital. And she didn't care, except she shouldn't be allowed to continue her heinous job. She'd leave that task for her mother to sort out.

Tara would have been proud of her for reaching out to FGM organisations and refugee charities. Maybe she would even find a charity to help abused sex workers and shed light on their plight.

Scrolling through the FGM organisations, she found an African diaspora women-led organisation, working to end violence against women and girls, including FGM.

Then there was *another one*, also dedicated to ending FGM worldwide. They mentioned education. *Hmm, that sounds important – it could lead to eradication of the atrocious procedure.* If her grandmother had been educated about the heinous procedure, she might not have gone ahead with it.

The last organisation she googled was listed as an international human rights organisation, working to promote the rights of women and girls. The lists of organisations went on and on.

Yasmine closed her laptop and looked around her in the café where she had been sifting through information on FGM. Some tourists were busy placating a toddler who wanted to get up and run into the park outside.

No wonder the child wanted to run away. She must have seen the ducks and geese waddling along the park.

Yasmine looked at the trees in Regents Park. None of them were four hundred years old like the oak trees she had encountered in Kurdistan. The oak trees had been strong in adversity. *If only they could talk and share their wisdom.* She would come back as an oak tree.

Yasmine let her eyes glide over to the calm lake. It offered a glimpse of amazing birds such as waxwings and bright green parrots which the toddler had most probably seen earlier on.

It was time to get up and go for a walk. Yasmine picked up the rest of her croissant and put it in a paper bag. She'd give some morsels to the ducks in the lake. The toddler ran after her and tugged at the hem of her raincoat. Her mother ran after her and smiled at Yasmine apologetically. Yasmine patted the toddler's head and said that it was okay and that the little girl had lovely plaits.

Harry's image entered her mind briefly. She had mentioned children but he had brushed that idea away. They hadn't even talked about a long-term relationship.

Maybe she had been too naïve. He was far too young to commit to anything or anyone.

Yasmine walked out of the café, breathed in the cold air and decided to walk up and down the open parkland, hoping to see a heron and waterfowl. Harry had laughed at the pelicans and their large beaks. How easy it had been for him to embrace his roots and identity. Born and bred in London with a man and a woman as his parents and an accepting extended family. She stood at the edge of the lake, watching a pair of swans glide across it with purpose.

I have to end this grief for Tara so I can find myself. Yasmine followed the swans towards the other end of the lake. They mated for life; a symbol of timeless love, awakening a sense of spiritual evolution. The two swans she was following glided through the water leaving hardly a ripple behind. Hmm. She had been skimming the surface for a long time. It was time to leave her ugly duckling feeling and reach out to her inner self, bridging new powers.

She took her mobile out of her handbag and dialled the number of one of the FGM organisations. Her heart beat faster but she didn't know why. *I am merely joining an organisation, not participating in anything dodgy.* Yasmine waited for a voice to boom on the phone and thought why should female sexuality be controlled and suppressed? It is a flower that needs to bloom. FGM was an evil crime.

'Hello,' a quiet voice said, 'FGM survivor's centre. How can we help?'

'Um, I'd like to do some volunteering in your organisation.'

'That's very kind of you.'

The person waited for Yasmine to say something, but she couldn't speak for a moment. Damn. She was the one who had phoned the organisation.

'May I ask what brought you to us?' The woman at the other end of the phone sounded so calm and soothing. Just what she needed.

Yasmine hesitated and sat down on a bench to collect her thoughts. 'Yes, well, I visited my family back home in Sulaymaniyah and...' She looked around to make sure no one was listening. 'I was witness to a young girl being circumcised.' She covered her eyes with her hands.

'Yes, unfortunately this still happens in many countries.'

Yasmine snapped back, 'Yes I know, but it was my grandmother who did the procedure.' She started to cry. No one was around her to give her a hug or some kind words. She tried to say something else to the woman at the end of the phone, but her voice failed her. It was as if she didn't have a voice, never had.

'I'm so sorry to hear that.' The woman kept quiet for a moment. 'Would you like to come in so we can discuss this?' She sounded so gentle that it made Yasmine cry even more.

She cleared her throat after a moment and said, 'I'll do that ... But please, keep talking,' she stuttered. 'I need to get some relief.'

The voice was silent for a moment. 'Madam, is there anything else you want to tell me? Were you a victim of this mutilation?'

'Oh no,' Yasmine retorted, 'but my friend was almost

344

done and when she refused, she was abused by her uncle.' It was such a relief to voice all this to a stranger, yet she wasn't able to relay her guilt about Tara's immigration and death. Not yet.

'You don't need to feel guilty,' Warda said, after finally introducing herself. 'You couldn't have stopped all the procedures in the world.'

Yasmine felt like hugging her.

She must be attuned to grief and despair. Yasmine raised her head and looked around her. People were walking past, oblivious to the suffering and torture in other parts of the world. It wasn't their fault. How would they know if they weren't educated about it?

'It must feel terrible, Warda.' She held her head in her hands. 'How can people live after that?' She felt her stomach churn.

'I'm a survivor, Yasmine,' was the brief but gentle reply.

Yasmine gasped. Her mouth felt dry. Was she living in a dystopian world? 'I'm so sorry, Warda,' she stammered. 'I didn't mean to hurt you.'

'It wasn't you who hurt me my dear,' Warda replied softly. 'But you can help me.' She hesitated. 'I mean my organisation. Globally, more than 200 million women have undergone FGM, and figures from UNICEF show that 4.4 million girls are at risk this year unless we get to grips with the situation.'

'I will certainly try and help,' Yasmine replied, 'and will make an appointment to see you personally. I just need to walk around a bit. Will you still be in the office in ten minutes?' Warda replied that she would be around until the evening and that there was no need to hurry.

Yasmine heaved a sigh of relief and got up from the bench. Indeed, there was no need to rush about anything now. She walked towards the lake.

Tell my story. That was the last thing Tara had said before she had left her in Sulaymaniyah, probably aware that she would die soon. And that was precisely what Yasmine would do. She would weave her story as vividly as her mother's ancestors had woven their colourful kilims. That's what life was about, interlinking patterns and forming new designs.

She glanced at the honking Egyptian geese, native to the Sahara and the Nile Valley, now at the edge of the lake. In a few months, daffodils would be tossing their yellow heads in the wind, heralding spring and new beginnings. *I'm not alone,* she thought, flipping her entangled hair in the same whirling wind as the daffodils would do in a few months, just like the spinning dervishes Tara and herself had imitated a few weeks ago in another part of the world.

Somehow, all creatures, plants and humans were connected. They would energise each other if only they were given the chance.

Acknowledgements

Special thanks to the novelist and meticulous copy editor Mary Torjussen who believed in my novel and gave me invaluable advice.

I am also grateful to Debi Alper from Jericho Writers who facilitated a very good self-editing course.

I am grateful to my Kurdish friends who told me narratives that inspired me to write this novel and breathe life into untold stories.

This book is printed on paper from sustainable sources managed under the Forest Stewardship Council (FSC) scheme.

It has been printed in the UK to reduce transportation miles and their impact upon the environment.

For every new title that Troubador publishes, we plant a tree to offset CO_2, partnering with the More Trees scheme.

For more about how Troubador offsets its environmental impact, see www.troubador.co.uk/sustainability-and-community